MORTARVILLE

MORTARVILLE
A NOVEL

GRANT BAILIE

PUBLISHING

Brooklyn, New York

Copyright © 2008 by Grant Bailie

Printed in Canada
10 9 8 7 6 5 4 3 2 1

No part of this book may be used or reproduced in any manner without written permission of the publisher.

Please direct inquiries to:

Ig Publishing
178 Clinton Avenue
Brooklyn, NY 11205
www.igpub.com

Library of Congress Cataloging-in-Publication Data

Bailie, Grant.
    Mortarville / by Grant Bailie.
        p. cm.
    ISBN-13: 978-0-9788431-1-3
    ISBN-10: 0-9788431-1-8
    1. Fertilization in vitro, Human--Fiction. I. Title.
    PS3602.A556M67 2008
    813'.6--dc22
                                            2007043456

To Erica

BOOK ONE

I Am Invented

My parents died in a fire before I was born. Drs. John and Jonathon Smithee—no relation. It is a fate that befalls so many of our better mad scientists. Their notes, following tradition, were destroyed within the same flames, along with their laboratory and its accessories: the foaming beakers, the coiling tubes bubbling with primary colors, the digital displays, monitors, levers, conduits and test tubes. The giant-sized breaker switches and big red buttons. Everything crackling, popping like firecrackers, dropping like flies.

All that was left amidst the charred, shattered and dripping remains (the fire hoses had had their way) was the extra-strength, high-pressure glass aquarium tank that was my womb. And, of course, me.

You can imagine the surprise I must have been to all those non-scientific men in yellow slickers, plastic hats and air masks. One or two must have dropped his ax in amazement upon seeing my naked and not completely formed infant body suspended in thick orange liquid, like an insect trapped in Amber. Or a carrot trapped in Jell-O. A carrot shaped like a man. A man shaped like a baby. Wires attached, batteries included.

All the usual half sentences had to have been spoken: what in the name of…what the…my dear sweet mother of …

The government had to be called, and it was. Men in suits had to arrive, and they did. My aquarium and the unborn me were draped with a green army blanket and carried to the street, to be ferried away by black limousine, by black van, by black helicopter to some volcanic island base, uncharted on any map, where I would be tested and prodded and puzzled over by men and women in lab coats. They would keep me in there, simmering in my patented stew until I was ready. And then birth.

Pow, zoom, swish and I was released from the tank through

a giant spigot. Then down a silver slide that brought me splatting against a metal tray like a cafeteria omelet. My nose and eyes were sucked clear of the goo that had been my home and comfort. I took my first breath, a deep and rasping gurgle, prelude to a long and bitter scream.

What was it like? How white was my nursery or cold my metal crib? Did I teethe on rubber stoppers fastened to rubber tubing or did one of the more paternal lab coats helicopter off the island to pick up a small order of pacifiers, rattles and stuffed animals? And for that matter, what of my parents, Dr. and Dr. Smithee? Their lives? Their work? Their fiery demise? I seem to have so many half-memories and images of events that I should have been too young or non-existent to now recall.

And yet scenes and details come to me still. In flashes and sparks. I see my parents—their own lab coats more wrinkled and less white than the government ones of my post-birth infancy—as they gaze wistfully into their special, twin-view microscope. Or I see their faces lit by the blue light of a Bunsen burner, thrown periodically into brighter relief by a wash of artificial lighting from some atmospheric contraption in the corner. They were not handsome men, my fathers. Studying the weakness of one Smithee's chin or the hawkish nose of the other, the thick glasses of Jonathon or the grey flesh hammocks beneath the eyes of John, the wispy, flesh colored hair that hung across the pink forehead of Smithee number one like a thin and badly made curtain, or the greasy black strands that grew from the misshapen dome of Smithee number two—it is easy to see why they turned to science for their propagation. And easy to see why their science turned mad. What joy could there be in the physical world for men such as that? Pigeon-toed (strangely enough, both of them), paunchy (more one than the other) prone to nervous sweating, they longed like anyone for love and reproduction, but even the gloss of super intelligence and a mantle full of science trophies could only go so far. There are those that even fame and fortune cannot make truly palatable. And the Smithees had neither fame (not really) nor fortune, though they might have achieved these things if their studies had followed along more conventional lines. Playing God was even then a thoroughly discredited field of science. How many monsters must be chased into windmills, set fire to or lured toward high voltage wires before the shine wears off that particular discipline? Not nearly so many as fiction would have had us believe. Even seemingly benign sheep and improved cattle became a pariah once the artificiality of their parentage was proved and some dire consequence vaguely implied. Pantheist, monotheists, polytheists—even some atheists—could take offense to the idea of life not born directly of life. There were riots, with squads of men in black shirts and white collars breaking windows and throwing confiscated equipment and furniture onto the fires that they were building in the streets.

Men like my fathers were driven underground or into unmarked laboratories on the third floors of abandoned warehouses. And for security reasons, certain secret government agencies moved their base of operations to remote volcanic islands.

The exact details of the Smithee's work are a mystery, though I have a theory that these memories—these fleeting, sometimes nebulous, sometimes vivid images I see, have been planted in me by them. They are part of a design, triggered to go off throughout my life so that a part of them would live on in me. It is the hope of any father.

It happens most often with electricity—bad wiring, thick carpet, static, a storm. A spark occurs and one image or another, some memory, some idea, rushes over me. I am born backwards into the past. A scene unfolds in real time and I cannot tell if I am here or there. And when it is over, another piece has been added to my memory.

Perhaps my parents knew that someday the angry mobs of clergymen and environmentalists would sniff them out and destroy them. Why else the fireproof aquarium? Why else the protective layer of defenses—the lasers, alarm screens, sprinkler systems, etc.—that surrounded my little womb? Oh, but only if they had taken such precautions with the front door.

But they have set up, somewhere in my manufactured make-up, the devices that would keep them—in a sense—alive. The phrase "molecular switch" pops into my head often and unbidden. If I shuffle across a carpeted floor, close my eyes and touch the sharp corner of a metal table or the screen of a TV, I might see a blue field, with a red double helix being prodded and shaped by the unsteady silver point of a microscopic needle. Or I will see the coils flowing with red yellow and blue liquid. Or I will return.

When I sleep tonight, beneath high-tension wires, beneath dry clouds that rub together like malevolent hands, I am likely to dream of two, unattractive men in wrinkled lab-coats, fiddling with knobs and test-tubes, pressing their faces intently against the eye-pieces of a variety of scopes, or occasionally playing Ping-Pong. From these dreams, visions, flashes and unlikely memories, I have pieced together this Frankenstein's monster of my history. And know as certainly as I know anything that I was made from scratch. Without sperm or egg. In a third floor secret laboratory. By two god-like mad scientists.

The Early Years

Being so immaculately conceived, I was a natural threat—after my unnatural fashion—to numerous branches of organized religion, yet might even have been seen as a potential savior or second coming to others, had my existence not been such a closely guarded government secret. But two armed officers flanked every doorway of my infancy. A soldier always sat at the foot of my cradle, or stood by stern-faced as one of the lower ranking technicians wiped my bum and checked to see how my latest rash was doing.

Despite these special beginnings, I was a disappointingly ordinary child to the scientists. Every diaper they changed or burp they coaxed contained, by all appearances, the same shit and gas of any other child. I crawled no sooner or faster; I cooed no cuter or more articulately. I drooled, I teethed, I slept and cried and no telepathic thoughts emitted from my head, or deadly ray-beams from my eyes. For a short time, there was some excitement over a flaky, bumpy condition developing on my scalp, with some of the more optimistic of the group imagining it to be the first stages of my evolution into something more. What sort of skin could I be manufacturing through unseen nanobiological mechanisms to protect myself from today's weapons or tomorrow's deadly sunshine? Would I finally peel away this ordinary human carapace and emerge from my sterile nursery as The New Man, a golden skinned mutant that would be the hope for a generation fated to live in a harsher environment, battling superhuman enemies and colonizing Mars?

It turned out to be cradle cap. You can imagine the crestfallen looks as they lowered me back into my crib and tossed out the samples of my peeling flesh they had so painstakingly prepared for the lab. Nothing would ever come of any of the other bumps and ailments I would develop. All my colds and runny noses were just colds and runny noses. My diapers—though they may have reeked—did not glow.

The years, few as they may have been there, slipped by and I was now a toddler. I toddled. I said a few words to the amazement of none. I mangled "stethoscope," rearranged the letters to "EKG," and "DNA", slurred my way through "genetics," "encoding," and "bioengineering." "Nanny-biology" I said and no one found it impossibly cute or precocious.

I was given out-of-date textbooks to play with. I drew on half the pages and chewed on the rest. I threw tantrums at the daily prick of the needle. I would not sit still while the wired suction cups were attached to my chest and forehead and fidgeted within the great tunnels of honeycombed light I was regularly subjected to.

"Sit still," one scientist or another told me. "Don't do that. Put that down." And I could swear the soldier in the corner was quietly unsnapping the flap of his holster.

As I grow older still, their experiments took on a certain random, non-scientific desperation. Keep the kid in the dark for seven days. Keep him in light. Submerge him in water. Put him near fire. What happens when he is fed only by machine? What happens when he is subjected to this and tormented by that?

Put the kid in a cage with a mother gorilla, someone suggested, and they did. We got along very well, and I cried for days when they transferred my beloved Abigail to the Department of Communication and Accident Research.

They may have held out some small hope for puberty. Might I not grow my special powers then along with broader shoulders, pubic hair, a wispy mustache? But all that was such a long ways away. They were not a particularly paternal or patient bunch and when funding was cut and they had to decide between my further upkeep and a new couch for the rec. room, the couch won.

I can recall with a preternatural clarity being bundled in a rough, green blanket and strapped into an extra large-sized child-carrier—I was five by now. And then the steady rocking back and forth as I was carried like a heavy valise by a soldier (he was quite strong) down the long white corridor to the helicopter pad.

I remember the smell of rubbing alcohol, formaldehyde, ozone, and pine scented cleaner. And in my ears, even now, is the click click click of military heels, the muffled whir of the black helicopter.

I am Transported

On the outskirts of the city of Mortarville is a mile long divot in the ground, only noticeable by plane or from the top of a tall tree. It is a place where the land has collapsed—the hive-like structure hidden beneath having finally given way to the forces of gravity, decay and neglect. Overgrown now with grass and weeds, its history is unrecorded and carefully forgotten. But here and there, among stagnant water, moss, young trees, and mosquitoes, a rusted beam breaks through the broken surface, as if the world itself were suffering from, along with its sundry other ailments, multiple compound fractures. The dirt here sparkles with the min-iscule particles of broken glass. This is where I was raised. It is the rubble of my second home.

It was once more than a mile-long dent in the planet, though even then it seemed to be less. To the eye of some wayward hiker or picnicking couple, it was only a patch of young forest, a small, pastoral swath of land far away from the noise of the city, and nearly away from its stench. But beneath the ground, all access points hidden, were countless floors of prison-like rooms. It was the Secret Government Home for the Products of Mad Science. Our Lady of Misfits. The Subterranean Island of Dr. Moreau. It had numerous nicknames, so many, in fact, that in my years there I would never learn its official name. If it had one, I did not recog-nize it from the others as they were all spoken with bitter humor, resentment and very little reverence.

I was brought there under the cover of darkness, swaddled in the same green army blanket. The helicopter landed in a secret place between two artificial trees and was nearly silent, even in landing, making my screams in the night all the more unnerving.

"Shut that kid up," a soldier said, running his palm along the grip of his still holstered gun.

"Got a cork that big?" asked the more fatherly of my handlers.

I don't know why I cried. The place I had left behind had

no reliable comforts. The only emotional attachment I had made during my time there—Abigail—was now being used to test biohazards, crash helmets or hearing aids. But there was something frightening to a child of five or so to be in those meager woods at night, beneath those meager stars, with the city of Mortarville glowing in the distance, throwing its indistinct halo into the smoggy sky above it. I cried and one or two wild animals answered me with their own cries, which reminded me of Abigail again and made me cry louder.

"I'll friggin' shoot him, so help me," a soldier said, holding back a tear, as the ground opened, the grass rolling back like two window shades to reveal the gaping metal doorway beneath it. A light grew from within, a distant headlight moving closer until finally an elevator booth rose out of the earth. The door opened. I had stopped crying long enough to blow a spit bubble as I stared in amazement. What dragon would they feed me to now?

The dragon, it turned out, wore a knee-length white dress, white stockings and orthopedic shoes. She smelled vaguely of rubbing alcohol, vanilla and soap. Down, down, down past floor after floor—visible through the elevator's steel grate—past countless levels of unmarked doors, steel grids, bridges, catwalks and walkways. Past pillars, girders and gargoyles and into the shadowy and bottomless depths below. The walls, doors and all the vaulting bridges and walkways between them were varied in style from gothic to Greek revival, from baroque to Bauhaus, and it seemed as if several cities had been piled on top of each other or several dark ages crashed together like trains and then reassembled from the parts.

If I'd had any experience in the matter, I would have recognized it then as a sort of prison or sanitarium. An old one, designed and built by a committee of madmen. Or if I had been weaned on fairy tales instead of textbooks, I might have thought it very much like a castle or dungeon. But raised as I was, all of it was alien and indefinable and the only clear sensation I could muster beyond confusion was a growing fear of high and low places and of being buried alive. I held the hand tighter. So tight, in fact, that the woman who owned it grunted in discomfort, pried it loose and took hold of my wrist instead.

The elevator ground and clanked to a stop. She opened the door and we stepped out onto a metal walkway. I peered nervously over the edge as a cloud of steam rose from a still distant and unseen bottom. She pulled me away, tugged me hurriedly down through stripes of light and shadows, beneath saucer lights and girders. To one side was an endless wall of wood paneling. It struck me, even in my malformed youth, as incongruous. These walls should be iron or stone. There should have been an endless stretch of black bars, though I had no way of knowing what such things could mean then. Instead there was sheet upon sheet of thin and unnatural wood, the patterns of grain and knots repeating themselves every hundred feet so that it seemed that I had passed the same plank several times before we stopped and she said in a strong and clear voice: "Open number 23."

This took me by surprise—but she was not speaking to me, she was addressing the receiver of a radio hidden somewhere on her body or perhaps in the ceiling above us. A piece of the wall next to where we were standing clicked, inched slightly forward, then slid to the side to reveal a room behind it—a vague brightness that threatened rather than beckoned. I looked in, but from slightly behind the woman holding my hand. If there were monsters or lions, I wanted them to attack her first.

There was no monster or lion inside. It was only a twenty foot by twenty foot room, one wall of stone, three of wood paneling. There was a bunk bed attached to the stone wall next to a pink and blue dresser. On one of the wood paneled walls hung a painting of a clown.

"Here you go, kid," she said. "Home, sweet home number 23." She may have attempted to smile, but it was either unsuccessful or, in fact, unattempted. She handed me the green army blanket she had been carrying and gave me a pinch on the chin that actually hurt for some minutes afterwards. Then she walked away, leaving me in the empty room, the door—though ostensibly wood—clanging metallically shut behind her.

Home, sweet home number 23—I would live there for the

next ten years. Two bunks, a clown painting and a dresser.

Both bunks were empty, the mattresses bare. I sat on the bottom bunk for a moment, staring at the clown in the painting. His eyes were black, framed in white circles, with one blue teardrop permanently spilling from the left one. He was smiling, but the red outline painted around his mouth was shaped in the form of a frown.

I climbed the steel ladder to the top bunk and lay there for a moment looking up at the ceiling, at its cracks and the naked yellow bulb burning in the center. The cracks formed no picture of comfort or solace. Then the light bulb clicked off and I was left in blackness. I wrapped myself in the army blanket and went to sleep imagining the rough fiber of it to be the rough, bristled gorilla chest of the only mother I had ever known.

What did I dream that first night in that strange new place? The night passed and dreams must have come and it seems to me now that those dreams would have been somehow relevant to this history—a window into the heart of all my hopes and fears at the time or a foreshadowing of things to come. But, despite my supernatural memory, despite the clarity with which I can see my early traumas, despite the fact that I know, somehow, that that dream was important, I can recall no plot or images for you now.

If I were to invent one, maybe it would be of the clown in the painting springing to life and chasing me through dark corridors. Maybe my fathers would resurrect themselves from the ashes and save me, or I would suddenly develop the ability to fly, shoot deadly eye-beams, or climb up walls. Or Abigail would swing down from a convenient vine or tire swing to beat the evil clown with her enormous hands until real tears poured from his eyes and the plastic flower on his lapel squirted blood.

The First Day

The light clicked on and it was morning. This was morning; the crack of dawn, cracked open and poured out all at once, a rotten egg exploding into the face of a frightened boy.

I would later learn that the building's lighting system had been designed to function differently: the glow of light bulbs—hidden then by attractive globes—was meant to build gradually, mimicking the real dawn, with the piped in sounds of native birds growing louder from discretely placed speakers. But all of this had broken down years before my arrival, along with about half the automatic doors and a third of the thermostats. As a result, all the lights clicked on at once and this was the new day. A heater clanked, but no birds sang.

I sat up and waited for someone collect me, to show me my purpose in this new environment, or to poke at me with yet another sharp, sterile laboratory stick. But nothing happened. An hour or so passed and no one came. I stared at the clown. He stared back. More time passed and it was impossible to tell what part of day it was or was becoming.

Now I was hungry. I climbed off the bunk, paced the floor, opened the drawers to the dresser (empty), looked under the bottom bunk (no monsters or lions). I tried the door, but there seemed to be no way of opening it from the inside; it had become a part of the wall, with only a thin seam distinguishing it. I put my eye to the crack but could see nothing.

After awhile, I took a nap on the bottom bunk—less from fatigue than a lack of options—and awoke again some indefinable time later to resume pacing. I kicked at the wall until the ends of my toes became numb, picked away at the loose paint of the bunk frame until my fingernails were black and I had exposed a small section shaped like a continent or country I had seen once in a textbook.

Sooner or later, I realized, I would need to go to the bathroom and having had this thought, the need grew from there. Where would I go? In the corner? In an empty drawer? In my pants? It became my dominant thought, replacing hunger, confusion, loneliness and all the unlabeled others. I yelled but heard only my own voice. I banged on the part of the wall that was still a door. Eventually, I soiled myself with both elements and felt them grow cold around me. Then the light turned off again and I crawled back up to the top bunk.

Now I slept, not fitfully as might be expected in the strangeness of my environment and the discomforts of my own waste, but fully, completely. The first, I think, of my transports back into the cushions of memory—a molecular safety mechanism to protect me from a harsh present and an uncertain future, though a faulty one that could just as easily drop me in the middle of a past trauma far worse than whatever my current circumstances might be.

Abigail holds me in her arms. Her arms are muscular and hairy--the hair is like wire, but there is comfort here. She pushes soft, thick lips against the top of my head and her breath is warm and smells of chewed leaves and baby food, which they feed her as a treat sometimes, or when they are out of fresh fruit and the bag of dried gorilla chow they keep in the pantry is running low.

She loves me and tells me so with the petting of her enormous black hand and the low and comforting alien words she makes from somewhere deep in her massive throat. She checks my hair for bugs and lice. When they had first placed me in her glass home, two men in lab coats remained for a moment, waiting to see if the gorilla might tear me apart. She was playing with her tire swing—not sitting in it but rather sitting on the floor beneath it, making it sway back and forth with the idle shoves of her prehensile feet.

She looked up with mild interest at their entrance and stopped her activity with the swing when she saw that they had something new for her to play with. They set me down in the far corner of the room, near her water dish. I did not cry. A gorilla meant nothing more or less to me than a lab assistant or a couch, and though I might have felt some trepidation based on some of the previous experiments they had conducted on me, I recognized immediately that the creature in the room was, at the very least, neither a vat of water or a pit of fire.

She moved closer by degrees, with a sort of loping crawl more sophisticated and deliberate than my own, pausing at intervals to sit and study the situation. She had been given a kitten once. She had liked it, but crushed it in her sleep one night by accident. Sometimes she tried to draw pictures of it with the art supplies they occasionally left in her cell.

Finally, she was next to me and reached a long and tentative finger toward the tip of my nose. Her own face loomed closer, wide nostrils sniffing to see what I was, enormous dark eyes darting up and down, looking for flaws or threats. The scientists were already backing quietly from the room, locking the door behind themselves with several bolts.

Abigail covered my face for a moment with one hand—one of her hands was more than enough. She tugged lightly at the sleeve of my shirt—a brightly colored and ill fitting cast-off from someone's grown children—and sniffed her fingers for some clue or explanation. I was a patient, passive baby boy and made no moves of my own, but only sat there, looking back, waiting to see what would happen next.

She retreated to the tire swing and looked at me from there. Not coldly, not aggressively or even distrustfully, but cautiously. Who knew what tests they might have subjected her to prior to my arrival? She may have had her own memories of water and fire to contend with—to say nothing of the trauma of a dead kitten.

Finally, I crawled to her on my own. Slowly, awkwardly, cooing my adorable coo that had no effect on scientists or their assistants. But Abigail responded. She opened her arms to my approach. She lifted me tenderly and placed me in her hairy lap.

I slept there in her arms for the first time that night. The next day we were fed the same bowl of mangos for breakfast and spent the morning crawling along the floor of her habitat as she introduced me to all of her belongings: a red ball, a water dish, a doll, a set of wooden blocks (slightly chewed) and a tire swing.

The days that passed were unnamed and uncounted. We were always fed the same meals in the same steel bowl—or maybe I was fed no meals at all and only survived by the graciousness of my host. That may have been the experiment: to test her selflessness. They could not test or measure, of course, the happiness I felt in those heady days. Though my stomach may have growled on occasion, and a diet of too much fruit may have played havoc on my youthful digestive system, I felt loved in her arms. I cherished the scent of her and the warmth of her breath. I was attentive to all the primate lessons she tried to impart upon me.

On art day she painted a picture, showed it to me, pounding the still wet paint with the tip of her giant, slightly curled finger. A blueish-blackish blob—her dead kitten. Whether the form on the paper was misshapen and mangled beyond easy recognition in an attempt to convey the violent tragedy of its death or if it simply represented the limits of her artistic ability, I had no way of knowing, but I could see well enough the sadness and regret in her eyes.

I cried like an animal the day they pulled me from the room, the experiment ended, my home and heart broken. Abigail pounded the glass walls, tossed blocks, balls, steel dishes and tire swings in mournful fury. She threw herself against the window, stretching herself to her full height against the glass, her long arms above her, the black pads of her hands laid flat and slapping repeatedly in some sad and futile gesture for mercy, for understanding, for me.

They took me away, down the hallway, to the sound of Abigail's muffled cries and rage. I pounded my chest and bit the fingers of my handler.

And now she holds me in her arms and I sleep like a baby, too content to even dream.

Home for the Ill-Conceived

The light clicked on. Another nameless day, but this time the door slid open and a large man dressed in white and holding a small stack of neatly folded sheets stood there. He seemed surprised to see me there on the top bunk.

"Oh crap," he said. "How long have you been here?"

"I don't know," I told him and started to cry.

They cleaned me up—not the man who discovered me, his job was laundry and he had his own problems to worry about—but two other men in white—white shirts, white pants, white shoes. They looked like nurses or janitors in hospitals or low-level assistants in secret government labs. They too were large men, half muscle, half fat, with big sweaty hands that led me out of my cell and down a hallway to a room with tub sinks and cleaning supplies.

They stripped off my clothes and threw them in a plastic bag, then put me in one of the sinks and turned on the water. The water ran cold, then warm, then hot as they scrubbed me with brushes and warm water and a new bar of soap that was still sharp at the edges. One of the men held his nose and the other laughed at him.

"You've smelled worse," he said and the one holding his nose said, "*You* smell worse."

When they were done, they handed me a towel and a stack of clothes. "Put these on," the one who had been holding his nose said. He handed me a gray sweat suit and a pair of gray slipper socks. I put them on and the two of them walked me back to my cell. Their shoes had rubber soles and squeaked against the metal grating of the walkway. They did not hold my hand, but walked close on either side of me, one or the other's large hand occasional touching my shoulder to guide me along.

"You hungry?" one of them asked and I nodded.

"Well, we'll bring you something to eat soon. OK?"

I nodded again.

"You need to go to the bathroom again?" the other one asked and I shook my head.

"You sure?"

"Yes," I said and my voice sounded impossibly small among the beams and arches and catwalks and walls, the rising clouds of steam, the shadows and gargoyles.

"Twenty-three," one of them said and the wood-paneled door slid open. There were sheets on both bunks now, and pillows. I sat on the bottom bunk. For variety. Sometime later one of the Men in White brought me a bowl of macaroni and cheese.

Mr. Grindlier

The next morning the door opened on a man in a brown suit. He was a small and officious looking, and his suit was tight, particularly around the middle where his stomach pushed out disproportionately. He attempted a welcoming smile that created odd and unsettling wrinkles around his mouth.

"You will pardon our confusion earlier," he said as if I were someone much older. "We're still setting up around here. Working the bugs out, you see."

He stepped cautiously into my cell, looked around and nodded at the clown painting like it was a coworker.

"Cheery," he said and I could only stare at him open-mouthed. He cleared his throat, touched the corner of the clown painting's frame, pretending to straighten it. "Quite cheery."

"Anyway," he began, "would you like a brief tour of your new home? I imagine you're curious…"

"Yes," I interrupted. And I was curious, of course, but also resigned. In my short history I had been submerged, encased, and isolated enough times without explanation to expect one now, let alone a tour of the facility. He held out his hand for me to shake. I had not shaken a hand before so I only stared at it, wondering why it was being extended with no shiny treat or tasty reward inside. He gave up after a moment and patted me on the shoulder instead.

"My name is Paul…Paul Grindlier…Mr. Grindlier. I'm the Administrator here. You can call me Mr. Grindlier. Or Administrator if you prefer."

"Administrator," I repeated. The word was new to me, though I think I repeated it back well enough.

"Do you know what that is?"

"No."

"It's kind of like a principal…do you know what a principal is?"

"No."

He smiled—sympathetically, I think. Or pityingly.

"I'm in charge."

"Like a scientist?"

"Sure," he said. "Like a scientist. But, you know, without the lab coat. Or the science."

I nodded.

"And your name is?"

And what was my name? I had been called many things in my short life, but none with enough regularity or affection for me to recognize it as my own. Was I John Doe? Was I John Smithee? Was I Wonderboy or Superman; Frankenstein or Frank? I had been Aquaboy for a few days and Adam for a few more. I had even been known for a week and a half as Bobo, which had been started for no discernable reason by a lab technician, picked up by several of his colleagues and then dropped after it had apparently run its course

"I don't know," I finally answered and Mr. Grindlier only smiled as if he understood, as if this happened all the time, as if it had even happened to him once or twice in his childhood.

"Well, we'll have to come up with something then won't we," he said. I nodded and felt something like hope.

But he didn't come up with anything right then. Instead he walked me out of the cell, a hand on my shoulder for comfort or guidance. Outside of my cell, we stood for a moment at the railing of the walkway. I looked down at what seemed an infinite depth of steel floors and bridges, stone walls, wood panels and shadows, steam rising from the blackness in mysterious, soul-shaped puffs.

"Something, huh," Mr. Grindlier said.

"Yes," I said.

"No one knows it's here," he said. "Can you imagine that? All this, hidden beneath a sheet of grass? All of us just going on with our little lives and them up there having no idea. Maybe someone is having a picnic over our heads right this second. Imagine that."

We both looked up. An infinite rising of steel floors, bridges, stone walls, wood panels and shadows. It was impossible to imagine a world of sunlight and grass above it. And I had no idea what a picnic was.

"Uh-huh," I said and he looked down at me with something like surprise, as if remembering suddenly that he had not been talking to himself, but instead a five year old and nameless child.

"OK, son," he said, patting me on the shoulder and stopping just short of ruffling my hair. "Let's give you that tour I promised you, eh?"

He gave me the tour, across catwalks and up and down several flights of steps, rising and falling in the elevator—he did not seem very organized and would often repeat himself, covering the same ground on the way to something he had inadvertently neglected. "See that gargoyle," he might say three different times, pointing to the same mossy stone monster in the shadows of a distant corner. Or: "That's where they take the laundry from your floor." Or: "That's where they cook the meals."

He told me that I was among the first, and that was part of the reason things were still so chaotic. But more were coming—new samples of the scientifically spawned generation were being shipped in daily and soon our chatter and laughter would echo through these dank hallways, bringing joy to this dark hole in the world.

"It has been rough for your kind," he said as the elevator rose or fell to yet another floor. "I know that, we all know that. And it's not your fault. You didn't ask to be the product of science, did you? It isn't like you jumped into that test-tube or Petri dish or whatever. But things will be better now. You'll see. This is a start, I think. We'll make amends. Right? I like to think so, anyway."

He showed me the bathrooms on every floor and tried to explain the lack of them in most of the rooms.

"It was designed for something different. This place. A long, long time ago. A kind of home for bad people. Very bad people. People who could not even be trusted to go potty on their own. Can you imagine someone that bad? Boy, that's some bad people, isn't it? But that was a long time ago. It's going to be something better now. Much better. A nice place. A place where you can learn and grow. Won't that be something?"

He looked down at me again. He was smiling and there was the hope and fear of the future in that smile. It was the kind of smile people give to new cars they have spent their whole life saving for and behind the smile, the small fear of everything that could go wrong and all the problems a clever salesman might have hidden with gum and tape and sawdust.

"You know, we might put bathrooms in later on," he said.

We walked on beneath archways, between columns, black walls sprouting brass curling vines that once might have held gas lamps, though nothing was in them now—they ended in empty holes, decapitated flowers. On mossy stones, I saw carved letters of forgotten names, the numbers of long past years. Who were they, the authors of these shaky symbols scratched into mortar and stone with coins or nails or pieces of metal or teeth?

Mr. Grindlier brought me back to my cell. He said the number and the door opened.

"Things will be better now," he said. "You'll see."

"OK," I said.

"But we still haven't given you a name."

"No."

"Have you thought about that? Is there anything you'd like to be called?"

"Bobo," I suggested, but he frowned at that.

"How about John?" he said. "At least until something better comes along."

"OK," I said.

"John it is then."

"John," I said.

"John," he said.

I Meet My Fellow Inmates

The next day I ate my meals in a cavernous mess hall two floors up and several dark corridors over. Long metal tables with attached benches crossed the room in three rows. A dozen or so boys my own age and dressed like me in gray sweat suits and slipper socks sat at the tables. Every third one of them, it turned out, was named John.

We chewed joylessly on cereal in the morning, macaroni and cheese in the afternoon, macaroni and cheese with peas and tuna fish in the evening. Steel beams arched over our heads and two stone centurions flanked the doorway, with two real-life men dressed in white leaning against them, watching us.

An impossibly pale boy sat next to me at supper-time, matching blue veins bulging from his temples and neck as he chewed.

"Are you the product of science?" I asked him.

He shrugged, forced something from mouth to throat to stomach and said: "I guess."

"You two!" one of the guards shouted from the doorway.

I looked up. The pale boy did not.

"Just eat," he said to us.

I ate. The meal ended, the plates were cleared, we returned to our cells where night fell with a click.

The next day repeated itself. Waiting in my room. Called to three meals. Cereal in the morning, some incarnation of macaroni and cheese for the meals after that. It would turn out to be the base ingredient of all my lunches and suppers. Macaroni and cheese with peas, with tuna fish, with pale hot dog wieners sliced into discs. It was boiled, and fried and baked. It was served in piles or pressed into cakes. Sometimes it was even served for breakfast, with eggs and flecks of something that might have been bacon. On very special days, there was a side of applesauce or a square of Jell-O with incongruous bits of carrot shavings suspended inside.

Gradually, some amount of entertainment or edification was added to the structure of our days. We were periodically rounded up and taken out on field trips, though not really out and not really into fields, but rather into elevators and up stairwells and down corridors. To an art room where we were given old computer paper and crayons of discontinued colors. To a zoo containing white mice, hamsters, guinea pigs and a dog. To a library where every book was missing its cover or some crucial page inside.

Our numbers grew until we filled the tables of the mess hall and the sounds of our sobs and pacing emitted through the thin wood panel walls of our cells.

At night, in blackness, I heard the squeaks of my fellow inmates, the sighs and snores, the bad dreams as I drifted off to waiting hairy arms.

One day, at lunch, a boy at the far end of my table rose up, and threw his bowl of macaroni and whatever at the nearest wall. It was not very near and the bowl fell several yards short, clattering across the floor.

"Do you know who I am?" he screamed, or maybe it was more of a cry. There was a vibration in his throat, like a small motor whirring inside against muscle and chords. His bottom lip quivered.

"Do you know what I am?"

We looked up from our meals, stared and waited to see what would happen next. The guards ran from their place by the door, fumbling for the sticks—like sawed-off broom handles—that they now kept strapped to their belts. The Men in White had started carrying the sticks when the boys filled all three tables in the lunch room. First one guard and then another and then all of the Men in White, as if it were not so much a change in policy as a fashion that had caught on.

"Do you know what I can do?" the boy yelled. The two men, though large, hesitated, stopping a few feet short of the boy and glancing nervously at each other.

The boy squinted at them and the men seemed to brace for the inevitable death-beam that would follow. But nothing happened. A tear and then another leaked from the boy's scrunching eyes and he began to bawl. They rushed forward now, lifted him up by the arms and carried him kicking and screaming from the room.

He was gone for the next three meals and when he returned he was quiet. One day I sat next to him at lunch. He chewed without speaking, without even making a sound.

"Who are you?" I whispered. "What can you do?"

He didn't even look up or stop chewing when he answered: "Same as you."

See Dick Run

Run, Dick, Run. And Dick is running. Dick in his striped shirt. Dick with his sunny smile and brown hair—a perpetual sun in the corner of the sky just for him. His dog is running along side him, smiling too, pink tongue hanging out. Boy, does Dick like to run. And golden-haired Jane is happy to see Dick run. Apparently, she can watch Dick run all day. She stands in the lawn watching like she will watch forever.

The books they had given us were in varying states of condition: bent, stained, misshapen, spines pounded into mush, pages falling out; some not so bad as that, some worse, none of them new. On the front page of my copy, stamped in black ink, was: *Property of the Mortarville Public School System*. Beneath that were several lines with different names written in different childish scrawls—*Darren Fowler, Heather Burdy, Sam Merold*—they had all owned this book before me, for whatever brief and distant period of time. They had held it in their small alien hands, blurring the print and bending the corners with their sweaty grips before their hands had moved on to hold other, bigger and better things.

And inside, Dick and Jane and their mutual dog were still running through a world of sunlight and green grass. These were the basic elements that surrounded them and they were euphoric and content here, never plagued by shortness of breath or muscle cramps. I dream of that world still—a world of endless and unencumbered movement.

They taught us in the cafeteria or sometimes, in one of the other rooms. The Men in White would tell us the letters, would make us stand up in turn and recite the alphabet, spell out simple words, count to ten. They wrote things on chalkboards that were placed in the front of the room. Some of them wrote better than others, but none of them wrote well—they all had large hands with thick fingers that were not made for writing.

They showed no great love or passion for the task they had been given, and often were seen checking a piece of paper for what to do next. They yelled when we got the answer wrong, hit us in the back of the head for talking in class.

Time passed—without the rising and setting of a sun, without clouds skidding by, without an invisible hand ripping away the pages of a calendar or the hands of a clock spinning into a circular blur like a gray dinner plate hanging on the wall.

I did well with reading. I liked the letters of the alphabet—in my mind each one took on its own personality. The letter A was wise and patient. The letter B smart but untrustworthy—he would forget things and get confused and was constantly losing his umbrella. C was somewhat dim and D a sweet girl who collected leaves in a scrapbook. E was slow but loyal. F had his eyes on J— romantic designs, but G, who was clumsy, loved J as well. H may have loved G but would never say so. I was aloof and mysterious, sometimes moody, sometimes changeable. K was evil. L through P were adults who worked in the same lab, mixing chemicals and inventing new things. R was their boss, and seemed nice enough, but was pushed to do less than honorable things by his controlling wife Q. R through Z were members of the same shadowy group that controlled the workings of the world; they sat at long tables in dimly lit rooms and spoke in whispers.

But from the depth of what well had I pulled this cast of characters? My knowledge of people and their interrelations should have been too limited; I had been raised by scientists, bureaucrats and a primate. The Men in White, who gathered us from our cells for meals and guided us up stairways for field-trips, were faceless and indistinguishable, though now and then they might carry on muttered conversations with each other in a corner, or share a joke with one of the boys. But they never spoke to me. So was this the gift of my late fathers? Had there been tucked, hidden between my cells, a summary of human behavior—a primer of people and their predilections? It seemed an odd gift and even now, I cannot see its purpose. All things considered, I would have preferred death-ray emitting eyeballs.

I am Given a Roommate

I was sitting on the bottom bunk one day when the door to my cell opened and there was Mr. Grindlier—bags under his eyes, thinner, grayer hair, worn down a little more by pressure and time. Standing next to him was a boy I had not seen before. The boy was taller than me, blonder and better formed. He had broad shoulders, a straighter nose, a stronger chin. "John," Mr. Grindlier said. "I have a new friend for you. A roommate. This is Sterling Jones. Sterling, this is John Smith."

Sterling Jones was busy examining the knuckles of one of his well-formed hands. He looked up only for a second, but in that second he seemed to take me in completely. He half smiled, then returned his attention to his knuckles. Mr. Grindlier nudged him on the shoulder and said: "Jones." The boy glanced up at Mr. Grindlier, and it seemed to me that Mr. Grindlier stepped back a little, as if the glance exerted force. Then Sterling Jones turned to me, smiled slightly—as slight as a smile can be and still be called a smile—and held out his hand.

"Hello," he said.

I shook his hand in awe, squeaking out my own feeble: "Hi." Even his hand... What better science had his creators practiced? What better brand of chemicals, test tubes and Petri dishes had they used? Maybe he had been formed in a gold or silver mold rather than a fish tank—a boy shaped mold—but broad-shouldered and already nearly the shape of a man.

I offered him the top bunk. It was all that I had to give.

"If you don't mind," he said, lifting a duffle bag from the floor behind him and carrying it to the bed.

"Well," said Mr. Grindlier. "I'll leave you two to get acquainted then," making his exit.

I watched Sterling unpack: gray sweatpants, gray sweatshirts, gray slipper-socks, a coverless book.

"My name's Sterling," he said and even his voice was better than my own—deep and mature. Even the shape of his lips, the whiteness of his teeth, the blueness of his eyes.

"I know," I said. "Mr. Grindlier just told me."

"Sorry. I hadn't been listening."

"Did you just get here?"

"No." He turned to face me, smiled broadly. "And you?"

"Me what?"

"You just get here?"

"No. No, I've been here."

"Me too."

"Uh-huh."

"Not *here* here, of course. In another cell. Upper floor. Closer to the *girls*." He smiled knowingly. But I didn't know. I stared back blankly as his smile changed from sympathy to pity to wonder to comfort to promise to knowledge, and to welcome. Then he said: "You have a little macaroni and cheese in the corner of your mouth."

"Thank you," I told him, wiping my mouth and trying to smile back.

Preliminary Studies

One day, before lunch, they lined us up outside of our cells and led us to the lunchroom in single file. This was unusual—we never had class before the afternoon and never ate lunch this early.

We took our seats at the long tables.

"What is this, brunch?" Sterling whispered.

I whispered back: "What's brunch?" but was slapped in the back of my head by a Man in White before I got an answer.

Another Man in White began passing out sheets of thick, colored paper, crayons, dull scissors, sparkly bits of plastic, Popsicle sticks, cotton balls. A third Man in White placed a mysterious hunk of white glop on a brown paper towel placed every few feet on the tables. We took turn passing it around, poking it with our fingers, sniffing it, trying to figure it out.

"Minty," one boy said and licked a bit of it off the tip of his finger.

"It's paste," Sterling said.

"That's stupid. Why would they make paste minty?" someone asked.

Mr. Grindlier entered the room, stood at the front and said in a loud voice for all to hear: "Do not eat the paste. The paste is to be shared among you. Do not smear the paste on yourselves or each other. You have each been given one pair of scissors. Do not poke each other or yourselves with your pair of scissors. You will be allotted two sheets of construction paper. If you ruin the first sheet, you may ask for the second. If you ruin the second, you will have to make do with what you have. Do not stick the sticks, cotton balls, or sparkly bits into your mouths. They are not good for you to eat and you will not be given replacements."

Next he held up a small box. "You will be given a shoebox. You will only get one shoebox. If you ruin your shoebox, you will not be given another. So please make do with what you have."

One of the Men in White began handing out the shoeboxes while Mr. Grindlier continued.

"Today you are going to make something called a diorama. You are only going to get one chance to make a diorama, so make this one chance count."

We all picked up our shoeboxes, looked at our materials. The one kid was still licking the finger he had stuck in the paste.

"The theme of your diorama," Mr. Grindlier said, "is a happy home. We want you to imagine a happy home. A place you might like to live. Maybe it is a place you have read about in a book. Maybe it is a place you remember from your past. I want you to picture that place in your head now. I want you to recreate it with the materials in front of you. Are there any questions? Does everyone understand?"

No one raised their hand.

"You may begin," Mr. Grindlier said.

The kid who had been licking his finger leaned toward me and whispered: "If they didn't want us to eat the paste then why'd they make it taste like mint?"

A Man in White slapped him on the back of his head.

I closed my eyes and tried to imagine a happy home. I imagined blue-construction paper skies with white cotton ball clouds, but that did not seem like enough and besides, what sort of structure could I assemble from sticks, shiny bits of plastic and mint flavored paste to go with it?

Sterling was already pasting a sheet of gray construction paper to the interior of his box. He asked for his second piece of paper, cut, rolled and pasted it into a small cylinder with a + at the top and a − at the bottom written in crayon. He pasted the cylinder into the center of his diorama.

"Home sweet home," he said before being hit in the back of the head by a Man in White.

I was still having trouble with my own diorama, but started pasting blue construction paper to the inside of the box anyway. Maybe something would come to me. Maybe I could make the image of my fathers with Popsicle sticks, maybe I could recreate their lab with a shoebox, paper and plastic, but would any of that be a happy home? I did not have the material to make even a replica of a glass cage with a tire swing. So I pasted my blue paper, pasted my cotton ball clouds, then pasted a small pile of Popsicle sticks into the center of the box and called that a home.

A Bully/Savior Story

In line one day, a boy in front of me turned and rapped his knuckles on my skull. It hurt.

"Hey," I said. I rubbed my head where he had hit me. It felt like a lump was forming.

"Just checking to see if you were ripe," the boy said.

I had seen this boy before—usually stepping on the backs of someone's feet or flicking their earlobes or knocking on their heads. He was a thick, brutish kid with a vestigial mustache and a wide, blank forehead. The most charming thing I had ever seen him do was turn his eyelids inside out, and I could see how a sharpened pencil would be a dangerous thing in the hands of a kid like him. It was probably the reason we still worked primarily in crayon.

"He seems ripe," the big boy said to a smaller boy in front of him. The boy in front laughed unenthusiastically, uncomfortable with being so randomly cast into the role of the bully's cohort. "Yeah. Ripe. Funny," the small kid muttered.

The big kid's joke was an allusion to a recent filmstrip we had seen about shopping for produce. It featured a smiling woman in the market, thumping on cantaloupes and watermelons with great abandon, listening carefully to the sounds they made like she was cracking a safe. After the filmstrip was over, the teacher had passed around a small honeydew melon so we could have a try at it ourselves. But you could tell without even touching the thing that it had passed ripe by a week or two already.

The big kid turned back to me.

"You're ripe," he told me. "You hear me? You're ripe."

"OK. I'm ripe," I said. I didn't know what else to say. What else could I say?

He took offense to this and shoved me on the shoulder, knocking me into another kid, who shoved back—more from instinct than malice, I think—into the big kid.

I was starting to wonder when the Men in White would take notice of all this unsanctioned shoving. They should have been there already, breaking things up and slapping the backs of our heads, but it was Sterling Jones's well formed hand that appeared over my shoulder to save the day. He shoved the big kid back—hitting him squarely in the chest and I could swear, for a moment, that I could hear the hollow thumping that was supposed to tell me when a melon was ripe.

The big kid staggered for balance, the people in line in front of him stepping out of the way as he stumbled backwards, his eyes wide and blinking like a cow's eyes, like the cows Dick and Jane had pet on their trip to the farm.

He clutched at the air for a moment before finally falling. No one tried to catch him. He hit the ground with a reverberating thud.

Sterling stood over him now, like a giant astride a hill—a hill that was breathing heavily and beginning to sob.

"Why don't you pick on someone your own size?" Sterling said as the Men in White finally arrived. Or maybe they had been there the whole time, observing, taking notes. One of them grabbed Sterling by the back of the neck and said: "OK, pretty boy, that's enough unsanctioned physical activity from you for one day I think," then led Sterling down the hallway while three other Men in White gathered around the big kid. They had their wooden batons out and one of them used it to poke the kid, like he was something that might explode or stick to their hands. And at the moment, he did look a little like something that might explode: his cheeks were puffing in and out, his lips were fluttering, his forehead and random patches on his face were turning bright red in the shapes of continents and countries.

"OK, OK," they said. "That's enough of that too. Whatever it is. That's enough."

But none of them stooped to help the big kid up. They nudged him with the ends of their sticks and the points of their shoes and it seemed that they would have preferred to just kick him down the hallway to wherever they wanted to take him.

Eventually he stopped making noises, his face returned to a color something like normal, and he struggled to his feet on his own accord. The Men in White led him and Sterling down the hallway to an elevator while other Men in White herded the rest of us back into a line.

We ate supper. It was an uneventful meal and when I returned to my cell, Sterling was there, sitting on his bunk.

"What did they do?" I asked him and he just said: "The usual. Nothing they haven't done before."

The next day, the big kid came up to me when no one was looking, cornering me between a wall and stairwell while the Men in White were distracted by a kid with a nosebleed at the front of the line.

"Look," he said. "I'm sorry about the way I acted yesterday. I have issues and stuff. 'Cause of the way I was raised and all. That's what they said. It's not my fault. It's the issues."

"Sure," I said.

"I don't really think you're ripe or anything."

"OK," I said.

"You know, like a fruit, I mean."

"OK."

Sterling appeared, as if from nowhere. "Didn't you learn anything yesterday?" Sterling said shoving the kid backwards again. The kid fell. It occurred to me that for a bully, the big kid had an unfortunate lack of balance.

"I did," the big kid said, and already his eyes were thick with tears. "I learned I have issues. That I am lashing out at others 'cause I don't feel good about myself. 'Cause of how I was raised and everything."

"Oh," Sterling said. "Sorry."

The big kid wiped his eyes with the back of a hand and reached forward, but Sterling didn't help him up. I tried, but I was too small and he was too big—the physics of the thing was all wrong. Eventually I knew he would manage it on his own, but it was too painful to watch so I left him there.

He never picked on me or anyone else again. He became older, taller, thinner. He became quiet and awkward. His mustache grew full, and his hairline receded before we finished puberty.

Unsanctioned Activities

At night, I heard Sterling adjusting himself on the mattress above me, flailing his limbs and torso and trying to get comfortable. There were squeaks and groans, an occasional sigh. Once or twice, I think, he punched the pillow.

"Are there really girls?" I asked him, speaking to the underside of his mattress as it swelled and receded above me in the darkness. The mattress stopped moving.

"Are there really girls?" It was not hard to hear the incredulousness in his voice. "Is that what you're asking me? Are there really girls?"

"Up there, I mean." I had seen pictures in old biology books. I had read things; even Dick had his Jane. Girls existed, but what did I know of the reality several floors above? "Sure," said Sterling's disembodied voice. "Of course they are. Where else would they keep them?"

I thought about this for a while as his breathing became deep and steady. Where else would they keep them?

At lunch the next day he mentioned the girls again, with a reverent tone and an inadvertent glance upwards, as if he could actually see the pretty bottoms of their feet walking above us.

"Girls smell better than we do," Sterling said. "And they have smoother skin."

I didn't want to be smacked on the head but I had to ask: "How do you know?" Sterling's own skin looked smooth enough—it was hard to imagine smoother.

He leaned toward me. "They're smarter too," he said. "Not at everything, but some things. We're better at math. Which is something. Math is important. But it's not everything."

A Man in White smacked him in the back of his head.

"If you're talking, you're not chewing," the Man in White said.

Sterling said: "Maybe I was talking with my mouth full."

The Man in White stopped in his tracks, turned slowly back. Everyone else in the room went still—forks frozen halfway to mouths, mouths full but not chewing. Nothing like this had happened since the boy who had failed to produce death rays from his eyes. The Man in White leaned down close to Sterling's face. I could see the individual dots of hair where he had haphazardly shaved in the morning. There was small Band-Aid on his chin, where I imagined he had cut himself. The Band-Aid had tiny flowers and butterflies on it. The man said quietly to Sterling: "What did you say, Jones? I didn't quite catch it. Would you care to repeat?"

Sterling swallowed. "I was just saying it's possible I was chewing and talking both. I could have been talking with my mouth full. That's all."

"Yeah," the man said. "That's a good point, Jones. Maybe that's true." The Man in White straightened up, ruffled Sterling's hair with the palm of his enormous hand. "But maybe you shouldn't be doing that so much either, kid."

The gesture did not seem particularly vicious at all, but something in Sterling's face hardened. He swung his head around and stared at the man in a way that looked lethal or, at very least, unhealthy.

Even the Man in White seemed a little stunned by it, taking a small step back to consider the matter. "Yes?" he said. "Is there something else, Jones?"

Sterling's face softened suddenly, as if a button had been pressed or released. He smiled and returned to his meal as if nothing had happened at all. The Man in White stood there for another moment, not knowing what to make of it. He glanced at a few of his colleagues in the corner. They shrugged back at him.

I turned back to my own meal, ate the rest of it quickly without looking up, without saying anything, without even tasting a bite.

At night, in our bunks, Sterling said: "It's hard to believe an ape like that could go home to a nice soft wife at night."

"Do you think he does?"

"They all do."

I thought about it for a moment but could not convince myself it was true.

"Anyway," I said. "I knew an ape once who was very nice."

He leaned over his bed so his face appeared upside down above me in the darkness.

"I wasn't talking about real apes, doofus."

Sterling's inverted face withdrew, returning to his pillow, to his tossing and turning, to his struggle for the comfort of dreams.

I closed my own eyes, tried to sleep, but could not shake the image of the Man in White returning from a hard day at the Home for Failed Experiments, hanging his wooden stick on a hook by the front door, kissing his wife, messing up the hair of his little boy with the palm of a hand the size of a slab of meat.

It was a few days later that Sterling began his tunnel. His digging woke me in the morning. The light of day had already clicked on, but sometimes I could close my eyes tight enough to keep it out for awhile longer before they collected us for breakfast. Not this morning. Sterling's legs were sticking out from under my bed. There was a scraping sound and when I asked him what he was doing, he squirmed out from underneath and sat next to me, smiling. His face was sprinkled with bits of dust and rock. There was a small scrape on his forehead. His skin did not look so smooth today.

"I'm digging a tunnel," he said. He showed me the plastic spoon he had been using, explaining how he had strengthened it through some homemade alchemy involving toothpaste, dirt, periwinkle crayons, processed cheese and a mysterious fifth ingredient he would not name.

"The formula came to me in a dream," he said. "And it works. What do you think of that?"

I looked under my bed. There were tiny bits of stone on the floor and more dust than usual around it. The wall itself looked as if a small animal had been scratching at it in one place, trying to get out.

"I dream about girls sometimes," I told him. "And apes."

"You should try dreaming about formulas some time. It comes in handy. But girls are good. All my dreams are about girls sooner or later."

The cell door opened, accompanied by the sound of all the other cell doors on our floor opening simultaneously. Sterling brushed himself off.

A whistle was blown and a man's voice shouted: "Breakfast time!" And then the sound of a hundred slipper-socked boys shuffling sleepily out onto the walkway.

We ate our breakfast. We were returned.

Digging

While I tried to sleep, Sterling grunted and bumped beneath me, his elbows poking against the mattress on the upswing.

"You want the bottom bunk now?" I asked. I could see how this activity might get old fast.

"No thanks," he said from beneath my bed.

I closed my eyes, tried to ignore the activity taking place beneath me, but it was impossible, of course. And it seemed what he was doing was an impossible task as well. The stone walls were old, but they were still made of stone. The plastic spoon may have sharpened and fortified by magic, but it was still a plastic spoon. After he had been at it for at least an hour he emerged sweaty, smudged and holding a handful of gray dust like it was a pile of gold in his hands. He smiled proudly.

"Only a matter of time," he said

"A lot of time," I said.

"Which we have plenty of, right?"

"I guess."

"Don't you want to see where they keep the girls, John? Isn't that worth a little effort?"

"I guess."

"And it's not even your effort. It's my effort. You're just watching."

"But it'll still take forever to get through that wall with a spoon."

"It won't take forever," he said. "Nothing takes forever. I don't think you fully grasp the concept of forever, John."

"A long time, then."

"Which we have plenty of. The girls will be worth it. Trust me."

And a long time did pass. Meals and classes. I offered again and again to take the top bunk, but Sterling seemed to like having someone to talk to or jostle while he was whittling away at the wall with his spoon. Usually he said something like: "Sooner or later," and "Only a matter of time," or if he had bent a thumbnail back while digging, "Shit," which was a word he had learned from one of the Men in White.

He went through several spoons. We grew older. We went to our lunches and field trips, sat in dark classrooms learning and relearning our alphabet, words, numbers. Sterling usually sat next to or behind me and when the Men in White were not looking, he would talk in a hushed and excited voice about the wonderland he imagined on the other side of the wall. After supper, we would return to our cell and he would return to work.

Every evening he crawled out from under the bed with a handful of gray dirt and sometimes a broken spoon. He always smiled and I learned to nod and smile too, so he would not think me a naysayer, discouraging him from his noble purpose. I even offered to dig for a while but he never let me and I did not press the issue. I didn't really want to dig for a while. It looked to me like a lot of work.

And anyway, what would be on the other side? Another wall? Another cell?

The Mediocre Escape

And one day, Sterling actually got through the wall, emerging from under my bed not with his usual handful of dirt, but instead a whole square stone that he had to drag across the floor with both hands.

"It came loose," he said, grinning broadly. His hair was gray from the particles of stone and cement.

"Wow," I said. What else could I say?

We heard someone pass by on the walkway outside of our cell and froze. The footsteps came and went.

"I better hide this," Sterling said, and pushed the stone back under the bed, but off to the side. I sat on the floor next to Sterling, looked under the bed at the black rectangular opening he had made in the wall. No light, no sign of anything on the other side. It could have been a portal to hell or a laundry chute for all I could tell.

"I bet we can make it through," he said

I looked at the hole again. I knew I could probably work my way through it, but Sterling, with his noticeably broader shoulders, was a more questionable fit.

"Where does it go?" I asked him.

"Who knows? Let's find out. Out of here, anyway, right? Out of here and maybe up. Maybe we'll see where they keep the girls."

"I don't know," I said.

"What don't you know?"

"I don't know."

"That's no reason not to try something."

"It isn't?" It seemed to me like the best reason not to try something, but he was already squirming under the bed, grunting, scuffling, scrambling, trying to force his better-made self into the opening he had made. He was doomed to failure of course and eventually conceded to the laws of physics. He pulled himself out, his face red and dusty. "I can't fit," he said. "You'll have to go without me."

I looked at him. I had not even decided that I was going with him; going without him seemed entirely out of the question, but he put his hand on my shoulder, ruffled my hair, smiled and said my name softly.

"OK," I said.

"You'll do it?"

"OK."

"Thatta boy!"

I shimmied under the bed, squeezed through the hole with little difficulty and felt the cold cement floor on the other side, smelled dust, dampness, mold, but saw nothing. A dull shaft of light emitted from the hole behind me, but that was it.

"It's dark," I called back to Sterling. "I can't see anything."

"See where it leads."

"I can't see anything," I told him again. "It doesn't lead anywhere." I felt like crying, turning back, or both. If this was an escape, I was not ready to leave. If it was a violation of rules—and it had to be—I was not ready to be punished. Sterling's hand reached through the hole, holding out a cigarette lighter.

"Take this. Tell me what you see. See how far it goes. Just go a little way. I'll stand guard."

"Where'd you get a lighter?" I asked, but he ignored me, and really, it hardly seemed the point.

By the small flame, I could see it was a passageway of some sort before me, about three feet wide and infinitely long. It was tall enough for a grown man to stand in, and being considerably less than a grown man, I stood up and took a few tentative steps forward. The floor did not give way, the walls did not grow spikes and close around me. About ten feet ahead of me I could see steps going up.

"There are steps going up," I half-whispered, half-shouted to the small rectangle of light behind me.

"Go up them!" the rectangle called back.

I went up them.

How far up? Should it be measured in feet, footsteps or minutes? Up is all I knew, up into the darkness with only the tiny, disposable lighter clearing a small spot through the gloom. Behind me, the dim rectangle of my latest home disappeared and I was alone. Though Sterling still called out periodically to see where I was, his voice grew more distant and less frequent until it was gone completely. I did not turn back. I kept going, until the narrow stairway ended and I was plunging down another black hallway and then up another flight of steps. Picture my little face, lit by the cigarette lighter, golden and disembodied like the winged heads of a particularly disturbing brand of cherubs I have seen since in museums, books and churches. A frightened cherub ascending.

The steps ended. Another hallway. The lighter became hot in my hands. I let the flame die and stood unmoving in the darkness for a moment, waiting for it to cool. The darkness seemed complete, but after a while I began to see things in it—black shapes against something slightly less than black. Were there doorways up ahead? Other hallways? Ghosts or monsters?

The lighter cooled. A flick of the thumb, a spark, and my way was lit again. The shapes were pipes descending from an unseen and unpromising heaven and ending in a dimly lit floor.

Another stairway, steeper and narrower than the last. I went up again. Up and up. Was it a slightly fresher breeze I felt upon my face? The smell of something beyond this world of rust, stone dust and mildew? Was the dim glow ahead something like sunlight? Up and up. Up and up. Up and up. My legs grew tired and the dim light grew brighter. Above me, a black circle rimmed with gold and I was reminded of pictures of the solar eclipse I had seen in my infancy, in the obsolete textbooks I learned from and chewed on in the secret island facility those many years ago. How many years ago? I no longer knew. "Circle," I might have said to a guard or nurse or scientist of those distant days. Or, not being an overly bright child, perhaps: "Square," or "Triangle" or "Pretty Bird."

"Solar eclipse, kid," the guard or nurse or scientist might have said back.

And now I was there. I could reach out and touch it. It hung no more than a foot or two above me. It was damp and felt like cold, rough steel. It gave slightly as I pushed on it with both hands. I pushed harder. My arms were young and thin, I was feeble but perhaps, at that moment, I was given some superhuman strength, perhaps my fathers had foreseen such a need and had tucked within my joints and muscles some extra reserve of strength. The metal hatchway gave, swinging open on creaking hinges. Sunlight and air rushed in.

I pulled myself up through the hole and crawled out onto a field of green beneath a blue sky and a yellow sun. A black bird flew by overhead. I lay there on my back, rubbing my eyes in the brightness, breathing fresh air, smelling life around me. Life smelled like mud and flowers. Mud and flowers smelled like I had always imagined. I lay there for a long time, nearly falling asleep from comfort and happiness. The grass bristled against the back of my neck like coarse fur and I felt safe and content again at last, as if held in the mothering arms of the entire world.

I forgot about Sterling, about the Men in White, Mr. Grindlier and the hole I had left. Time did not exist for those few moments—I lived and died a happy lifetime right there in the grass, while birds were singing in the trees and the sun was pressed like a mother's hand against my face.

Then they came running over a hill. Two wide brim hats. I could see their steel blue eyes, even from here. I sat up, squinted. Forest rangers, I thought. I had seen pictures; Dick and Jane once visited a park. The two men wore olive green uniforms and each had a walking stick that they moved up and down in the air like batons as they ran toward me As they grew closer, I could see their cheeks puffing rhythmically in and out like pink bellows, matching the pumping of their legs, their arms, each other's legs and arms.

But why were they running toward me? Was I sitting on some rare wild orchid or endangered spotted snipe? I prepared to apologize and throw myself upon their woodsy mercies. I would very much like to be raised in cabins now, I thought, or in tents or lean-twos by these two manly men, far from the pale faces and damp dust I had left behind. Feed me meals of nuts and berries. We will eat them by firelight, at rough-hewn wooden tables, as we laugh boisterously at some earthy joke involving a funny, industrious squirrel and a difficult nut.

But closer now and I could see the small blue sparks emitting from their faux-wooden walking sticks. They held the tips toward me as they ran and the sparks leapt out and I was enveloped in a sudden, blackening pain.

Temporary Confinement

They shocked me with the points of their walking sticks, dragged me through grass and mud, into secret elevators, down steps and hallways. They locked me in a closet and stood outside the door while I sobbed. I could hear them shifting on the balls of their feet, leaning against things, checking their watches.

"How long do we have to wait here?" one asked the other.

"As long as it takes," the other one answered.

It took a while.

I sat in the darkness of the closet, crying until I couldn't cry anymore, until I couldn't even remember why I was crying. I was in a dark closet, but so what? I had been dragged through grass and mud but I had been dragged through worse. Even being shocked with sticks was not a particularly new experience.

I closed my eyes and tried to sleep, but there was something sticking into the small of my back. A shoe. I moved it aside but that did not really make me comfortable. The wall was hard. The floor was hard. I missed the grass, blue sky, sun, birds, flowers. I had known them for all of maybe five minutes, but it was the first five minutes in a long time that had seemed like something more than just another five minutes.

Sitting in the closet, I felt surrounded and buried in all the other gray and sunless minutes of my short life gathered there from the past to suffocate me now.

How long was I in there, in the dark, with the smell of shoes, mothballs, woolen coats, and mildewed umbrellas around me? More than five minutes. More than ten. More than a hundred.

"Jesus," I heard one of them outside say. "Do they think we've got all day?"

"This is getting a little unreasonable," the other one said.

I curled into a ball and sniffed at the knees of my pants. I had brought the smell of grass and mud back with me. At least that was something.

Two Men in White finally arrived and I was dragged from the closet to a series of small rooms: a holding cell, a debriefing room, a discipline room, a punishing room. I was asked questions I did not understand by faces I could not quite see—large fleshy discs that hovered vaguely over me like flying saucers emitting a warm and sour exhaust.

Tempest

"You didn't happen to bring my lighter back," Sterling asked. I had been in our cell for a few days by now, mostly sleeping or trying to sleep. I was still sore and in no mood for talking. I had wine-colored welts along my back and side, and my liver and spleen hurt, or at least those nebulous parts inside of me that I imagined to be my liver and spleen. I had not managed to bring his lighter back.

The stone had been cemented back into the wall, and the bunk had been moved to the other side of the room—for security reasons. I was in the top bunk now. Sterling insisted on it. I think he was trying to make amends.

"Do you have any idea where it might be? My lighter?" he asked.

I grunted and turned over, looking at the new wall my bed was now up against. It looked very much like the old wall.

"You have no idea what I went through to get that cigarette lighter," Sterling said.

He was right—I had no idea what he had gone through. And certainly a cigarette lighter would be a difficult thing to acquire. Maybe he had stolen it from one of the Men in White or had done some extra chore for them—something horrible and unpleasant that they would not want to do for themselves. At least Sterling had given me a few days to recover before asking me about it. But I didn't have it—it was in dust or grass now, being destroyed by the elements.

"So what was it like?" he asked when he had finally given up on the topic of his missing lighter. "What did you see? Girls? The girls' shower? Does it lead to the girls' shower? Could you see into the girls' shower?"

Do the girls have showers, I wondered vaguely. Of course, they did; *we* did. But were there even girls? I had seen none. I have seen only hallways, stairways, sunshine and sparks before being dragged back down, back below ground, back home sweet cell #23.

"You did see the girls' shower, didn't you, you lucky bastard," he said, punching me in the shoulder before finally climbing up into his own bunk. I winced, then I slept. Fitfully. The pain of my capture and interrogation was still there, but exhaustion won and I was finally able to will away the brightness of the overhead bulb—my own personal sun—and draw dark curtains across it. Thick theater curtains. Eyelids. The vapors of a dream. I dreamt.

Green hills and blue skies and in the distance a city, a vague and promising city, shrouded in the fog of myth and industry. My future waits there. It waits presently…patiently…sings a soft song to me, calling me toward it. Over green hills, under blue skies. I should move like a ghost, a black bird, a shadow. Float toward it like a spirit. It is the gentle soothing voice of a mother who pats the fevered brow of her much-loved son with a damp cloth. Pat pat against the fevered freckled brow.

Mommy, mommy, asks the boy in chirping voice. Chirping like a bird this little boy blue. Do the girls have showers too? Like we do?

Of course they do, Johnny. Little John. John-John, Jack and Jon. They have showers the same as you and your friends. Why wouldn't they? Doesn't everybody need to keep clean? Isn't cleanliness next to something or other?

I suppose so. But I've never seen them. I've never seen the girls at all.

The girls exist too.

They do?

Of course. Otherwise, why shower? Otherwise why keep clean? Why bother?

The pretty mom tucked the boy beneath his quilted comforter. She turned the edges over neatly at the top, ruffled his feathery hair, kissed his cheek, each action as if it were part of a recipe. How to Tuck in a Boy. Preparing Casserole of Well Rested Son. Tuck, ruffle, stir, then bake. Bake to a golden brown in a large aquarium or casserole dish. Check with a fork or small pointed stick.

The mother was pretty, but her hands were unusually large, with several dark, coarse hairs rising from the knobby peaks of her knuckles. The nails were black and jagged. Her thumb was long, nearly reaching to the end of her forefinger.

The freckled, feathered boy smiled from out of his drowsy comfort. Smiled dreamily, with two dimples. The mother clicked off the sun and closed the door softly as she left. In the kitchen her husband, one of the boy's fathers, sat drinking a smoking gin and tonic from a beaker. He asked: "How's the wee one?"

"An angel, as ever," she said, sitting down across from him at the table.

"My little man," the father said proudly, wiping a tear from behind one thick lens of his black-rimmed glasses. "My little man," he said, adjusting the microscope. On the slide, lit by the reflected light of the small mirror beneath it, he observed the cells darting about within the drop of his tear, the wet feet slapping against the tile floor, the smell of soap, steam and water pouring down. Musky smells even after lathering, rinsing, repeating. Prancing about with their mysterious and enviable parts dangling. One-eyed monsters pierced out of the fog like steamships, like freighters, like aircraft carriers, like gunner boats. Grey towels snapping—loose lines in a stormy wind. Sea storm. Loose ropes on deck whipping about. Sailors lose their eyes. One eyed-sailors staggering out of the fog.

Prometheus Remembered

L et us say that the days passed quickly from there, flipping by like a stack of pictures snapping by to show the illusion of movement. The picture of a boy growing into a young man. Let us say that all my bruises healed, and rough hair began to grow in patches on those mysterious parts of my body. All our voices broke and deepened. We were young men now—or nearly so.

The Men in White seldom came into the classrooms anymore. They patrolled the hallways and walkways, periodically checking the cells for signs of suspicious activities. Sometimes they would pick one of us at random from a line, frisk him, or bring him to another room for questioning and examination.

Sterling was hauled away with greater frequency than anyone else. I asked him why. "I guess I just have that sort of face," he said.

"What sort of face is that?"

"Guilty...pretty...I don't know. You tell me. What kind of face is it?"

"It's a good face," I said.

"Yes, I've been told that," he said. "But thank you."

"Do you do something to them? Do you say something that they keep picking on you like that?"

Sterling said: "Just what they want."

Every other day was shower day and on shower days, I often thought about the girls—the mythical girls that Sterling still liked to talk about in quiet moments. He had many theories about their location and composition, and about the logistics that must have been involved in keeping them from us for so long. One of his theories had them showering on the even days while we showered on the odds. Maybe they used the very same showers, he said, and were brought down quietly while we slept or ate, were in class or visiting the zoo. Maybe they giggled and spoke in singsong voices, used slender pink soaps that smelled of flowers. And when they were gone, the Men in White would move in with hoses and squeegees to remove all signs of them.

"It's a theory, anyway," Sterling said.

The cell door opened and Sterling and I took our place in line. Gray towels were handed out along with small gray bars of soap. A whistle blew and we all marched forward down the hall. No one had ever asked us to march. It just, somehow, over the years, seemed like the thing to do. It was probably the whistle that made us think so.

"Do you remember when you lost my lighter?" Sterling asked while we stood in line and the Men in White counted our heads. "Remember when we were kids and you decided to go poking through a hole in the wall and took my lighter with you and then came back without it?"

"I remember it a little differently," I said.

"You would. It wasn't your lighter."

We took our showers. I avoided looking anyone in the eye.

Zoo Story

Sterling and I were cleaning out the zoo. It was a punishment, but what was our sin? We had discovered an unlocked stairwell and had gone up three flights past our authorized area. No one had ever told us what our authorized area was, but we knew we were past it the moment we started.

Finding the unlocked door had just been a happy accident, (though admittedly a less happy one now), and we had traveled several levels without resistance, expecting at any moment for someone to notice until so many moments passed without anyone noticing at all that we began to hope it would go on like that forever. I began to smell, or imagined that I smelled, dirt and fresh air and sunlight. Sterling thought he could hear the laughter of girls in the distance, like the breaking of small, glass things.

But in the end, we only found dust and cigarette butts. Sterling wanted to try one of the cigarette butts, but we didn't have a lighter. He blamed me for this, of course, and we had been arguing when one of the Men in White heard us, pulled us out of the stairwell and brought us down to Mr. Grindlier.

We had to wait in the lobby to his office for half an hour while he was shouting at someone on the phone behind his pebbled glass door. Something to do with the electric bill or water bill or heat bill. Something necessary and expensive like that. We had heard him shout this before too—for an underground facility the place was surprisingly drafty.

We were missing classes, which neither Sterling nor I minded too much. All we had missed so far was Algebra and Outside Prep classes. Algebra gave me a headache and Outside Prep was mostly just some teacher or Man in White droning on about the accepted practices, traditions and fashions of current society. Sometimes they showed pictures, sometimes a filmstrip or a movie. The filmstrips and movies usually featured someone named John or

Johnny—depending on his age—as he went about his daily routine of having breakfast with his family, driving to work or taking the bus to school, raising his hand to be called on by the teacher or the chairman of the board. They had titles like: *My First Bus Ride* or *Punctuality and You* or *Wash Your Hands!* The stories in the filmstrips were usually told in brightly colored drawings. Everyone had round or square faces that showed either enthusiasm or thoughtfulness. *John takes the bus to his office downtown. He pays the driver his fare and always says thank you.* And then the machine would beep and the frame would be advanced.

When it was a movie, the faces were real, but the color was faded and the surface scratched and jumpy. The people and atmosphere seemed of a different world, a yellow and green planet with a bright and bleaching sun. The voices were muffled and warbled, as if coming from somewhere under water. Sometimes the film would stick and melt against the projector bulb or it would break completely and the loose end would flap rhythmically on one reel while the other reel spilled its contents onto the floor until the teacher woke up and scrambled to fix it.

The idea behind these presentations—and the class itself—was not to make us long for what we did not have, but to teach us the culture and habits of the species we were a part of and to prepare us for our inevitable release back into the wild. We would have to fit in and it would not be in our best interest to bore, confuse or alienate others with stories of our strange creation and nurture.

If we had been missing Biology instead, Sterling would have been more upset—they were just getting to the part about ovaries.

My favorite class was Popular Communications, but that was only on every other Thursday. It had replaced Language. We already knew how to read and write; now we had to learn the finer points of understanding a TV schedule, the relevance and impact of the ratings system, and the development and evolution of the sitcom. We did not have TVs in our rooms, but every other week Mr. Melvin wheeled in an enormous set and showed us tapes of things that we would presumably know if we had been raised in a normal living room with a normal mom and dad fighting over the remote.

Some of the shows were funny enough, though it was sometimes hard not to recognize familiar patterns emerging. There was always the strange, comical neighbor who borrowed things and raided the fridge. There was always the husband's doomed schemes, the wife's thwarted ambitions, the friend of questionable morality. There were misunderstandings of fidelity, sexuality and motives. There were family vacations to Hawaii where the family luggage is mixed-up with the suitcase of a bungling pair of secret agents.

In the Administrator's lobby, Sterling and I waited patiently on a brown leather couch. The couch was ancient and brittle and crackled beneath us. There was a coffee table full of old magazines and pamphlets, all of the same theme: *try harder, get along, take pride in yourself and your part in the system, you are special, but not as special as all that so don't go getting a big head about it.*

Mr. Grindlier hung up the phone—we could actually hear him hang it up—and we were ushered in. We took our place across from him at his large and cluttered desk.

"Hello boys," he said. "Doing a little exploring were we?" He smiled. He was trying to be friendly, sympathetic, understanding in the ways and needs of young men, but the smile ruined this. His lips were cracked and bloodless and his coffee stained teeth worn nearly transparent at the edges. His mouth seemed much older than himself—worn, beaten and eaten away by time, even the warm breath it exuded smelled like decay. How does a guy get a mouth older than his face? Was it transplanted? Taken from the face of some elder unfortunate and applied—lips, tongue teeth and all—seamlessly to his own? I had heard of weirder science.

"So boys will be boys, I guess, eh?" he said, cocking an eyebrow and letting his mouth settle into a more natural expression. "But you're not really boys anymore, are you? You're practically young men now."

Neither Sterling or I said anything.

"No," Mr. Grindlier said. "You're not little boys anymore. We expect more of you now. And you should expect more of yourself. You want to explore? Explore a book. Explore the mind. Explore your classes. Explore Algebra, Business, Chemistry, History, Outside Prep, Biology." He paused, turned a page over on his desk, as if considering something—though it seemed a page turned at random. His desk was strewn with papers and none of them seemed to be about us.

"Maybe not so much Biology," he said.

Sterling and I continued to look at him without saying anything. It was not our first visit to his office and we knew by now how little was expected of us.

"And don't go crazy with the chemistry either," he said.

"I like Popular Communications," I told him and Sterling shot me a look of annoyance, as if I had just added half an hour onto the conversation—which, in fact, I might have.

"That's good. Popular Communications is good. Kind of a fan myself. Popularly communicating. Anyway, my point is, there's no reason for you two to be wandering around in stairwells, or poking anymore holes in the walls. Before you know it, you'll have your fill of the outside world, believe me. For now, study the outside world from in here. Where it's safe. Your time in the sun will come. Literally. About the sun, I mean. You get that? Is any of this getting through to you two?"

We both nodded.

"Well, there you go. I'm glad we had this little talk. You think you've learned your lesson this time?"

We both nodded.

He looked at me then—just me. He knew my record—that was what his look meant. He had not forgotten. I nodded again—just me this time, so he knew that I understood.

Then to both of us: "And you won't do it again?"

We both shook our heads.

"Now what should we do about punishment? I think some punishment is in order here, despite your sincere repentance, don't you boys? Some task to fix this moment into your minds, right?"

He stared at us. We stared back for a moment because these

questions did not seem to be the kind that required a response from us. After an uncomfortable silence and some reconsideration on our part, we nodded.

"Very good," he said. "Very good. Now let me see…"

Cleaning the zoo mostly entailed transferring the animals from their cages into shoeboxes, emptying the cages of their accumulation of neatly compacted fecal matter and soiled wood chips, and then cleaning and refilling the cages with clean wood chips. A few of the larger cages—the guinea pigs, the chinchillas—needed to have their floors scrubbed, and in a sudden burst of enthusiasm for the task, I decided to clean their running wheels as well.

"They're not really that dirty," Sterling pointed out, but I polished the chrome with spit and a paper towel anyway. I thought it would make the animals happy. I thought it would make the confusion of their temporary transfer to cardboard boxes seem worth it to them in the end. *Look*, I could imagine them thinking in their rodent-like way, *something is better, shinier, cleaner. It was all worth it.* I know I would have wanted it that way if someone had pulled me from a cage only to put me back in the same cage a little while later.

"Their poop looks just like their food," Sterling said. "You ever notice that?" He was, at that moment, dumping the last of the discards into a large plastic garbage can. And it was true. Their shit did not even smell. Their pee was another matter, of course.

"They're highly efficient animals," I said.

"I bet we could just put their poop in their food dish and they wouldn't even notice the difference. We could feed them their own poop, and they would poop it and we would feed it to them again. Think of the money that would save. Grindlier'd love that."

Sterling currently liked the word poop. He knew how to say shit, but preferred poop, particularly in regards to the waste of small animals.

"They probably like the taste of their food," I said. "It probably doesn't taste the same as their poop."

"Really? Why don't you try some then?" He held out a small,

dark pellet. I could not even tell which it is.

"That's shit," I said.

"Same difference," he said and tossed it over his shoulder.

When we had cleaned the cages and replaced the wood chips (and I had kidded myself into thinking the running wheels were cleaner looking than when I had started), we began transferring the animals back from their boxes. But one box was empty.

"This box is empty," I told Sterling. He shrugged. He was holding a white rat by its tail, dangling it over the opening of its cage. Normally I would have told him not to do that, that the rat probably didn't like it, and he would argue that rats don't have feelings one way or the other, and at least not in their tails and anyway that that was how the father rats would carry them around in the wild. But I didn't tell him not to hold the rat by its tail this time because I was holding an empty shoebox in my hand and it worried me some.

I looked around at the floor, checked under my feet, the soles of my shoes. Sterling laughed at this. "I think you'd know if you'd stepped on it," he said. "I think it would have made a sound."

"Help me find it. It has to be around here somewhere."

"A popping sound, I'm guessing," he said. "Maybe a little squishier. And crunchier. And, I mean, there are bones involved."

"It has to be around here somewhere."

"Sure it does. It's probably one of the mice, so it's not like he could just crawl away into a mouse hole or something. Oh...wait a second..."

I almost hated Sterling at that moment. He no longer seemed the golden, well-made man/boy. His handsome mouth seemed cruel, his clear eyes indifferent.

"Which cage was it?" I asked him. "*Was* it a mouse?"

He looked around at the cages, at the boxes he had not transferred over yet.

"Actually, I think it was a hamster. Which is not much different, I guess."

"Crap...help me find it."

"I'm looking," he said, not really looking. He nudged the pile of empty boxes with the tip of his shoe.

"You should be more careful," he told me.

"Help me find it."

"If we had a snake, we could let the snake find it. Snakes eat rodents. This zoo needs a snake."

"Help me find it."

Eventually he helped a little. We looked everywhere, under boxes and tables, in all the dark and hidden corners of the room, but the walls of the room were old with countless spaces between molding and floor, between stone and stone, where a small animal could enter. In the end we had to give up. Sterling made a pile of wood chips in the empty cage and we hoped that it will fool them—make them think that there was something sleeping in there.

At night, in the darkness of our cell, Sterling asked: "Where do you think they get those animals, anyway. Are they from a pet store, you think? Or a lab like us?"

"I don't know."

"Maybe they catch them in the basement."

"What basement?"

"Pick a floor. This place is nothing but basement."

"They wouldn't find hamsters in the basement."

"Why not?"

"Because hamsters don't come from basements. Or gerbils or guinea pigs either. They come from pet stores. Maybe rats come from basements, but not white rats, I don't think."

"I came from a basement," Sterling said. "People don't come from basements, but I came from a basement."

"How did you come from a basement?"

"My dad's lab was in a basement."

But I was thinking about the hamster—I was pretty sure now that it was the hamster—and was hoping he had found a way out of here. I went to sleep imagining him lying in soft grass, a bright sun warming his little hamster face and making him sneeze.

A Hard World for Little Things

Morning clicked on. While making my bed, I found a small, dark pellet in the sheets. I held it carefully between two fingers and sniffed, but it did not smell of anything. It could have been shit or food or a piece of plastic.

I hung my head over the side of my bunk and looked at Sterling. He was finishing up his own bed, tucking in the corners, fluffing the pillow. Sterling was fond of playing small pranks—hiding one of my slipper socks, tripping me in hallways, dropping bits of dirt into my food—but maybe he was innocent this time. He showed none of his usual signs of amused guilt: the avoided glance, the artificial look of complete absorption in some small task, the whistling of some chirpy, non-existent tune.

He looked at me staring at him with my inverted face.

"You look funny," he said.

"Did you do something?" I asked. I could feel the blood filling up my brain.

"What?" he asked.

"Nothing. Never mind."

The day went by without further event, though Sterling and I expected it at every moment, a sudden siren that would declare the mysterious decrease in the zoo population by one. How long could a pile of wood chips shaped like a sleeping hamster really fool them? Indefinitely, it turned out; in a loveless world, it would seem, an empty cage was as good as a pet.

In Outside Prep we learned about tax forms, the right to vote, and the institution of marriage. We saw a movie where rice was thrown at a happy couple in white and black and tin cans were dragged behind their car as it drove away framed by the shrinking outline of a heart.

In Algebra, we learned something about how many Xs meant how many Ys if Q equaled something or other.

In Health, they postponed explaining the location and purpose of ovaries to us again and instead showed a movie about the wisdom of washing your hands before a meal.

And then it was bedtime again, the ceiling above me like a blank screen clicking into darkness. I stared up at it, waited to see what image might appear, then heard a soft tapping—like tiny feet clad in hard shoes—inside the ceiling. Then a scraping sound, an awkward scrambling descent down the space between the walls, and a small thud at the bottom. I peered over the edge of my mattress at the floor in the darkness, like the bottom of an ocean. Could I see anything? Did a small white object emerge from the corner? Did it dart into the center of the room and then hesitate? I climbed from my bunk as quietly as possible, taking great care not to squeak or to step on the face of my roommate. I crawled slowly on all fours to the center of the room. The white object did not move, or moved imperceptibly, and I wondered if it was not just some discarded sock or jockstrap. Sterling could be a thoughtless and slovenly roommate.

But with my face close now, I could see its shining eyes, its pale fur and whiskers, its pink mouth, like a blurred shadow on its ghostly rodent face. I could smell its breath, which came in quick nervous pants. Vaguely sweet, like dirt. I whispered to it comfortingly. Good girl, I said, though who can really tell the gender of a hamster, especially in the dark. She did not run away. Perhaps she remembered my scent, perhaps she remembered the care I took in cleaning her cage, in making even the spokes of her wheel shine. I laid my hand out palm up in front of her and she stepped tentatively onto it. Good girl. I named her Abigail and took her back with me to bed, where she slept in the crook of my arm until morning.

Assembly Line

"I myself come from a long line of artificial ancestors," Sterling told me one day, after that day had clicked off and we laid staring up into our respective nights. "My father invented his father, and his father invented his father before that."

I grunted. Though it was a topic that usually excited me, I was tired from a long day of peeling potatoes and mopping floors. We were older now and with age came menial labor.

"In a lab, I mean," he elaborated. "Neither one of them had navels, which is always pretty much a give away, isn't it?"

"I have a navel," I said, checking, though I already knew it was there. I had seen it before; I had played with it and contemplated it.

"Maybe you had a plastic tube or something connected there. It would leave the same mark, I think."

"Maybe."

"Anyway, having one doesn't mean that you aren't. I just mean, not having one is a pretty good sign that you are."

"Uh-huh." I closed my eyes.

"I have one, but it was just added for appearance sake. It's not a real navel."

"Uh-huh."

"On my Mother's side, her great-great-great grandfather invented the Mayflower..."

He continued to talk and his story became the dream I dreamt. I see it projected onto the flesh screens of my eyelids, divorced of his words, his voice, it is the image of a water-spotted black night, a dark sky above a stormy sea. Ship sails made of lab coats unfurled, the ship rising and falling on mountainous waves. Lantern-jawed captains standing at helms, sprayed damp by the sea. Through storm and mist the shore of a Promised Land emerges, seen through the rain-speckled lens of a telescope: a circle of vague and mottled movement against a field of black. Are these trees swaying along the shores of Plymouth Rock, storm clouds moving in or out, or cells darting back and forth, meeting, merging, dividing? It could be Sterling's Greatest Grandfather forming his first pseudo-pod, stepping upon the stage of a microscope slide to do his little dance, his shy shuffle before an adoring panel of fathers and the reserved but enthusiastic applause from the students in the gallery.

My esteemed colleagues, the distinguished scientist begins, pausing to stroke his Vandyke in a thoughtful and personable way. From these elements…these elemental ingredients, these tiny bricks, this bricker-brack of pre-life, we have made, you see here with your own eyes, life. And from here, from here on out, for here to eternity, we have become Eternals.

Less reserved applause now: it comes like thunder and waves. The students in the gallery rise to their feet. They too, good grades permitting, have been promoted to gods. Sterling's greatest grandfather is among them—the top of his class. He is chosen, thanks to a glowing letter of recommendation from his professor, to be the protégé of the distinguished scientist. He will clean his test tubes, bring his coffee and watch silently over his shoulder as he scratches out his latest brilliant equation, theory or formula on the blackboard. He will run to the store for more sulfur or borrow a cup of sodium trichloride from the lab next door. He will clean the blackboard. He will observe and learn and build upon the work of his mentor, making his own recipe for primordial soup, bubbling his broth in his own test tubes, create his own son, in his own image, from the clippings of his own fingernails and a lock of his own thinning hair.

The boy is conceived in a beaker, grown in a dish, coddled in a cradle of goo. He coos then caws then forms a hand. He forms a fist. He moves, he crawls, he walks, he lives. But he lives too quickly. He is a difficult toddler within the first week. He is a rebellious teenager within three years, terrorizing the other scientists with prank phone calls, leaving the tops off of important experiments, borrowing the car without asking. He stays out till all hours with the dean's favorite daughter.

"You are so fascinating," she says, batting long eyelashes like the wings of the rare butterflies that are pinned to a green mat in the biology lab.

He shrugs. "I suppose."

"What's it like?" She moves closer. She lays her head on his shoulder and looks up lovingly, ignoring the one or two nose hairs she can see from this angle. "What's it like to be...what you are?"

"I don't know." He turns on the radio, but does not turn it up loud enough to drown out their soft words. "I've never been anything else."

"Neither have I."

"Sure you have. You've always been something else."

She pouts. "That's not what I mean."

He shrugs. "Then what am I?"

"You're fascinating."

She wants him, of course. She is attracted to him: he is tragic and vaguely forbidden. Also, he will not be around that long. He will not be like some later boyfriend who will break up with her shortly before graduation but then send her emails ten years later, letters from his current and disappointing life to some past ideal, completely oblivious to the passage of time and the inevitable effects it would have on that ideal.

"What's it like?" she asks him. "What's it like to know where you came from?"

"You don't know where you came from? That's some school you go to."

"You know what I mean. From a test-tube..."

"A beaker, actually. The professor had it bronzed. He keeps it on the mantle. Sometimes he puts flowers in it."

"How sweet."

And he will not live to see her grow old. His own vision will fail before the first line appears upon her face. His own skin will sag before any part of her falls an inch.

He is a candle burning quickly and melting, she thinks romantically, and leads him by the hand into the house, into her father's mansion, into the coatroom where they lay down on makeshift bed of her mother's faux-furs.

She will always be young to him, imbedded like this into the cataract mist that will form over his eyes. Her flesh is soft and perfect, round and unaffected by gravity. He cups her in his hands and already she is receding, as she will recede further, back into the obscuring mist, an angel taking her bow and leaving, stepping backwards between heaven's curtains as his hands grow thin, become knobby and roped with veins.

A few months later, he is an old man stooped over the worktable provided for him in his creator's basement. Beakers are bubbling, bright colors are flowing through spiraling tubes, and a device more atmospheric than practical sends thin fingers of electric arcs crawling up between two poles.

"What are you doing down there, if you don't mind my asking?" the professor calls down. The creator is younger now than the creation and finds himself often torn between the opposing inclinations of parental suspicion and respect for his elders.

"None of your business," says the rebellious young old man.

Eventually he must move to his own apartment off-campus. His rent is paid for in part by the Government Grant for the Funding of Creative Life Sciences and by the generous endowment of the professor's guilty conscience. He also works part-time in the library, pushing a cart of books very slowly down the aisles.

He makes the kitchen his laboratory and continues his experiments on a yellow Formica table. He boils his formulas in pots on the electric stove and saves his more promising results in the ice cube tray in the freezer.

He is an older man still some short time later when the lobby buzzer rings and he rises slowly from an unintentional nap in front of the TV. He moves toward the intercom with the swiftness of a glacier and when he finally arrives the caller has left. He does not see the dean's lovely daughter—still lovely and young, swollen now with new life. He does not see her sobbing as she walks to a waiting cab.

I awoke to the switching on of morning.

"Good morning, sunshine," Sterling said.

We got up, dressed and went to our daily chores. We mopped and peeled and sweated our way through another day or decade.

Class

Sterling did not like Popular Communications and drew pictures of Mr. Melvin during class. He nudged me, trying to get me to look, trying to make me laugh. In Sterling's drawing, Mr. Melvin's glasses were like two dinner plates, his nose was like a penis and his chin was nonexistent. Occasionally this sort of thing made me laugh—the first five or six times, at least. Now I would rather watch the show.

"What a bore," Sterling would sometimes whisper to me during class, and I knew he was talking about the teacher more than the subject. I did not share Sterling's disdain for Mr. Melvin, though Mr. Melvin sometimes fell asleep in class, leaving us watching nothing but static until someone got up to wake him, and his breath usually smelled like coffee and cherry cough drops. But he had a love for his subject, or at least, an enduring interest. I had heard him laugh during a show he must have seen a hundred times before and gasp at some shock that could no longer have held any real surprise to him. He seldom gave us homework or tests, but instead would ask questions in class and would smile and seem pleased if we got the answer right. "Why was Sally pretending that James was her boyfriend when she ran into her boss in the restaurant?" he would ask. Or: "What is the significance of the rookie cop being a vegetarian?" I always tried to answer. I liked him to think that he was getting through to me.

Sterling's favorite class was Biology. He was fascinated with the mysteries of sex, and though we had learned in Popular Communications all about the bedroom farce, the hopeless crush and the art of the double entendre, we had learned little about the act itself. Biology was our presumed salvation, but so far it had only been three weeks of tackling the mating habits of the segmented worm. There had been some vague explanations of the physical changes of puberty, but these things had already occurred in most of the class already—beneath gray blankets, in the dark and semi-privacy of our cells. What we needed was details, focus, motive.

I found these things for myself in Popular Communications and the pretty girls that lived on screens, next door to happy families with rollout lawns. There was a particular dimpled, black and white girl I would sometimes dream about. She lived in a big city apartment with her successful widowed father. She wore blouses, skirts, white socks and saddle shoes, and in my dreams, I would knock on her door and her father will let me in. I would sit on the couch while she got ready in the other room. Her father would fix me a cocktail and chat with me from his large, leather easy chair about his hard day at the office, the dog-eat-dog world of advertising, and the difficulties of raising children in a single parent household.

That was my dream but Sterling wanted something more—something concrete. He wanted illustrations, a clearly labeled map, a chart of all the essential working parts. He wanted scenarios that did not end discretely with a kiss at the front door, or a bedroom door closing shut, a lamp on the night table turning off. He had never given up hope of finding the girls, and still talked about secret passageways, forgotten corridors, peepholes and unlocked doors. We would find it, he said, and was always on the lookout for an opportunity to arise, and for us to break out and begin our holy quest of biological necessity, like salmon swimming up stairwells.

At night, all Sterling wanted to talk about was his quest, which, by virtue of my being his cellmate, seemed to have become our quest.

"Think about it," he said. "They have to keep the girls somewhere. It can't all be hairy men with big hands and chewed off fingernails. Someone must have invented something softer that doesn't smell like sweat and piss."

"I guess," I said.

What I wanted—which I guess was not all that different—was to will pleasant dream into existence. Something about my long skirted white-socked black and white angel. But he went on and on and his words infected my dream so that in it I was trapped in a secret passageway with my angel and we were climbing through dusty, narrow stairwells, brushing away cobwebs, lighting torches with Sterling's lost lighter. A skeleton lay sprawled across the floor—a pile of grinning bones, a pirate hat on his head, a yellowed map clutched in his bony hand. My girl was frightened and held my hand tightly. In my other hand, I held a gun. My pocket was bulging with bullets, and they spilled out as we walked, clattering against the floor.

"We can use them to find our way back," my girl said. "Like breadcrumbs."

"Exploding breadcrumbs," I said because now they were firing from behind us—flashes of light and noise that threw the passageway, the tunnel, the cave we are in into a bright and fading relief, like flashbulbs.

"Photographers," said the girl, rolling her eyes, sighing with resignation over the rigors of fame. The press called out to her, asking who her latest escort was. Is he an actor too? A star like you, Ms. Cochoran (her name)? Noreen (also her name)! Look this way!

Her hand felt good in mine. There was a sort of comfort and rightness to it. The gun was gone and my arm was around her soft waist, but I awoke to Sterling's voice. He was still talking.

"Anyway, I have a plan," he was saying.

"What's your plan?" I asked him. My dream was gone now; I might as well hear his.

"I'll tell you tomorrow," he said and a minute later he was snoring. Now I couldn't sleep. Abigail appeared on the edge of the mattress and took her usual spot in the crook of my arm. I would say that this was love or loyalty, but sometimes I saved food from lunch and put it there at night so she would come. She would be gone by morning.

The Second Attempt

The next day Sterling told me his plan. Or as much of it as he felt was safe for me to know. He had a map. It was drawn with a blue ballpoint pen on a brown paper towel. He would not tell me how he got it, though I got the impression that one of the Men in White was somehow involved.

"Never mind how," he said. "It's a map. That's the important thing. Don't tell anyone. It's our secret, John. This is our way in."

"You mean out," I said.

"I mean what I mean," he said.

Another day passed. Classes. Segmented worms. If X equals. The hairstyles of action villains of the last decade. The mystical pattern of threes in dramas and comedies. In the evening, before the day clicked off, Sterling took out the map again, unfolded it carefully and smiled.

"Tonight," he said.

But the door was locked and my fear of punishment was greater than my desire to know anything beyond it.

"The door's locked," I told him.

"Not to me." And I thought for a moment that he would exhibit some feat of superhuman strength, maybe laser beams would shoot from his eyes and melt away the bars and wood paneling. But that didn't happen either.

"I don't know. It seems pretty locked," I said.

He just smiled and walked over to the door, pressed against it for a moment, bouncing the palms of his hands lightly, until something clicked and it started to slide open. He pulled it back close, but not all the way.

"There was a screw loose," he said. "In the lock. I took it out this morning."

Outside the door, we heard one of the Men in White whistling as he approached. He was not whistling any tune—just one note over and over again—interrupted by his breathing. It grew louder, then passed, then faded away.

We climbed back into our beds. The lights went out. In the darkness, I could hear Sterling's excited breathing.

"Just wait," Sterling whispered. I did not know if he was whispering to me, himself, or the world in general. "Just wait...just wait...just wait."

We waited. I did not sleep. Abigail did not come. Maybe it was an hour later when I heard Sterling say quietly in the darkness: "It's time, John. Let's go."

I climbed down from my bunk reluctantly, but what could I do? If I stayed and he was gone in the morning, I would still be punished. Boys had disappeared before. We never knew if they were moved to another floor or disposed of in the furnace. Clouds of steam still rose periodically from the depths of the unseen levels and it could have been escaping souls of the lost, caught and incinerated.

Sterling opened the door slowly, his eyes gleaming in the darkness like something wet. We stepped onto the steel grated walkway outside the cell, closing the door carefully behind us. It did not click shut. Because of the missing screw.

On the platform, the dim platter-shaped lights above us were set to twilight and I could see the filaments within the glass bulbs glowing a dull orange. I could also see the rows of dim lights in the cellblock above us and the ones above that, but they were faint and disappeared quickly into the blackness. If I walked to the edge, I was sure I would see the same below, floor after floor of dim lights fading into darkness. But I did not walk to the edge; we stayed close to the walls, Sterling squinting at his map as we proceeded slowly forward.

"This way," he whispered. I followed him past cell door after cell door, all closed and silent, all containing our comrades who were fast asleep and dreaming safely behind wood panels.

We rounded a corner, went down a spiral staircase—down, further down, down into darkness and a rising cloud of steam. We descended past black, rough-hewn stones and rusting I-beams and reached a bottom filled with shadows and dampness. There were no cells here. Only black walls, enormous and ancient, streaked with water and moss, mortar crumbling between the stones. The walls opened into a dozen hallways leading in all directions, where the lights were few and far between, large and naked bulbs from another era that hummed with electricity and flickered like candles. Every third one or so was burned out—burned out a decade ago and left there to collect dust.

"See, they knew we would think up instead of down," Sterling told me, as if imparting to me some great bit of secret wisdom. "That's what they thought. Because they're girls, right? That's where girls would be. Because they're angels and above us. They teach us that. But that's not where they are. They really put them down below. That's where they keep them. It's a trick, see?"

I didn't see, or didn't believe. And what was the trick exactly? That they tell us they are above us or that they hide them below? Or did he mean something larger? That they were not better than us?

We walked on into a passageway where the stone walls formed an uneven arch above us. Our feet splashed in shallow puddles. Now and then something mysterious crunched beneath our soft heals or scurried past in the shadows. How could my angel or any angel be here? Though this was indeed a colorless world, and my own particular feminine ideal was at that time black and white (and dark haired and dimpled), I knew she was above this dungeon. She hovered where it was light and airy. She flew, her long skirt and ponytail blowing, from antennae to antennae, a chorus of studio laughter singing her praise, calling her name: Noreen.

"This isn't very promising," I said, looking at all that crumbling darkness.

"Not much farther. Down another hallway then another stairwell."

"OK."

We went down another hallway and another stairwell. Then around another corner crawling with what I imagined to be cockroaches or rats, but I could not see, could only hear—or almost hear—the small, scratching.

And then we opened a door and everything changed. A glowing hallway was before us, empty and infinite, with white walls and florescent lights and two parallel lines of white doors with white frosted windows. We squinted, as if caught in a searchlight, waiting for sirens to go off, and I remembered a certain show where a hallway like this had heat sensors on the floor and an elaborate grid of laser beams crossing invisibly from one wall to the other.

"Should we move?" I whispered.

"We can't stay here, can we?" he said.

We moved. Slowly. Creeping. Our feet—our gray slipper socks—wet from the previous tunnels and squishing as we walked. No door alarm sounded, no door opened. I heard the vague and muffled sounds of machines. Clicking, like typewriters. Whirring, like the wheels of computers. Were there voices? If there were, they seemed thin and metallic, as if they too emitted from machines.

"Are girls in there?" I whispered, though I hardly cared—I wanted to be back in my bed, with Abigail warming the crook of my arm. I knew this could not end well.

"Not according to my sources," he said. "The end of the hall…"

The end of the hall was a long ways away—we would have to squish quietly past a countless number of doors, any one of which could open—alarms, flashing lights, cattle prods. I could feel the world rearing back, preparing to strike.

But we made it to the far end without anything happening. Then another hallway—less bright, less white, with fewer doors, ending in one ominous door marked: HEAD ADMINISTRATOR.

Sterling smirked and nudged me and said. "Ha! Look at that. Grindlier's not even the top Administrator."

"This doesn't look like anyplace they keep girls," I said. Sterling looked around, considering.

"This is where I was *told*."

We crept onward to the end of the hallway. There was an un-marked, windowless door to the right of the one marked HEAD ADMINISTRATOR. Sterling turned the handle and we both entered a small closet, squeezing in to fit between the mops and brooms and shelves of cleaning supplies. He closed the door and it was dark now except for one circle of light coming from the wall. Sterling pressed his eye to the circle and sighed.

"Yes…" I heard him say and I knew he had finally found the thing he had been looking for.

"What?" I whispered, but he did not answer.

"What is it?" I asked him again.

He pulled his eye away from the hole and shifted himself within the small space to allow me room.

"Look for yourself."

I placed my eye to the opening and saw, framed in the peep-holes blurry edges, an office, a desk, and behind it, a woman. A woman, not a girl. An office, not a girl's shower. We had been misinformed, though Sterling did not seem disappointed.

She wore a brown suit, like a man's but with bigger buttons and a white billowy shirt beneath it. A mass of yellow hair was arranged behind her head in some professional configuration and she was chewing on the end of a pencil while flipping through a small stack of papers. There was a glass of wine on her desk; she removed the pencil from her mouth and took a sip. The glass had a red inverted arch where her lips had touched it.

She was beautiful, I suppose, or close enough. Red lips, large eyes, smooth skin. Pretty enough to play the youngish business-woman on a TV show—the tough, pragmatic female who hides her softness and passion from her coworkers, but reveals it one day at an office party, in some after-work bar, or trapped in an elevator with the man who fixes the copy machine. She lets her hair down in romantic or emergency lighting and there she is: a woman.

But this was still not the girls' shower and I had seen a woman before. I had held the cold hand of that sexless beast that had brought me there—who rode with me in the elevator from the earth's surface those distant years ago. I was not impressed.

There was something else on her desk: a jar. A large jar filled with an orange liquid. I did not notice it at first, but I saw it now and looked at it more than the woman. There was something floating in the jar. A vague shape. A malformed pickled something or other.

"What's that?" I whispered, but did not relinquish the peep-hole so that Sterling could see what I was referring to.

"What's what? Is she undressing?"

"Why would she undress in her office?" I asked. It struck me as a ridiculous notion—flying in the face of everything we had learned on TV.

"I don't know. It's a *private* office…"

Maybe it was a pickle in the jar, but weren't pickles usually green? No—anything could be pickled really, so maybe it was a pickled tomato or pepper or carrot. But I saw two dark disks, like buttons, roughly where eyes might be if the tomato or pepper or carrot was actually a pickled baby.

Maybe I gasped, or flinched. Maybe Sterling knocked over a broom. Or maybe we had whispered back and forth once too often. At any rate, a noise was made and the woman at the desk was startled. She jerked her head in my direction—like the woman in a scary movie who has heard the slithering footstep of a monster in the shadows. But she was not like that woman at all. She was not soft, vulnerable, or frightened. Instead, she stared at me, at where I was behind the wall, at my little eye pressed against the hole, stood up, and in doing so knocked over the glass of wine. It spilled on to her papers and ran off the edge of the desk. Little droplets that I could not see had apparently splashed onto the front of her blazer; she brushed her hands across it furiously, as if knocking away a crawling spider.

"Shit," she said and for a moment I thought she had forgotten about the noise she had heard. But my thinking this seemed to remind her, and she looked suddenly back towards the wall.

She walked closer, squinting at the wall. I could not move, though Sterling was still trying to nudge me aside to get a look.

"Shit," I said very quietly, with mostly mouth and no throat and very little air, but given the fact that she was coming towards us already, that she had heard a sound and was investigating, it was perhaps an ill-advised thing to do.

She was close now, and all I could see was her white blouse, its brass buttons, the little droplets of wine against the white. She knocked against the wall.

"Come out come out whoever you are," she said.

Bad Experiences with Doctors

The Head Administrator shouted "Security!" in an unnaturally loud voice that seemed to come from everywhere at once and bounce off everything else. It rattled the walls of the closet, vibrating through the floors. Things began falling off the shelves even before she began smacking the palm of her hand against the wall.

"I think we have rats!" she yelled and it was like the voice of an angry god.

Then she repeated it, with each word counted off with a smack of her hand against the wall.

"I! Think! We! Have! Rats!"

A broom fell against the back of my neck. Sterling was struggling with a collection of coat hangers that rained down from above when the door was thrown open and we were yanked kicking and screaming from the closet by the large and faceless men in the usual white uniforms. I mostly kicked, Sterling mostly screamed.

"Get your hands off me!" Sterling yelled. "Get your fucking hands off me!"

There was a pause after he said that—a dramatic pause where everything seemed to stop and consider itself for a moment. The Men in White exchanged looks—then one of them punched Sterling in the face.

"The mouth on this kid," the one that had punched him said to the other one.

They dragged us down the hallway by the collars. I don't know what I did or said next—I may have cried, I may have told them I was sorry.

They shoved us into an elevator, shoved us into the corners, then stood back and stared at us.

"Anything else you want to say to us, Jones?" one of them said.

"Any other suggestions for treatment, you'd like to offer us?"

the other said.

Sterling just glared them.

"How 'bout you," one of them asked me, but I got the impression he was only asking me to be polite—as if they wanted me to know that they hadn't forgotten about me. I shook my head.

The elevator opened onto a green hallway I had not seen before. There was a yellow line painted on the floor. We followed the yellow line to an intersection of hallways, where the yellow line split into two separate lines—one black, one blue. We followed the black line to another intersection where it split into two more lines going in opposite directions—one red and one purple.

The Men in White paused.

"Which way?" one asked the other.

The other looked to the right, the left, and then back the way they came. "Jeez..." he said.

We followed the red line for several hundred yards. By now the Men in White were tired of dragging us so we all walked, though once in awhile they would smack me or Sterling in the back of the head.

The Men in White stopped walking, looked around.

"I don't think this is right," one said.

"I know it's not right," the other said.

"If you knew it wasn't right, maybe you should have said something before we went this way."

"Maybe I didn't know then."

We turned back, followed the purple line this time instead until we came to an unmarked door. They opened the door and threw me inside.

"Sit still and shut up," they said. Then they left, closing and locking the door behind them.

I looked around the room. It was small, with cinderblock walls painted a color that seemed almost to be no color at all. A pale brown or a gray or a green—it didn't matter and could have been any of these depending on the mood. There was a folding chair in the middle of the room and nothing else. I sat still. I shut up.

They placed Sterling in another room not too far away. I could hear his screams—there may have been a vent or airshaft between us. They were tinny, like the voice in a soup-can telephone.

His screams finally stopped and I heard scuffling, a door opening and closed. After that there was nothing. I sat and thought about my sins, imagined my punishments, prayed to Noreen Cochran for hope and guidance.

Some time later, the door to my room opened again. It was Mr. Grindlier. He came in, began circling the room, touching the walls, sniffing the tips of his fingers and now and then glancing my way.

"So here we are again," he finally said and I looked around, not quite understanding.

"Not *here*," he clarified. "You've never been *here* before, of course. I know that. I was referring more to the situation. You transgressing and me trying to set you on the right path, as it were. We've been *there* before, haven't we, young man?"

I nodded.

"And here we are again."

I nodded again, but mostly I was wondering how long until we got to the part where I started screaming.

"And I don't like being here," he said, as if considering the room now instead of the situation, studying the brownish-grayish-bluish-greenish walls. "I rather thought you would have learned your lesson last time, but maybe that's my fault. Maybe I'm too easy on you men. It's a weakness of mine, you know. Compassion."

"Yes, sir," I said.

He cocked an eyebrow.

"Oh? You agree with me then? You think compassion is a weakness?"

"Um...no?"

"Are you asking me?"

"No?"

He smiled. It was not at all a comforting smile. His ancient mouth. His coffee-stained teeth. He walked around my chair. I did not know if I should follow him with my eyes. Would it be rude to do so? Would it be cocky not too?

"That sounded like a question too," he said.

"I'm sorry sir." Apologizing seemed like a safe bet. When in doubt, apologize—I had learned that much.

"Yes. I think you are. In truth, so am I. I think we made an error in putting you with Sterling. He's a strong character. You're a weak one. These things were bound to happen. Please, don't take that the wrong way. It's nothing to be ashamed of. Your weakness." He placed a fatherly hand on my shoulder. It smelled of gasoline. I couldn't figure that out. I still can't.

"Of course, it isn't anything you should be particularly proud of either," he said.

"I'm not proud, sir.

"No. No. As you shouldn't be. But let's not call it weakness, shall we? Let's call it *malleable*. Now malleable, that's a good thing, isn't it? We can work with malleable, can't we? That's the whole point of it...malleable...being able to work with it. I'm not so sure about your friend Sterling, of course. I wouldn't call him malleable. I doubt there's much we can do with him. But you... You follow. You can be molded. You've just been lead and formed by the wrong person, but we can fix that. We can fix you. We're the right people. But do you want to be fixed? That's the question now, John. Is being fixed something you think you would like?"

"Yes, sir."

"Do you want to be saved?"

"Yes, sir."

He ruffled my hair. "Thatta boy," he said and left the room.

I sat there waiting for I don't know how long, until the Men in White came in again, wheeling a gurney between them. A small black bag was on the gurney. The second man opened the bag and pulled out a needle filled with an orange liquid. It looked thick—as thick as jam; it didn't seem possible that it could be squeezed through a needle.

"Roll up your sleeve," he said. "It'll burn a little at first but then it will all just be a pleasant dream."

I was doubtful, of course. I did not roll up my sleeve right away. I stared at the point of the needle, the small, orange drop growing.

"Your sleeve...roll it up."

I did not move. I wasn't trying to resist exactly, I was just momentarily unable to move. One of the Men in White stepped forward, grabbed my arm and yanked up the sleeve. Then he held onto me with both arms around my chest, even though I wasn't struggling.

The needle went into me. It burned a little at first but then it did become just a pleasant dream.

My Show

Even without sparks and molecular switches, without the miracle of atomic memory, modern science and the apron strings of my fathers pulling me constantly backwards into the past, I can recall the cold steel table, the TV false-life, the bright and mysterious chemical sustenance piped directly into my veins. I recall these things from within a fog, as if they were the details of a remembered, but perpetually fading dream.

I was strapped to a metal table, a tube running into one arm, various wires taped to my head, chest, stomach, penis, legs, feet. My head was held in a sort of soft vice and above me, a wide screen hung from the ceiling, lowered toward me and bent inward so that the sides of the screen filled my peripheral vision. The screen became everything.

I do not know how long I laid there on the table, or if I was being observed or monitored, though it is hard to imagine that I was not. If doors opened and closed around me, they did so quietly. The footsteps were silent.

On the screen, a blonde woman floated above me. Her face was pretty but angular. She was reminding me to wash my hands before eating.

"Wash your hands," she said. "You don't know where they've been."

They were my hands, of course. I knew where they had been, but when I tried to raise them in front of me to look at them, I remembered that I was strapped to a table. It was peculiar how quickly I had forgotten.

And yet a pair of small hands appeared on the screen in front of me. Small and dirty hands. They were younger than my own hands. But maybe they were my own hands. Maybe I was confused. I imagined flipping them over, to check both sides, and on the screen the hands flipped over.

"That's right, young man," the blonde woman said. "Cleanliness is next to Godliness."

Where was I? I thought of moving my head to the left and right and the image on the screen shifted to the left and the right, showing a kitchen with bright yellow daisies on the wallpaper.

A man approached from the kitchen doorway. He was smoking a pipe, wearing a sweater with patches on the elbows. On him it made sense. It was somehow both confusing and comforting to see that sweater.

"Hello, son." The man said. He had the sort of pleasantly bland face that seemed almost the average of all faces.

I moved my lips but could not bring myself to force a sound.

"Cat got your tongue," the man said and laughed.

Then I appeared to be walking——out of the kitchen, down a hallway—into a bathroom. I was turning the faucets—H and C. I was holding my hands under the faucet and could feel the water running over them. Too much C. Not enough H. I made an adjustment. I used the small bar of pink soap at the side of the sink. It smelled like artificial flowers.

I returned to the kitchen table. Pancakes were being served. A small stack was set in front of me, and I found I could cut them, pour syrup on them, spear the dripping pieces onto the prongs of a fork and lift it to my mouth. And I could taste them, chew them, swallow them. At first it seemed mostly an act—I tasted and pretended to chew, pretended to eat, but I eventually began to feel the solidity of this imagined food forming in my mouth. I swallowed and felt the pancakes go down my throat. This was better than macaroni and cheese. It was even better than the bits of mango Abigail had sometimes placed in my mouth when I had been a baby

I enjoyed the meal, the kitchen, the show. The man and woman ate pancakes from their own plates, chewing happily, taking sips of orange juice between bits, wiping syrup from the corners of their mouths and smiling.

"Our son is rather quiet today," the man said to the woman.

"Oh, he's just thinking," the woman said to the man, but

they were both looking at me as they talked. Chewing, smiling, sipping.

"You know him," the woman said. "He likes to think. He likes to live in his own world."

"Imagination is a splendid thing!" the man said. He put down his knife and fork, let loose a merry belch and said: "How 'bout some coffee hun?"

"Coming right up, sweetheart!" she said rising from the table and beginning to assemble a chrome device out of a small pile of shining parts on the counter.

The kitchen became dimmer—as if outside a cloud was passing over the sun. But the cloud did not pass. A second cloud overlapped it and it was nearly night. In the darkness I could still taste the syrup in my mouth. I heard the woman screwing metal parts together. No one switched on a light.

The picture faded to black, the black wavering for a moment before shattering into a storm of dissipating gray dots. The screen, a perfect blank again, straightened and ascended back into the ceiling.

I looked around, blinking at the jarring whiteness of the room and for a moment could not figure out where I was, who I was, or guess at what would happen next. An elephant wearing a sport coat could have entered the room next and it would have made as much sense as anything else.

A door opened, heels clicked softly toward me, a woman's face hovered above me. Dark eyes, pale skin, yellow hair. Pretty in an angular way. The woman. *The* Head Administrator. She smiled and placed a soft hand on my forehead.

"You seem hot," she said. "Are you running a fever, dear?"

"I don't know," said I. "Am I?"

She laughed. Tenderly. Not tenderly.

I must have been feverish. I saw spots and then everything faded to black again.

Part of this Complete Breakfast

The Man and Woman served me orange juice, buttered toast, a bowl of cereal. The cereal was round and shaped like little smiling faces—but faces that had twisted holes for eyes, twisted holes for noses, twisted holes for mouths. They were supposed to be happy-clown faces but looked more to me like faces that had been torn off, baked, frosted, and made part of this complete breakfast.

My little hand held a big spoon. Interspersed among the faces were mini-marshmallows, and the spoon sought these out first, then poked disinterestedly at the faces left behind. They were not frosted enough. Their smiles seemed forced. I imagined the sort of tragedy that would burn the faces from a hundred clowns.

"Don't play with your food," Mom said, and Dad looked up, letting the spine of his newspaper break a little so he could see over the edge.

"Don't dawdle Jack," he said. "Time is money."

"Yes, sir," I muttered.

"And speak clearly."

"Yes, sir," I muttered louder.

He gave me a look. I knew that look. I ate the rest of my breakfast quickly.

"Imagination is all well and good," he said. "But lets not forget the real world too. And in the real world you're liable to miss your bus."

On the bus I was older, as if five years had passed from breakfast till now. Was I a teenager? The boys and girls around me were older. Wispy hair appeared above the upper lips of some. Strange new forms pushed out against the shirts of others. Much talking and laughing and passing of things back and forth. An object was tossed at the head of one boy and the boy scooped it up and threw it back hard.

"Pussy," he said.

Laughter.

Cut again, this time to school. A class. World History. Mesopotamia, or The Rise and Fall of Rome. Some empire or another is always rising or falling. I sat in the back, trying to remember who I really was, where I really was. The teacher called on me.

"Jack," the teacher said. He was tall and faceless. Truly faceless. His face had been torn off, baked, frosted, and served in a bowl just that morning. "Jack, could you do us the favor of reading number seven out loud?"

But the desktop beneath me was empty. The teacher waited.

"I haven't got a book," I said and it seemed for a moment that the world paused—the faces around me, the faceless teacher, the grain that made up the air and light, frozen in place as if waiting for a switch to be thrown, another tape to be started containing the appropriate scene.

"Read from your neighbor's book then," the teacher finally said and I looked to my neighbor. He was a boy my own age, but taller, better formed, more golden. The cinematographer had been kind to him. A book lay open before him on his desk. He smiled encouragingly or sympathetically or mockingly and glanced down at the pages, tapping his finger on the number seven.

I read number seven. "Ea, the skillful and wise poisoned Apsu and Mummu, causing them to fall into a deep sleep. Ea then killed Apsu and strung a rope through Mummu's nose. Then he built his house on top of Apsu's corpse, and moved in with his pregnant bride and new pet."

That was number seven. I looked up. The teacher was still waiting.

"That's all," I said.

"Do you care to answer it for us, Jack?"

"It's not a question," I tell him, and again the world paused to consider. But what world? Did my back rest against a plastic school chair or a metal laboratory table. Was I naked or clothed. *My name is Jack*, I think to myself, and try to go on from there. *But is it*

Jack? Or is it John? Or is it Jon? I am playing with blocks. Red and blue and yellow. Triangle and rectangle and square. I am trying to build a structure I can understand. John or Jack. My name is Jack. Who am I? Jack? Where am I? I am playing with blocks and rubber test tube stoppers. I am Jack. In a class. Underground. Teething on test-tubes, nursing from beakers. In a crib. No. On a table. Alone. Not alone. Alone. A rope through my nose. No. A wooden table. No. Steel. Lightening. Steel and rubber stoppers. Bright blocks and fire.

The tape moved forward in a sudden jerk—the teacher's mouth was blurry and red. I could not see his eyes.

"Answer the question, Jack."

But I couldn't. He was not real and it was not really a question.

The lights came on. The screen ascended. Mr. Melvin entered the room looking sheepish and apologetic. He pulled up a chair and sat down next to the metal table, next to my head.

"I don't like these methods," he told me in a quiet voice, like we were friends, like he understood. He was my favorite teacher. He was the good cop. "You're better than this, Jack," he said.

"Am I?"

"Of course." He brushed a few strands of hair from my forehead.

"Much better."

He had something on his lap—a stack of something, I could just see bright colors from the corner of my eye. "Hey," he said. "I brought you something. For when they're done with you here."

He held it up for me to see. It was a stack of comic books. He spread them out like an enormous hand of cards. Superman. Aqua Man. The Electron.

"Your homework," he said.

Solitary Confinement

After the steel table, I was given a white paper robe and a room of my own. The robe was opened in the back, tied together loosely by a string I had trouble knotting. It crinkled when I moved. The room had a bed and plaster walls painted white; no stone, no wood paneling disguising an iron-barred door, no painting of a clown. I knew that cell was still somewhere, waiting, but for now I was here. Here did not seem that bad.

I sat on the bed in the corner, read the stack of comic books and filled out the worksheets Mr. Melvin had included with each one. What was the major conflict between The Magenta Avenger and ShockWave? How did their similar backgrounds play into this conflict? In "The Shape of The World," how did the hero Crumb use his ability to shrink to prevent The Matter Transformer from changing all the steel in Centralville into rubber?

I filled out the worksheets with the small, inch-long number two pencils provided for me.

An essay question asked: describe in your own words the message behind issue twenty-three of *The Electron* and how it might relate to current society. How might this be relevant to the expected audience of a comic book?

The story in issue twenty-three of *The Electron* was titled: The Gun. On the first page, two teenagers from the wrong side of the tracks hold up a liquor store. During their getaway, they toss the gun over a fence. It falls into the playground of a school. The next day, a six-year-old boy named Tommy finds the gun. He hides it in the pocket of his jacket and takes it home. At home, he shows it to his older brother, Johnny. Johnny has blue-black hair, and thick eyebrows that speak of dark forces at work. A good kid though. Just troubled. He is not doing well in school and some of the other kids pick on him. His parents are concerned by his moodiness. They do not understand him, but to Tommy he is a hero.

"Isn't it neat?" says Tommy with wide saucer eyes eager to please.

"It sure is, kid," says Johnny. "But you better leave this to me. A squirt like you could get in trouble."

Johnny takes the gun to school. He won't use it, he thinks in balloons hanging over his head. He doesn't want to hurt anyone. Just scare those bullies a little.

At recess he takes it from his backpack to show his friend Rusty. "Holey Mackerel," says Rusty. "Let me borrow it. Just 'til lunch."

Johnny is reluctant ("Gee…I don't know…"), but Rusty is his only friend and how can he say no?

Behind the gym, Rusty shows the gun to Butch and Terry. Butch wants to hold the gun. He doesn't think it is real. "No way," says Rusty, but he relents. Maybe Butch is his only friend.

Butch holds the gun in his hand. It glows with thick black lines signifying its dangerous importance. Butch radiates lines signifying impending doom. Rusty's red brows are knitted and there are lines on his forehead showing concern.

"Don't be such a wimp," Butch says, taking aim at nothing. "I know what I'm doing. My Dad's got a gun like this at home."

But the gun in his hand goes off. BANG! The bullet is off and flying toward a blonde, pig-tailed girl skipping rope on the playground.

Fortunately, The Electron—who at that moment is in fifth period study hall—has overheard their conversation and the subsequent shot. The bullet is pulled off course by a discreet blast of electromagnetic power (under the desk, when the teacher isn't looking—a yellow zig-zagging bolt—ZAP!).

And then the gun itself is attacked—drawn from the hand of the surprised Butch, it flies through the blue-dotted air, past trees and clouds splashing (SPLASH!) into an ocean. It sinks to the bottom as curious fish look on and you might think the story ends there, but here comes a kid in mask and snorkel. He picks up the gun from between rocks and discarded tires, and soon he is walking out of the sea holding the gun, beaming with excitement and promise at his new discovery. The End. Or is it?

It was a pretty bad issue. Where is the super villain? The great conflict? The resolution? The Electron himself does not even leave study hall, never changes from his guise as a typical teenager, until one frame at the very end where he points to the reader and advises them of the dangers of firearms and the proper procedure for disposing of them. Call the authorities immediately, The Electron says, though in every other issue the authorities were trying to bring The Electron in for questioning.

I wrote my essay. The dangers of guns. The proper authorities. All that.

Eventually they came and got me again—the usual large, silent, smiling Men in White. I was given a gray sweat suit to put on again then escorted down the hallway, up a set of stairs, then down another hallway to the elevator.

When I got back to my cell, Sterling was gone. Four days later, he was still gone, and I began to resign myself to him not coming back. Did I miss him? I think I did, though it was easier to sleep nights and it was nice not to have to hear him digging, planning his next great escape, or waxing poetic about what lied beyond, above, or below us. I could dream of Noreen Cochran without his voice intruding on the soft black and white of my dreams. I could enjoy my solitude, and my freedom from anxiety. And what was so bad, really? I was fed and sheltered. I was not free, but I had never been free. Freedom did not hold the same sway on me as it had on Sterling, who always imagined a brighter and better place beyond these walls and dirt.

Abigail the Hamster slept with me most nights. She had done that less when Sterling had been there. His snoring may have bothered her, though sometimes I suspected him of shooing her away or worse, capturing her between his own sheets, forcing her to sleep with him, his hands clutched over her squirming body while I, in my own bunk, waited in vain.

But now she was in the crook of my arm. Her tiny breath and whiskers. We dreamt together.

Sterling did come back. The cell door slid open one morning and there he was, standing with a small box of stuff, a pale and dazed look on his face. Even his shoulders seem less broad as he looked at the floor and shuffled over to the bed. He sat the box on the floor and himself onto the bed and began to quietly weep.

Comparing Torture

Sterling barely talked to me anymore, though sometimes at night he would make small animal noises while he slept. Not quite sobbing—more like gnawing, like he was gnawing in his sleep, but at what? The imaginary binds that tied him? His lower lip? And some mornings, his mouth would be bleeding. He would wipe away the blood with embarrassment, as is if it wasn't his blood at all and he had no idea how it had gotten there.

Several times I woke up at the click of day to see him balled up on the floor in the corner. He would still be asleep, his clothes twisted on his body, sometimes half off, the sheets of his bed strewn across the floor like wreckage.

I remembered a story we had watched in class once where a man became a monster at night—from the influence of the moon, or a bite, or a scientific formula involving test tubes, beakers and smoke. The man was normal by day, had a job, a wife, a child and a dog, but at night he did terrible things that he would not remember in the morning, and then would be horrified to discover a strange bit of polished fingernail between his molars while brushing his teeth. The man thought he had been having nightmares. He did not know the crimes he committed at night were real.

"Do you have nightmares?" I asked Sterling one day.

He stared at me for a long time before answering.

"I guess," he muttered.

"Wouldn't you know?" I asked.

"I don't know," he said. "Would I?"

It was the most he had said to me in a week. I thought maybe I was onto something, but did not want to scare him away. I tried to make my voice calm and authoritative, as if I were a doctor or scientist with many degrees on the subject.

"You would know if you had nightmares," I told him

He shrugged and said: "Whatever."

From then on, I studied Sterling the way researchers in nature specials study the habits of mountain primates. I watched as he ate his food without noise or pleasure, watched as he sat silently in class. He did not even draw in the margins of his papers anymore. In the evening, he paced our cell until it was bedtime, sometimes pausing in front of the clown painting, staring at it as if it were a living enemy, a mirror, or both. Once or twice, I heard him mutter something at the clown but never clear enough to know what it was.

"They made me watch TV," I told him one night, after the light had clicked off, but before he was asleep; I could hear his breathing—it was not yet the strange gnawing sounds of his dreams.

"I was strapped to a table with a giant TV in the ceiling," I told him. "They showed me some show about a father and mother. Not a lot of plot. No credits." I suppose I wanted to encourage him to open up about his own trauma, maybe to let him know I had suffered too, that he was not alone, but even while I was telling him what I had gone through, I knew I was being less than forthcoming with my description. The show had been much more than that.

"Must have been horrible," he said. Sarcastically, I think. Bitterly, maybe. "They made you watch TV," he said. "How could you stand it?" Sure. Bitterly. Sarcastically.

"I was naked," I said, wanting to make it a little worse now and wishing I had a greater facility for lying. If I did, I would have added electrodes and barbed wire to the story. I remembered his own screams coming through the walls and it was hard not to imagine knives, sharp sticks, car batteries and clothespins somehow being involved.

"The table was cold," I told him. "It was a cold metal table and they fed me through a tube or something. In my arm. In a hole in my arm."

He didn't say anything.

Visitors

I was trying to sleep, hoping for the comfort of dreams, when there was a metallic click and the door to our cell slid open. I turned in my bed to see the silhouette of a Man in White, his arms stretched out above him, large hands clutching at the top of the frame. It was a gesture that struck me as particularly gorilla-like, and yet filled me with no sense of comfort or nostalgia. I closed my eyes, or pretended to, still peeking out through the blur of my eyelashes.

The man in the doorway tapped his fingers lightly against the frame—it sounded meaty, like a series of pork chops landing on a metal table.

I noticed that Sterling's own nighttime sounds had stopped, then I heard the less random squeaking of him rising from his bed, the pad of his feet across the floor. He stood there, nearly as tall as the Man in White now. He leaned close to him and soft words were spoken between them, impossible for me to hear. Viewed from between my eyelashes, with the light behind them, Sterling and the Man in White looked like two aliens standing at the entrance of their space ship.

Was he escaping again—without me this time? I felt an emotion I could not identify but seemed related to jealousy—a first or second cousin, perhaps. I did not want to be part of another escape attempt, nor did I particularly desire visits from Men in White during the night, but still I felt a hard to define resentment.

The door slid shut again and I opened my eyes. I was now alone in my cell. I tried to sleep but couldn't. Abigail crawled onto my bed and nestled herself into the crook of my arm, but it was of no help that night. I felt her small breath, the beat of her tiny heart, but was too distracted to find comfort in it. I was thinking.

The Men in White did not, as a rule, fraternize with us young freaks of science. Their job was to herd us, capture us, torture us, but Sterling had always been a little different in that regard. They herded, captured and tortured him too, yes, but they also patted him on the top of the head, smiled at him in hallways, and singled him out for the occasional friendly nudge with the tip of their beating sticks. I feel certain now that it was from a Man in White that he had gotten the cigarette lighter used in our first attempt, as it had been a Man in White who had provided him with the map for our second attempt. I would see him chatting with them at the ends of lines, in the back corners of classrooms, in the cafeteria.

He knew their names. I never did; I could never tell one from the next, or keep their faces from blending into each other in my memories or nightmares. "Which one?" he might ask me, back when we still talked, in regard to some story or another involving a Man in White. "Was it Bob or Richard?" he would ask and I would inevitably answer: "I don't know." He would try then to elicit some sort of descriptive detail from me. Was it the one with the black or the brown hair? The one with the broken nose? The one with scar across his upper lip? The one who smelled like raw potatoes? I could not tell. I could not remember.

It was a source of some frustration for him. He would rattle off a list names, hoping one would be recognized. Tom, or Sam, or Butch, he would say and I would stare at him and blink dumbly.

"Jesus," he would finally say. "Your powers of observation are uncanny."

"I can remember things," I told him. "That's my power. I can remember things from before I was born."

"That's great," he would say and roll his eyes.

But if Sterling had been quiet lately, if he had been quiet for months or years, it was possible that he had only been quiet to me. I was no longer his confidant or co-conspirator. Maybe the Men in White—or one of them at least—had replaced me.

I had the sudden and overpowering sensation that a world had been taking place outside of me, outside of my knowledge—that plans were being made, passions formed, enemies and friends decided upon, without a word to me. I was not, in fact, very observant. But I could still remember the aquarium-womb of my gestation and the spigot of my birth, and that should count for something.

A Sort of Ending

We were sitting in class and Mr. Melvin was struggling with the projector—a piece of film had jammed itself somewhere in the mechanism. There was the smell of burning plastic. Mr. Melvin tried to shove his fingers into places not meant for them to go and received some sort of shock for his efforts.

"Shit," he said, recoiling and waving his fingers in the air in front of him. A few in the class laughed, but not many, because we were young men now, and had heard him say shit before, and could say shit ourselves on a regular basis and with the practiced ease of grown-ups.

While Mr. Melvin worked on the projector, I went over my notes from the last movie, which had been about a man haunted by ghosts. The ghosts were not scary—they did not rattle chains, float through walls, give cryptic warnings or even say "boo," but they crowded the man's apartment like guests at a party that would not leave, filled the streets he walked on, the grocery store he shopped at, the office building he worked in. No one else saw the ghosts and the man did not let on to anyone that the ghosts were there. It was as if he lived in a world several times more populated than the world of anyone else, and though more than half of that population was non-corporeal, the man did not feel right about walking through them as if they did not exist. He avoided them instead, walking in crooked paths through rooms and down sidewalks until people began to doubt his sanity.

"There is no clearer indication of our mental health state than the way we walk," Mr. Melvin had said in the darkness, while the movie continued. "Remember that."

"Will it be on the test?" someone asked.

"No, but you'll have to walk places at some point in your life, so it would behoove you all to not walk like crazy people. That's what I'm saying."

"So it won't be on the test?"

"Just watch the movie, please."

It was a foreign film and it ended without a clear resolution. The man went on living with the translucent mob of the dead that surrounded him, telling no one. Though now he was abandoned by friends, family, love. He lost his job. He slept in a cardboard box at night and spent his days sitting on the sidewalk, asking for donations of food and money. Now and then, he would make a mistake and ask a ghost for food and money. The ghosts would not look at him. They would avoid his gaze. They seemed embarrassed in their translucent way, and would walk quickly away.

The second movie had just started when something went wrong with the film. It was impossible to say what the movie was going to be about—only that it began on a faded summer's day near the ocean, the waves coming in and seagulls dotting a pale sky. The credits had not even run—not even the title.

Mr. Melvin could not fix the projector and had to wheel it out of the room. A Man in White stepped in while he was gone and stood by the doorway. I saw Sterling look up from his desk with something like attention for the first time that day. He had slept during the first movie, stared blankly during Mr. Melvin's analysis of it, and laid down his head again as soon as the second movie had started.

Now there was an exchange of knowing looks between him and the Man in White, a wink, a nod, a one-sided grin. The class talked quietly amongst themselves. Sterling tapped the end of his pencil against the top of his desk; it was the biggest display of energy I had seen from him in months.

The Man in White came over, leaned down, whispered something into Sterling's ear. Sterling laughed. The man straightened up, smiled, nodded. They seemed like old friends, sharing an inside joke, and I wondered how a thing like this could have happened.

He was still exchanging whispers with the Man in White when Mr. Melvin returned, pushing either a new projector on the cart or the same projector repaired. Sterling and the Man in White looked up and Mr. Melvin paused in the doorway, as if he knew something horrible was about to happen.

And it did. It all happened quickly—not in slow motion like in the action movies we had studied, but in fast motion, like a comedy, like a silent movie or cartoon. I could not fully understand the events that occurred or even now place them in their proper order. The world itself seemed spliced together, a shutter was malfunctioning, film was stuck and would repeat and burn.

The Man in White said: "It's all fixed now, Professor," and lifted the projector over his head.

"What?" Mr. Melvin said, his eyes widening, darting from the man's face to the projector, as the Man in White lifted it over his head and said: "It's all fixed now, Professor!"

"What are you..." Mr. Melvin said.

"It's all fixed now, Professor..."

"What are you..."

The Man in White swung the projector down, crashing it on top of Mr. Melvin's head. There was blood on the floor, on the wall, on the knuckles of someone's hands. A chair hit me in the arm. Someone was overturning tables. Someone was throwing chairs and they shattered against walls. There was blood on the floor. A desk was thrown against a wall. It splintered into pieces. Mr. Melvin was bleeding on the floor. Sterling was standing on a desk shouting something. Mr. Melvin groaned.

Sterling shouted: "Huddled masses unite! You have nothing to lose but your chains! Give us liberty or give us death!" I did not know what these things meant. Maybe we saw them shouted in a movie once or in several different movies—they appeared to have made a greater impression on Sterling than myself.

Someone was crying in the corner, but where was I? My arm was bleeding. There was blood on the floor. "It's all fixed now, Professor" the Man in White had said, grabbing the projector from the cart, raising it over his head. "What are you doing?" Mr. Melvin had asked before he was lying on the floor, a halo of blood growing beneath his head. Why had these things happened?

The door was thrown open and we poured out onto the landing. Fire appeared before us—burning papers and books thrown through the air and tumbling down into the abyss. I thought I smelled potatoes but had no idea why. It may have been the sweat of the boy pressing against me or the tears of the boy behind me, his damp face slammed hard against my shoulder.

The Man in White was on the landing—or was it a different Man in White? He was holding Mr. Melvin in his arms and Mr Melvin seemed small—smaller than normal—almost child-sized. The Man in White lifted Mr. Melvin over his head like he had the projector.

I was pressed hard against the railing now, wondered if it would hold. It groaned with the strain of us. The heat of bodies and breath and fire surrounded me. I glanced down into the bottomless depths, clouds of steam rising up. A column of black smoke ascended from below. The air had become thick and no longer like air at all. The smell of boiled potatoes—roasted potatoes—wafted up from somewhere. Someone threw the projector over the railing. Mr. Melvin followed it down. He did not scream. Someone screamed. Others screamed. I was dragged from the railing, sucked in by the tide of people, carried forward, crashing against walls; an angry mob that shouted "Freedom!" or "Girls!" We flowed up hill, upstream, up stairs, swelling as we were joined by other rooms and cells pouring forth, emptying into us, pushed upward, through hallways and tunnels, shoving and moving on, rolling and trampling on itself, wet with its own spilled blood, slipping on its own spilled blood.

I could not even tell what actions were my own anymore. Did my own feet move or did the force of others carry me along entirely? Did we have feet at all? We continued upward like that.

Even Sterling, who had led us for several floors, could not stay ahead of us, could not stay apart from us. He was absorbed by our mass and rolled under our force, trampled under our feet, under our one foot to be drowned and crushed at once. He was liquefied and we moved on, with him on our heels, smearing the floor.

Give us liberty, we shouted or only thought as burning bodies and books fell around us.

Smoke and flames, and the sound of things cracking and crumbling, columns toppling and metal beams sagging, TV guides fluttering down like flaming moths. The shouts and screams and hacking coughs. The smell of things burning, wooden desks, books, meat. The smell of plastic burning like film against a projector bulb.

Alarms were blaring, mixed into the screams of people and the groans of structural supports. A foul water poured down on us but could not extinguish us. We smoked and hissed and moved on.

Finally we burst through the ground, tearing at the sod that had entombed us for decades. We erupted with all our heat and smoke released, and spread out thinly across the green fields, collapsing, cooling, hardening on the soft grass and dirt. We coughed up bits of ourselves into the wild flowers.

The sky is blue.

The sun is yellow.

Our faces are black.

We were no longer a force but individuals again, sitting on top of a planet we knew only from books, TV shows, movies and per-haps some dim and overused memory.

I sat on the grass and it seemed as if it was the exact same sun in the exact same sky as before. My lungs hurt. I coughed and gasped, but even in my ragged breaths I could sense the difference. This was real air, heated by a real sun.

The ground beneath us began to tremble. A patch of it sank and fell inward, like the crust of a pie collapsing, taking several people with it—boys, prisoners, Men in White, too exhausted to even scream. A gaping, smoking hole remained. Another piece of grass swelled then burst with a sudden belch of fire and a tree was shot from the earth like a rocket, flying high into the blue sky before plummeting downward again, a trail of smoke behind it.

I could not even move. No one could. We just watched the tree rise and fall without saying a word.

A few moments later the silent black helicopters were landing and black vans were speeding toward us in the grass and mud.

Soldiers slid down from the sky on ropes, poured forth from the gaping mouths of various vehicles and ran towards us from all directions. We were surrounded. They nudged and kicked us back onto our feet, then prodded us with the points of their guns and sticks until we were gathered into small and manageable groups.

My First Bus Ride

We were divided into still smaller groups, a half dozen or so, and herded through swamp and woods. Mud sucked at our feet and one or two of us lost a shoe.

"Keep going," the soldiers said. Maybe they would shoot us if we fell behind, though they did not seem interested enough to expend the energy or the bullet. They were making jokes quietly to each other behind us—I could make out the words but did not understand the jokes. They laughed. A branch flew back and hit one of them in the face. He swore, and the others laughed some more.

We did not laugh. We knew better than that.

These are trees, I thought to myself as we trudged on. *This is the world: this mud, this sky, this is fresh air.* It was as if I was trying to convince myself. It had been so long, I had seen and imagined so many images in the meantime. I had read so many books, that already the outside world was falling into a familiar groove in my brain. *This is the world and it always was. These are trees. This is mud. This is sky.*

We reached a clearing, another muddy field and across from it a road. The road was black and straight and without lines. It went on to the ends of the world in either direction. We crossed the field and stopped at the side of the road. We did not cross the road, but stood there, held together by soldiers and our shared sense of uncertainty. We were waiting for something. We looked around at the world, took tentative sniffs at the atmosphere.

The two soldiers relaxed a bit, barely pointing their guns at us at all. We were not a very threatening lot. We were wet. The air became less bright around us and some of us began to shiver.

I did not know the people in my group. I had not sat in lunch-rooms or classrooms with any of them, or hadn't noticed them if I had. They seemed thin and remote to me, one very much like the other, as if they had been the product of the same assembly line. Two of them had only one shoe each; they shivered more than the rest.

The soldiers looked up and down the road. One of them checked his watch. There was no sign of traffic, no sign that there had ever been traffic or ever would be—except that there was a road here, and roads were invented for such things.

"Smoke 'em if you got 'em," one soldier said to the other, and they each took out a cigarette, lit it, inhaled, exhaled. The rest of us watched. *We haven't got 'em.* We stood there and watched them smoke, then squash their cigarette butts into the gravel by the side of the road.

A wavering spot on the road's horizon grew into a bus, its motor roaring toward us.

"Is that it?" one soldier asked the other.

"What else could it be?" the other soldier said.

The bus squealed to a stop in front of us. It was all black with tinted windows that reflected the sky. The door opened with a hiss.

The soldiers prodded us into the shape of a line, and one by one, we climbed the steps leading up into the cool, dark unknown of the bus's interior.

I sat near the back. The seats were tall and soft. They smelled new. One soldier sat in front and the other stood in the aisle facing us. The bus started, lurched forward.

I looked out the window at fields sliding by, trees, a water tower. They did not look like they looked on TV. The fields were gouged into muddy lines. The water towers bled rust and I studied the rust, wondering if I might find a message in them—an image of hope or salvation. These things happened.

Patches of snow stretched across the fields, smudges of blank spots that made the world look like nothing so much as an unfinished drawing on unclean paper.

We drove for a while—I don't know how long. The scenery did not significantly change. It was all just fields and trees and more water towers and now and then in the distance a small house.

It could even have been the same scenery passing by two or three or a hundred times, like in a cheaply made cartoon.

No one on the bus spoke, not even the soldiers. We all stared out the windows, clouding the glass with our breath and then wiping the clouds away with the palms of our hands.

Maybe hours went by. Finally the bus turned onto another road, traveled along bumps and ruts for a while longer before stopping in front of a small, mustard yellow, two-story house that leaned almost imperceptibly to one side. The door of the bus opened at the mouth of the house's driveway.

"Home sweet home, gentleman," one of the soldiers said and we were guided by gunpoint off the bus and up the driveway to our new home. There was a welcome mat in front of the door. I didn't know whose idea that was. It seemed almost a cruel joke.

Halfway House

We were assigned rooms, given clothes, food, modest entertainment. We spent our first days avoiding each other and watching TV. We spent the days after that doing pretty much the same thing. I napped a lot in the room that I shared with no one. We all knew that something else must happen and we patiently waited for it to come about.

The window in my room overlooked wheat fields, rolling hills, distant rooftops, and the more distant city. I sat in a chair some mornings or evenings and looked out toward the city— toward Mortarville—and imagined a better place. Under certain lights— when the sun's rays were like a far away golden rain or maybe Christ's own spotlight shining down—it seemed likely even. How could those faraway towers, those spires, obelisks and monoliths not be the home of hope? How could prettiness and promise not reside there, arm in arm, sharing a spacious loft or even a studio apartment?

But the hope of Mortarville was muted somewhat by the images of Mortarville that I saw on the TV—its murders, factory closings, poverty and occasional riots. Though the News Anchor Couples would smile and try to accentuate the positive—there was always some new plan and scale-sized model of the plan on the horizon—the city itself was crumbling. It looked nice enough from a distance, the grime and decay obscured as it was by a romantic haze of smog, but on TV it rusted and bled, it suffered and died in full color and high definition stereo.

A newspaper arrived daily, thumping against the door every morning, but what arm had thrown it? What paperboy, with his striped shirt, his bicycle, his baseball cap. I never saw him and any neighborhood kid would have to live miles away.

On mornings when I was up early, I would listen by the door, hoping to hear the paper land, hoping to catch sight of whoever had delivered it. But even when I opened the door only seconds after I heard it arrive, the street would be empty.

I carried the paper in, scanned the headlines, placed it on a table near the door. Later, it would travel around the house by its usual means: carried by a Doe to the kitchen, carried by a Jones to the living room, left by a Smith in the bathroom. The news of Mortarville, the opinions of Mortarville, the problems of Mortarville, the hope of Mortarville and the latest problem with that hope. It looked like a bad place to visit and I didn't particularly want to live there, but somehow I knew it was where I would end up. Maybe that was where we would all end up.

On the last two pages of the newspaper there were comics, and I read these religiously, following the interpersonal and legal relationships of Judge Morgan and his friends, the homey intrigues of Sister Perth, and the zany antics of Private Stockman, the worst soldier in the US Army. He was violently murdered by his superior officer—Sergeant Krank—every other week and left in a broken limbed pile on the floor, but would be restored, by cartoon miracle, to solid form by the next installment.

The kitchen pantry was fully stocked with macaroni and cheese. There were other things too—peanut butter, soup, crackers, bread, etc., but mostly, I just ate the macaroni and cheese. It brought me some comfort. There were frozen peas in the freezer and sometimes I added these to the mix for variety. I remembered something about the different food groups, and the importance of all that.

I preferred to eat in my room, sitting in a chair, eating from a bowl while I looked out at the wheat fields, the rolling hills, the distant rooftops, and the more distant city.

The Basement Sessions

We had been there, waiting, eating, reading newspapers, watching TV for a month or so when Mr. Rooney began making his weekly visits. He would enter through the front door without knocking, and find one of us—in our room, in the kitchen, in the living room. I guess he had a key.

He was a man of average build, average height, indiscernible age—though he somehow reminded me of the lead zombie in a movie I had once seen in Mr. Melvin's class. The dead brother returned from the grave.

There was something dark about all the corners and edges of Mr. Rooney's face, as if theater make-up had been applied. Maybe that's what reminded me of the zombie.

He wore grey suits and spoke with the sort of quiet, controlled voice that made one think that he had been different once, that some horrible rage hid beneath the surface, but a lid had been placed over it and screwed down tight.

When he entered the house, he did so silently, and moved across floors as if he held no weight. Sometimes you would not even know he was there—you would just look up and see him, standing in a doorway, leaning against a counter, waiting. Then he would say a name as if reading it from the top of a list, even though he had nothing in his hands.

Jones, or *Roberts* or *Smith,* he would say, (there were two of each—no relation) and the appropriate Jones or Roberts or Smith would stand up and follow Mr. Rooney to the basement.

The basement was painted pink, with beige carpeting. It contained a couch, a chair, and a water heater.

Mr. Rooney carried a briefcase. He sat in the chair.

"How are you doing today, Mr. Smith?" he would say. "Everything all right here for you? Are you comfortable enough? Are you being sufficiently provided for? Would you like to lie down?"

I told him everything was all right, but that I would rather sit up.

"Are you sure?" he would ask. "It's a very comfortable couch."

"I'm fine," I told him. "I'll be fine. I'll be fine sitting."

He would nod, smile, mark something down on a notebook he kept balanced on the end of his pointy knee.

"Some people find it's easier to talk lying down," he said.

"I'm fine."

Then he would ask me how everything was going in the house, and I would tell him it was all fine. I had my macaroni and cheese, a bed and nothing to complain about.

"Would you like to talk about anything?" he would ask next. "The fire? Your friends?"

"Not particularly," I told him.

"You parents?"

"Not particularly," I told him.

"Do you remember them?" he asked. "Do you remember your parents?"

"Yes," I said. "Very well."

He marked something else down in his notebook.

At first, he would always ask about the underground home for lost boys, about how I liked it there, and did I miss it now, but as time went on, the subject seemed to lose some of its interest for him. He wanted to talk about other things.

We began to talk of other things. He asked me about my parents again, but would correct me if I mentioned Drs. John and Jonathon Smithee.

"Not those parents," he said. "Let's talk about your other parents. Let's talk about your *Mom* and *Dad*." He raised his eyebrows and leaned forward in his chair, hoping I would take the hint, hoping that the lessons of my previous home had not been wasted on me.

It did not take me long to figure out that he meant the people I had seen on TV, the man with the pipe, the woman with the apron and pearls. I would tell him about them, to keep him happy.

After awhile, I would even begin to make stuff up—telling him about my troubles in school, the girls I'd had crushes on, the bullies who threw me in the dumpster, my favorite and least favorite classes. He would nod, sometimes jot things down in his notebook again.

"Tell me how it felt to be the son of your parents," Mr. Rooney would ask and I began to play along with these preparatory exercises or rehearsals. I invented an internal life to go along with the external one that had been suspended above me on a TV screen while I had been strapped to a metal table. I was afraid of my domineering mother, pitied my complacent but well-meaning dad. I loved the maid who would come twice a week to help with the housework and later loved the pig-tailed girl who moved in next door. I hated the bully down the street and remembered with a strange mixture of anger, regret and horror the time he had found a gun in the garbage and it had gone off in his face while he was showing it to the other kids at the bus stop.

"And how did that make you feel," Mr. Rooney asked. "How did it make you feel when you realized what had happened...that he was gone forever."

"Sad," I told him. "I cried."

Mr. Rooney leaned back in his chair.

"Very good," Mr. Rooney said. "Very good. Are you sure you wouldn't like to lie down?"

"I'm OK sitting," I told him.

But he still seemed happy. We were making progress.

Our Family

Six traumatized, semi-broken, slightly scorched young men went on living in the numberless house—carried on with something that bore a passing resemblance to life, and not speaking to each other beyond a few necessary grunts. We met each other's gazes only grudgingly, fleetingly. Squeezing past one another in doorways we might say, "Excuse me." More likely we would only mumble something approximating that.

Six months would go by and the place would never seem like a place to wait. Its walls and floors never settled into the grooves of the familiar and it seemed at any moment they could be disassembled and taken away by an unseen crew of stagehands. I could wake up any morning to find myself sleeping in a field alone and it would not have surprised me.

On rainy days, the roof leaked in the kitchen and someone took a pot from a cupboard and placed it on the floor. The water dripped, the pot filled, someone else emptied it. The seconds were counted like this. Time passed and was emptied into the kitchen sink.

I cannot say why we did not talk to one another—it is impossible to imagine we did not have something to talk about. Interesting conversation could be made from my beginnings in an aquarium, or my few happy months being mothered by a primate. And what of their stories? What fires were they forged in? What dishes, tubes, or kilns had been their wombs?

In the living room, the TV was always on. There was a couch and two chairs in front of it and there was always at least one of us there, watching. What did we watch? Whatever was on—we had no device for changing the channels and were subject to the whims of whatever antennae, cable or programmer controlled it.

Usually it was the news. The news of Mortarville and the

world beyond. The occasional drama. The occasional comedy. A war was being fought, a boy was in love with a girl, something new had been invented and a plane had crashed into a river. Things exploded, people tripped over ottomans, windows shattered in slow motion, stocks rose and fell. We watched a show about a man who flies over the city and sometimes crashed through walls rather than using a door or window. But the walls he crashed through looked flimsy to begin with, and when he went through them it was less like he had been flying and more like he was just stepping in from an adjacent room. Some of the bricks even bounced when they hit the floor.

When his semi-spectacular entrance was finished, the man stood with hands on hips, legs akimbo, chest puffed out, waiting for someone to tell him how he was needed—why he had been summoned by secret whistle, magic word or watch or whatever. There was a moment or two where everyone in the room only stared, adjusting to the fact that a man had just entered through the wall, and that he was wearing brightly colored leotards and a cape, while they were standing there dumfounded in their tweed suits, brown fedoras, sensible skirts and shoes.

We men of the house watched TV silently, sometimes chewing our meals there, staring at the man flying above a fake city, or the real world unraveling and building itself up again. The brave stories of this or that. The courage of men and women in the face of this or that. The tragic or comical misunderstandings between a man and a woman, a boy and a girl, a parent and child, man and humanity. I—perhaps all of us—had seen it all in some degree before. In class. Variations of the epic and common struggle of life. We watched, we ate, we remembered and digested.

The front door was open but we had nowhere else to go.

Pastoral

Some evenings, I would leave the numberless house to go for a walk. No one stopped me, but the sidewalk in front ended after only a hundred or so yards. If I went farther, I would have to continue on in grass and weeds or in the street. There were no neighbors, no other houses, no sign of life anywhere besides our little home.

The street itself traveled on in either direction, straight and unbroken, fading into the distance. On the other side of the street was a field of corn and on our side was a field of wheat or something that looked enough like wheat to call it that. If I walked far enough, the land began to rise a bit and I could see over the wheat to the rolling hills, houses and city beyond. I could not see over the corn no matter where I stood, and one day I decided to walk through it and see where it might lead, what might lie on the other side of it. It seemed almost like a green wall before me, with the space between each row a doorway leading into a narrow green hallway.

The aisles of green stalks seemed endless and smelled of life, of promise, of hope and, I suppose, corn. Maybe I could live here, I thought, beneath the sun and sky, surviving on my wits, rainwater and raw corn. But it seemed unlikely.

A plane buzzed by above me and I stopped, stood completely still and waited to see if the plane would shoot at me, drop bombs or perhaps swoop in low to unload its cargo of deadly gas or powder on top of me. But the plane was very high up; it did not seem to notice or care. It flew straight off into the distance, swallowed up by a blue that seemed particularly perfect and pure that day.

The cornfield ended and I was in a field of mud and stunted weeds. A line of trees was a hundred yards away and I walked towards it, wondering what was on the other side, while mud sucked at my feet and tried to pull off my shoes.

The buzzing returned to the sky. I looked up, saw the plane returning, lower now, determined, imagined its pilot, eyes squinting down, teeth bared, finger on some red button. There was the sound of gunfire, louder than it appears on TV, and bullets were plunking into the mud around me. I ran. Slipping, falling, scrambling across the slime while the plane roared past just a few yards over my head. I could feel the wind of its propeller, the pull of its wake and threw myself face-first into the mud. Behind me the plane rose and began its turn back.

I scrambled to my feet and ran for the trees. The trees would protect me, they would hide me. The field was too wet for the plane to land and he would have to return to whoever had sent him empty handed, with no bleeding body to report, no job well done, no promotion or medal. I heard it coming back, gaining on me, and the empty field before me seemed to stretch out, adding miles to my goal. I ran harder, the roar behind me, squinting, his finger on the button.

But the trees were just ahead, the plane was too low. The pilot abandoned his red button and pulled the throttle hard, the engines strained against the force of momentum, the wings and propeller fought clawing for some grip on the air.

We reached the trees at the same time. Me with ragged breath and beating heart, him grazing the top branches and returning to the safety of the sky, buzzing away into nothingness, obscurity and failure.

I stood for a moment, clinging to the bark of a tree. I was alive. I had made it. If I could catch my breath again, I would be fine. But I could barely see—the blood seemed to burst from my veins, pouring into the holes of my eyes, flooding my brain, covering the world. I felt the rough skin of the tree and saw nothing for a moment. The rough skin against my face. If I could breathe. It seemed as if the tree was breathing instead. Its rough, bristled skin was heaving, some massive gentle giant heart inside, beating slowly, a large black knuckled hand hovering above my head, wanting to pet my hair, wanting to comfort me.

The pounding in my head and chest subsided and there was

light again. The world was back. It was silent and peaceful. I walked on.

On the other side of the trees was the rushing brown water of river. A tree floated by in the river, its leaves still green, its pale roots sticking from the water like loose wiring. I watched it roll in the water and disappear around a bend.

And then, there was a man standing next to me at the edge of the river bank. I did not see or hear him come, but suddenly felt him there and turned to face him. He was dressed as a park ranger, with broad brimmed hat, the green shirt and pants, the walking stick.

He looked at me. His face was dark with black eyes and eyebrows, and deep lines that traced the skull beneath the flesh and muscle. Some muscle or nerve seemed to be pulsing along the line of his jaw.

He almost smiled. "You should be getting back now," he said.

"Yes sir," I said.

Release Date

A black van arrived in our driveway every couple of weeks. Mr. Rooney and some faceless others would get out, enter the house, call out a name. One of us—one of the six then five then four—would answer the call, follow the men outside, get into the van, and be driven away.

Smith or Jones or Roberts would never return. Those of us that remained might look out the window as they drove away, but we did not speak of the matter. There was more room on the couch now, more food in the pantry for the rest of us.

I watched TV and waited for my name to be called.

On TV there was another plant closing, another scale model of a new plan for downtown renovation, a small but violent disturbance during Mortarville Pride Day, where several people and windows were broken. The weather was partly cloudy with a chance of more of the same tomorrow and a local sports team had lost its third game in a row.

I began to dread Mortarville, but what future was there for me here in this temporary house? It was hard not to imagine being left behind, abandoned, the pantries left unstocked, the TV bill unpaid and shut off with the electricity and the heat. I would sit alone in the dark and starve.

There were only two of us left. Me, the last John Smith and him, the last James Roberts. We kept to ourselves.

Then the black van arrived and my name was called.

"How do you feel?" Mr. Rooney asked as we drove down the long, straight and featureless road.

"Fine," I said.

"Ready to conquer the world?" He smiled.

"I guess."

And then the new world appeared: the concrete wonders of Mortarville spread out across the front windshield like a broken toothed smile.

BOOK TWO

The Titular Hero Arrives

Here, at last, is Mortarville. A city founded upon the industries of cement, steel, glass; a city founded upon the industry of city building, and consequently it has been built from these materials to an epic scale far exceeding any need or use. No alleyway has been left unconverted to a four lane highway, no park unpaved, no obscure military hero or historical event that has not been cast forever into stone or iron to tower grim-faced above an intersection, glowering down at a rusting playground, municipal lot #7 or the brown and crooked river that winds through the city's neighborhoods and industrial parks, foaming at its banks.

There, on the corner, the inventor of the four-way stop sign, the twin razor or the snooze alarm points his patina-ed hand toward a promising and forgotten future.

And here, in the center of People's Square, roosted and shat upon by an impressive variety of pigeons, is the hero and patron saint of Mortarville. A ten-foot tall and smiling boy, his green and immovable bangs lifted from his eyes by a permanent wind, his parents, cast in stone and smaller than the boy, weeping stone tears forever at his feet. This boy once bravely carried the flute into battle against an invading force. The invading force was fully armed with things considerably larger and more dangerous than a woodwind instrument. Not surprisingly, the boy perished early in the battle. An arrow to the heart. But he did not perish immediately, and this was taken as a sign by the city's defenders. It was a miracle, of sorts. He was carrying a flute, and the first half dozen or so shots had missed him completely. Of course, a reasonable person might have deduced that even invading armies, no matter how barbaric, hold no special malice toward apprentice flautists and may have not been aiming for him at all. But never mind that. Heroes are not made nor statues built by reasonable people. It was a miracle. The defending army went on to victory, decimating the attackers, killing all the males, salting the earth, raping the women and subjugating the children. And upon the pedestal which the young hero forever stands, a plaque and the city's anthem:

O Mortarville, O Mortarville
Thy beauty of we sing!
Thy azure sky and water ways
Thy bubbling natural springs
That feed the mills of industry
Which pays for all these things

But most of the mills of industry have gone west or east or north or south, for parts and profits unknown, and most of the people have packed their things and followed after, leaving behind the monuments and towers built with their pride, sweat and taxes to rot now from weather, bird shit and neglect. Even the bubbling springs no longer bubble so much as gather in fetid puddles in dirt that sparkles with broken glass.

Now a nail salon inhabits one small corner of what used to be the third largest department store in the country. "The EZ-PZ Money Exchange" (in hand- painted letters) has replaced the The First Mortarville City Bank, its once grand lobby partitioned now by temporary walls and a drop ceiling. The stone and steel wedding cakes remain in the city's skyline, but in disrepair. It seems, at noon on a weekday, that these temples to industry and commerce were built by a vanished race of giants and are now inhabited by hermits, wanderers and parasites, moving into these roomy carapaces, these hollowed carcasses left behind.

And where am I now? I am here, at this desk, in this room, in this building, in this city. I am in Mortarville.

You cannot see the city from here. My desk faces a cinderblock wall in a windowless office. I am a grown man three floors beneath the street. Trucks rumble by above me, occasionally knocking white dust loose from the pipes and tiles overhead. It falls into my hair, onto the shoulders of my black suit. Sometimes, I notice people glancing at my shoulders. I follow the dotted line from their eyes to the specks of white dust.

"It's not dandruff," I tell them. "It's the ceiling." Sometimes they laugh, like this is some sort of folksy expression, but I point upward with one finger and if I'm lucky, a truck rumbles by on cue and a light dust falls upon both of us to illustrate my point.

I am older now, though not taller. I am gainfully employed, though not too gainfully. Our Lady of Scientific Mistakes is far behind me, but maybe not so far as that. I am technically free.

I am typing a report. The typewriter I am writing on is massive and old. A turret-less tank, it hums when I turn it on, and the lights of my office dim, as if someone were being electrocuted down the hall. Sometimes, when I hit shift and the letter "I," I receive a small electric shock. Sometimes I do this on purpose.

I am the Security Director of the last remaining downtown mall. No one here knows the secrets of my origin. I come and go, they learn my name or they don't, and they assume that I am a man born like them. "Where are you from?" someone might ask one day and I will say to them: "From Mortarville." And as time goes on, it feels more and more like the truth.

If I told them otherwise, would they care? The real truth no longer matters. The days when clergymen, neo-luddites and pantheists rioted in the street are long gone and forgotten, erased from our memories and left out of our history books. The newspapers that must have once carried the exciting events of those dark times have been misfiled, lost in suspicious fires or dissolved into dust. If I say out loud tomorrow that I was conceived in a dish, gestated in a tank, and born from a metal chute onto a metal tray, no great notice will be made, nor shock registered. A mild and blank discomfort might rise but it will be shrugged away. Move on. Nothing of interest here. Carry on with your shopping.

"At approximately 0730," I type. All my reports begin this way. It would seem that I never know the exact time of anything. At approximately 0730 something or other happened, as it always does.

The Assistant Security Director comes into my office and sits in a chair in the corner, between the wall and a banged up file cabinet. There is a nametag on the breast pocket of his white shirt that reads *Tom*, but really his name is Richard. He took the nametag from out of a box of nametags of people that used to work here but no longer do. He doesn't like the people in the mall to know his real name, he says. They might try and track him down. I point out to him that the nametags only have first names on them, and it is unlikely that someone would be able to find him from just "Richard," any more than they could "Tom." He is not convinced, or he has other reasons he is not sharing, or he is just being difficult, which would not be entirely out of character.

He sits in the chair and scratches the paint from a corner of the file cabinet with the tip of a key. He does this every time he comes to my office, and has scraped away a patch the size of a quarter and the shape of the state of Florida. Or maybe it is supposed to be a penis. This too would not be out of character.

He pauses, admires his work. Now it seems like neither a penis nor the state of Florida, but some other significant shape that I should recognize. I stare at it for a minute while he brushes away the crumbs of loose paint.

"What is it?" I ask him and he says: "A secret. So what are you doing, dick-less?"

And what can you make of or do with a man like that—a man inordinately fond of swearing often and without logic or reason. "Fucking cock," he might say while riding in an elevator or walking down a hallway. "Shit-balls." It is all apropos of nothing, and sometimes I will ask him why he is shouting "dick-licker," or "cum-guzzler," in my office when we were only talking about this week's reports or next week's schedule. He usually shrugs or repeats the statement louder. Or he calls me a pussy.

I could fire him, of course, but what would be the point? The parent company would just send me someone else to train and he would have his own quirks and problems. Maybe the problems would be worse. Maybe they would be better but why take the chance? I will endure. I will write my report.

"Writing a report," I tell him. "That's what I'm doing."

"The water leak?"

"Yeah."

"Keep up the good work, smegma," he says and I say: "Thanks."

Terminal Mall

That is the name of the mall I work in. In honor of what it used to be, in honor of all the working parts that have been filled in with concrete or covered over with brick and drywall. Once trains rumbled, tickets were sold, and commuters commuted from happy home to lucrative career. They walked up and down faux-marble steps beneath obscure Roman gods cast in cement, holding cement scale models of engine cars, dining cars and cabooses in their massive cement hands. The Gods of Industry and Transportation and Business. The Demigods of Traffic and Taxpayers. The steel tracks that once groaned with the weight of the masses have been plucked from the ground, to be bent and reassembled into an attractive sculpture on the center floor of the mall. The sculpture is of a man swinging a hammer. It signifies something, but does not really look very much like a man swinging a hammer and sometimes people—out-of-towners mostly—will ask: "What is that supposed to be?" A man swinging a hammer, we have been taught to answer. The sculpture is titled, "Man Swinging a Hammer." It was created to honor our glorious working past, back when things used to work gloriously.

When I stray from the safety of my office, up stairs, through the greasy haze and out into the mall, I will pause to gaze from an upper level balcony at this kingdom I command. Though command is too strong a word for it. As is kingdom. Mostly I move people around and try to keep the overtime down. I make schedules and then change the schedules when the workers tell me about doctor's appointments they have made, or funerals they must attend, or family reunions. And sometimes I think, if I kept better track I would be able to catch their mistakes and inconsistencies, point out to them that given the number of funerals they have found it necessary to attend in the past, any reunion now could be held in one booth of a local coffee shop. But I don't keep better track of things.

People still shop here, but mostly it is the derelicts wandering back and forth, filching a few pennies and dimes from the wishing well fountains placed in several corners of the mall. Their pockets are dark from the wetness of their stolen money. They carry shopping bags from purchases made half a decade ago.

There are guards on the floor, or at least, there ought to be. There should be one right there, making slow methodical circles around the sculpture of the man with the hammer. There should be another one on the level I am observing from, patrolling the circumference of the mall. Depending on the time of day, two more should be in the food court and a third should be making rounds on the top level, occasionally poking his head outside to make sure the exterior walls are not being defaced or falling down on their own accord.

But sometimes the guards are sleeping on boxes in the back corridors. Sometimes they are committing illicit acts in storerooms with their girlfriends or fellow guards or by themselves or with mannequins. The guards wear black uniforms with gold badges and red stripes. They carry guns, which is a fact that never fails to make me nervous.

I was a guard here myself once. Fresh from The Secret Home for Lost Abominations, I answered an ad in the Mortarville paper of record: *The Mortarville Straight Shooter*. Students and retirees welcome, the ad said, and this spoke to me of certain low standards of ability that gave me reason to hope. With nothing but a fraudulent resume provided for me by a secret government agency, this seemed, as much as anything, like the job for me.

I came to the interview in my one government-issued blue suit. It was still new then, with all of its original creases. I sat in the basement office, which is now my office, while my predecessor—a man named Kevin Fox—interviewed me from a list of company-issued questions. He stared down at his sheet of questions through most of the interview, only lifting his head once or twice to look me briefly in the eye while he talked, as if suddenly remembering then promptly forgetting a trick he had been taught at a business seminar. He explained to me about the exciting team I was joining. We were the Independent Security Division of United Conglomerates Incorporated being contracted out to the Property Ownership Division of United Conglomerates Incorporated. UCI was a pretty big company, with interests across the globe. You wouldn't know it from the benefits package. Kevin Fox gave me a folder explaining my Health Care Plan, my Death and Dismemberment Plan, my Vision Plan. The folder had a picture of male and female security officer on the front. They were looking up at something and smiling. Their uniforms were perfect.

"They seem pretty happy," I said.

"And healthy too," Kevin Fox said.

After the interview, I was given a uniform and a gun. Over the next couple weeks I would be trained to observe, notice and detect. This was The Independent Security Divisions motto. "It's our Holy Trinity," Kevin Fox told me, which made a kind of sense to me since as far as I could tell they were all the same thing.

I was taught to load and clean my gun. I was taken to a vacant field on the outskirts of town and shot seven out of ten bottles successfully, which was good enough to pass.

An ancient and shrinking guard gave me a tour of the facility, showing me—at his own shuffling pace—all the darkest and brightest corners of the mall. He told me the history of the building and the personal history of himself. But he had only three teeth, unreliable lips, and a thick gray broom of a mustache that filtered out all the softer consonants so it was not always easy to follow what he was saying.

"It used to be a train station," he told me no fewer than a dozen times. I told him I already knew that, but it didn't matter to him or he didn't hear me. He also told me that his name was Bob Longstreet and that the Longstreets had been living and working and dying in the city of Mortarville since before it was a city—since the days of log cabins, fruited plains and martyred flautists.

"Just keep your eyes open," he said, blinking his own eyes which were like black moons with milky clouds passing permanently across them. "Keep your eyes open and you'll see plenty around here, I'll tell you. I've seen plenty, believe me. You wouldn't believe the things I've seen here. Every day something's going on. Some crazy thing or another. I could tell you stories..."

And he did. Plenty of stories, but they never struck me as crazy or unbelievable. Mostly they were long and circular, with the ends looping back into the beginnings, toothless snakes gumming on their own tails, becoming bored, tired of the taste and distracted.

The city of Mortarville might not seem like much to a young man like myself, it was true. But once it was really something. Should have seen the mall when it was a train station. Should have seen Mortarville when the men wore hats and suits and carried briefcases and the women all wore long dresses and pearls....

The cell phone stand in the corner used to be a soda shop. Soda for a nickel. A big glass, too. Tall as your arm or shin. Wide as your head or hips...

By the time Bob Longstreet finished, we were standing at the highest point of the building, looking down upon the city. Mortarville in repose. Mortarville in decay. We were outside, above the observation deck and below a fluttering flag. The wind blew through the cloth of my shirt, rustled the hairs of his mustache, made the polyps of his flesh quiver. We leaned over the cement wall that held us back from a certainly lethal drop and looked down at the city far below, laid out in uneven squares and crumbling blocks. The crooked brown river seemed, from here, like a tear in a badly wrinkled map.

"That's Gypsum Avenue, Klinker Street, Quarry Road," Bob Longstreet said, pointing vaguely. "Millionaire Row, they used to call that," he said. "Was something then."

On the edge of the city, where the landscape dipped down toward the water, where the old buildings had already fallen, we could see the gravel piles, the conveyor belts and rusting water towers, the bins and hoppers that had mixed and poured this city. A line of cement trucks were waiting to be filled. The trucks were pocked with rust.

"Maybe we'll bounce back," Longstreet said. "Used to be

something, once." He mumbled something else that I could not make it out.

I could see my old home from here, the house without numbers. I did not point this out to Longstreet. It was a closely guarded government secret.

Bob Longstreet Teaches Me Basic Report Writing

"Always begin at the beginning," he said. "Always start with the time and date and then answer the five W's."

He waited for a moment for me to ask.

"The five W's?"

He smiled through his mustache. "Who, what, where and when," he said.

"That's four."

"What?"

"That's four W's. Not five."

He thought about it, did the math in his head, looked down at his knuckles, seemed to count on those for awhile.

"Hmm…" he said.

"Why?"

"What?"

"The fifth W. Is it why?"

"No, why's no good. Why's an opinion. No one wants your opinion in a report. Just facts. It's not why."

"OK."

"Maybe it's how."

"Four W's and an H?"

"Yeah. Who, what, when, where and how, OK?"

"OK."

"I could have sworn there was another W, though."

"Four's good," I said, not wanting him to feel too bad about it. "Four Ws. And an H."

"And no opinions," Bob Longstreet said. "Just facts in the order they happened."

He stood over me the whole time I wrote my first report, the one about the girl who had passed out in the women's restroom. The needle was still in her arm when Longstreet and I found her. Someone had already called 911 and security had been notified; that's why we were there. We brought the camera and I took pictures of some mysterious vials and drug accouterment she had left on the floor next to the toilet. Longstreet got her name for the report by constantly shouting for it while the paramedics checked her pulse, extracted samples of her blood and started an IV. "What's your name?" Longstreet yelled as her eyes rolled up into her head. "I need your name for the report. What's your name? You gotta have a name…"

She muttered something that was somehow both vulgar and incomprehensible and Longstreet turned his attentions to the paramedics.

"Did you get her name?" he asked them. "I need a name. For the report."

They shook their heads and carried on with their work. The woman stirred at the prick of another needle.

"I feel funny," she muttered. "Did you give me something? Did you just give me something?"

The paramedics found this amusing. They laughed and one of them said: "You gave that to yourself, honey."

Several other guards had shown up by this time. We were all milling about in the women's restroom while the paramedics did their work. It felt a little like a cocktail party gone horrible awry. And with no drinks. Just sinks, mirrors, stalls, and dispensers filled with pink soap.

"Find out her name," Longstreet said to the paramedics. Then Longstreet said to me: "You always need a name. Also a unit number and what hospital they're taking her to…even though there's really only one hospital…though now and then someone goes somewhere else…"

"You gave me something," the woman said. "What did you give me?"

"I'm out of film," I said. I had taken about seven snap-shots of the needles and baggies. I didn't take any of the woman when she was sprawled out across the toilet bowl, because we have rules against that.

One of the guards squirted soap onto his hands and ran them

under the water in a sink. He looked around for a paper towel.

"There's no paper towels," he said.

Another guard got on the radio.

"Command Center, tell housekeeping that the women's rest-room needs paper towels."

Eventually, one of the paramedics went through the woman's wallet and told Longstreet her name. She was transported to Mortarville General Hospital at approximately 1205 by EMS Unit Four. All secure. Someone from housekeeping brought paper towels and Longstreet and I returned to the Command Center.

I typed my report with all the approximatelies and the whos whats, whens and hows that Bob Longstreet advised. The type-writer hummed.

"Should I tell it in first person?" I asked him and he said that I should.

"First person it is," I said. I began at the beginning. But I have trouble beginning at beginnings. Not just hers but mine. The start of anything seems too far away and too clear at once. My entire life is a tangle of details and sparks and how do I separate what I am now from how I was made from what I will become? Or from what surrounds me? The world is big and strange and alien and familiar. The breath of Bob Longstreet presses against the back of my neck and carries with it the scent of damp soil.

Begin at the beginning and the big typewriter gives me a little jolt and I think of fire, angry mobs and breaking glass.

My Spectacular Rise to Middle Management In the Exciting World of In-house Security

A month or two later, a fire started in one of the service corridors. I was checking the area when I smelled the smoke. I liked checking the service corridors. It was quieter there and away from the crowds—such as they were (and they were not much). But even the relatively meager crowds of a failing mall made me a little nervous. In the service corridors, you met only delivery people and stock boys and clerks and you could nod sympathetically and grunt with one another in a shared language of resignation, misery and regret. It made me think of home.

I was in one of the longest, lowest and darkest corridors when I saw a man I didn't recognize. He seemed nothing like a delivery person, stock boy or a clerk. He was tall and thin, with dark, dirty hair that looked as if it had been styled by a series of small explosions involving some amount of grease.

He saw me, grunted, walked quickly past. It was not the grunt of a fellow worker, but a strange and alien noise. Then I smelled the smoke, saw a few gray wisps of it curling around the corner ahead of me, and froze for a moment. *Where there's smoke*...I remembered and imagined a painful ending, the agony of burning, the bubbling then blackening of flesh.

I almost ran down the hallway. *Almost* ran because I tried to never actually run at work. It was something like a personal policy—if I ran, my gun might spill out of its holster, go off, send a bullet through my brain or the brain of an innocent bystander. Or I might trip, or arrive too dizzy and out of breath to call for back up.

So I moved swiftly and efficiently down the hallway, a fast and somewhat graceless walk toward doom. A quick and anxious pace, and rounding the corner, a wall of fire, flames and smoke curling up against the ceiling, blackening and consuming everything.

Where was the nearest fire extinguisher? I tried to remember.

It had been part of my training. *Fire extinguishers are located at all...* but the end of the sentence escaped me. All hallways? All elevators? All fires? I got on the radio.

"514 to Command Center," I said, trying not to sound either too panicky or too casual. "I have a situation here...in the back hallway." If I was too casual, the Command Center might not bother hanging up on his usual phone fight with his wife to answer my call. If I sounded too panicky, he might spill his coffee on one of the panels again.

Maybe I had been too casual. Flames were crawling up the wall and smoke was blackening the ceiling and nothing came back over the radio. *This can't be good*, I thought. I actually thought that. *This can't be good.*

I could feel the heat of the flames—not so much that it was painful yet, but enough to know that there was a fire nearby, that it was growing, that it was consuming, which is what fire does. It consumes. It destroys. It leaves children without parents, then brings down the orphanages too. Fire is cruelly ironic. Fire is my personal enemy.

I repeated my radio message, more urgently this time, trying to suppress the vibration taking over my throat like a small motor set to fear. I added: "Code Red" to better convey the seriousness of the situation.

Just then the sprinkler heads went off in the hallway. The fire hissed and went down some, but not enough, and now smoke and rusted water filled the hallway. Alarms were going off, great whooping screaming sounds that drowned out whatever might finally becoming back to me over the radio.

I ran—actually ran now—back down the hallway, in the direction I had come from, away from the smoke and fire and fire-retardant rain, sloshing through the inch of dingy orange water that was already covering the floor, splashing and sloshing and coughing my way out. I didn't drop my gun. That much was good. And I did not trip and fall until I was out of the corridor and onto the main floor of the mall, surrounded by bewildered shoppers and bums. I imagine it was a little startling for them to see me bursting through the double doors like that, soaking wet and winded, trailing thick smoke. And it was startling for me to remember, as I plunged forward the three steps leading down from the corridor entrance.

The floor was gone from beneath me and I was flying face forward from the top of the steps toward the other floor several feet lower. In slow motion, as people who are interviewed on TV after accidents are fond of saying. The whole thing was like in a movie, they are also fond of saying, and like in a movie it served a purpose. The plot is advanced: I fall with all my weight and force into the wild and greasy haired man, and we both go spilling across the marble floor, smashing against columns, shins, and shopping bags, stopping against the hollow plastic neo-roman façade of The Lottery Shoppe.

My radio was squawking now. Nonsensically, with one electronic voice cutting off another and everything jumbling into clicks, whirs and static. Guards were appearing through the crowds of onlookers, shoving their way forward through shoulders and elbows. Someone helped me to my feet, while I managed to cough and gasp enough words out to give them the idea that the wild-haired man who happened to be beneath me was somehow a party in all this mess. A guilty party. He was helped to his feet as well, though not so gently. Two guards handcuffed him and brought him back to the holding cell, knocking him into several walls and corners along the way. The fire department arrived with hoses and axes and the fire was put out. An ambulance arrived and paramedics strapped a plastic cup to my face and shoved oxygen into my lungs, but I refused to let them take me to the hospital for further treatment.

I went back to the Command Center and wrote a report while all the events were still clear in my mind—though I changed the events some to make my actions seem less random and clumsy. I answered all the questions: who, what, when, where, and how. I was thorough, concise and checked all my spelling while the man in the holding cell was screaming about his wrists hurting because the handcuffs were too tight, and also how he was a personal friend of the mayor and would have all of our jobs for this, that he was being harassed and accused for nothing more than a lack of hygiene, and how really, he was the one who had been attacked.

It might have been more convincing had his pockets not been stuffed with rags, matches and a can of lighter fluid.

My report was a big hit. Mr. Fox brought me up to meet the heads of the Property Management Division—a long table full of old men high in the highest tower. It was a vast, ornate and dimly lit place, more like the home of a secluded millionaire than an office, with dark paintings of furrowed brows lining the wood paneled walls. The carpet was the color, consistency, even the smell of deep forest moss. The ceiling-high windows that would have overlooked the city's highest buildings were covered with thick curtains that let in only razor thin shafts of dusty light.

The air was hot and humid, as if adjusted more for the comfort of the fleshy leaved tropical plants that inhabited the numerous shadowy corners of the room than the men that worked at its massive desks and tables, or napped in its enormous chairs and couches by the dark wooden mantles of unused fireplaces.

And there they were waiting for us, expecting us, the old men, the Vice Presidents of Property Management, all blue-veined hands folded onto the darkly polished table, their dry, scaled-over eyes looking up.

"This is Jack Smith," Fox said. He said it quietly, as if in church. "The man I told you about."

A month after that, Fox was emptying out the drawers and shelves of his office into a small cardboard box someone had thoughtfully provided for him. His eyes were red and watery and now and then I heard a small wet sound escape between his lips. It could have been a sigh or a sob.

I stood in the doorway, watching quietly, trying to think of something comforting to say—but what had happened? I did not know, so what words could I offer now?

"You OK, Kevin?" I said.

"Just fine," he said. "Just fucking swell."

142

Two men I had never seen before were standing behind us at a discreet distance pretending not to be watching. They were solid looking men in a black suits, black shirts, black ties.

Fox picked up a file from his desk and one of the men said quietly but very clearly: "Is that yours?"

Fox put the file down. He picked up the box and shoved past me through the doorway, pausing long enough to say: "Watch your back, Smith. That's my advice to you. Watch your back."

I could not tell if it was advice or a threat.

The Men in Black returned for me a little while later, after they were done escorting Kevin Fox off the property or dumping his body in the river or whatever it was they had done with him.

One of them said: "The Vice Presidents would like to see you, Mr. Smith."

They brought me back to the top of the tower where the old men were sitting at the long table in the shadows as if they had never moved.

"We need a new Director of Security," one of the old men whispered. I could barely hear him. I had to lean forward. "We've heard good things about you," he said. I think that is what he said. Something like that.

I said: "Thank you."

And that was it. My entire interview. The old men fell into a silence that seemed almost like sleep and the two men in black who had brought me there escorted me back as far as the elevator lobby.

"Good luck," one of them said.

"Don't do what Kevin Fox did," the other one said.

"What was that?" I asked them.

"We're not allowed to say," they said.

Work

Work is work. Sometimes, when people ask for one reason or another, that is what I tell them. How is work, they will ask. Work is work, I will say. And it was. And it is.

And I will dream some nights not of my interesting past, but of my mundane present, no different than a million other presents. I will dream of schedules and reports, overtime analyses and expenses, billings, invoices, disciplinary actions and counseling. I will even sometimes complete projects in my dreams—long and complicated procedures in carbon triplicates, carefully wrought charts and figures—only to find them instantly undone by the alarm clock and the morning sun. It is disappointing, of course, but no more disappointing than the end of one week and the start of another, with time undoing everything, as if none of it had ever been real and nothing lasting could ever be produced in this world.

I sit at my desk and type, chart, counsel, reprimand. I answer the phone and listen to the complaints from mall tenants, visitors, clients, bosses and employees. I take pictures of broken ceiling tiles, damaged walls, leaking pipes and water logged wigs. I counsel Bleuler about his attendance and McElrath about his hygiene.

Sometimes the men in black suits, shirts and ties come by for a visit. Always in pairs but not always the same two. They work for the Vice Presidents. It is hard to say how many Black Shirts there are or what exactly it is that they do, but sometimes they come by, they sit in my office, they ask how things are going. They ask as if they already know the answer.

It seems impossible to me that this was what my fathers had intended in creating life from scratch. So much sweat and inspiration just to add one more soul to the world's endless army of middle management hacks. Though it is almost certain that this is what my keepers, teachers and caretakers at The Home for Invented Boys had intended. *Where the Products of Yesterday's Science are Molded into the Dull Young Men of Tomorrow* could have been their slogan. And they molded me well. They broke and rebuilt me almost completely. I tell no one of my special beginnings, my unique origin and oppression. Work is oblivious to the remarkable invention of me. I am like a superhero that never acts. I am silent and can almost forget.

But I am protected at the core. Or I am corrupted. Switches have been put securely in place, the cells cannot be erased. A storm brews, the sky boils, electricity hums and crackles around me, and I remember everything.

Richard enters my office and sits down in his usual place. He says: "Cheswick left his gun in the food court again."

"He did this before?"

"I told you about it, penis-breath."

"Is it still there?"

"Ha-ha, dick-wipe. No. A customer pointed it out to him. They said: hey, fuckface, you left your gun."

"So it wasn't really left then."

"Except the part where he left it."

"I'll have a talk with him."

"OK. Sure you will, pussy."

"I will."

"Uh-huh."

He resumes work with the point of his key on the paint of the file cabinet. He begins humming quietly to himself. I do not recognize the tune at first but then realized it is the theme song from a TV show that was cancelled a decade ago. A show I liked. A show I used to watch in class at the home.

"Maybe you should go out on the floor," I say. "You're a supervisor. Maybe you should be out supervising or something."

He shrugs, but finally gets up and leaves.

After he is gone, I look at the mark he has left on the file cabinet. The strange, half-remembered shape like some object from my dreams. Is it a secret message? Maybe it is just a penis, but this raises another question: what fuels his obsession with genitalia? There are obvious answers here too, of course—upbringing and latent feelings of whatever—but what of the less obvious ones?

Could it be some hint that he knows of my inorganic origins? He might be telling me, warning me in code, that he is aware of what little role the penises of my fathers played in the existence of me. They were blindfolded witnesses, my father's cocks, innocent bystanders to my sterile insemination. Did the Assistant Director of Security know or suspect this? Maybe—or maybe not. Maybe sometimes a penis is just a penis.

A Distant Relation

The owner of The Beauty Shoppe flops a wet wig onto my desk. It looks like a small, drowned animal laying there, bleeding clear blood—an exotic animal with blond highlights. I wonder for a moment if the wig is alive.

Living Wigs® had been all the rage about five years ago. Wigs made of actual living hair—though not technically hair, but some microscopic and well-organized group of cells that grow and need to be shampooed daily. They were popular for all of a month and a half before it occurred to people that one of the few advantages to wigs was that they did not grow or need to be shampooed daily.

I nudge the wet thing on my desk with the tip of a pencil.

"Is it alive?" I ask.

"Are you crazy?"

"So its not alive?"

He exhales, rolls his eyes, checks his watch, goes through this whole list of actions meant to signify his impatience.

"I need a copy of your report for Corporate Loss," he tells me. "This is the fifth time something like this has happened." It is actually only the third time something like this has happened, unless he is counting the time their employee toilet backed up, and I have my suspicions about that too.

"This is only the third time this has happened," I say and right away I know this is a mistake. He proceeds to tell me how even once is unacceptable, but this has happened to him at least five times, probably six and he is not going stand here and argue math with me, so just give him the goddamn report.

"You'll have to get that through Property Management," I tell him. "I'm not allowed to give out reports. I give our Loss Prevention the reports and they send them to Mall Operations and they give them to Property Management."

He rolls his eyes again and says something under his breath.

"This is fucking bullshit," is what he says. And not really so much under his breath.

He leaves the drowned wig on my desk. I try to ask him nicely to take it with him but he tells me that I was responsible for it being broken and therefore I, or Property Management or Mall Operations or whomever, has just purchased it. It is not a point worth arguing. Maybe Property Management will pay him for his loss and suffering, or maybe they will not. I use the tip of my pencil to push the wig off the edge of the desk and into the waste paper basket. It makes a splatting noise at the bottom of the can.

It is the end of the day. I turn off the typewriter and turn off the light. Another day done and I stand there for a moment in my office listening. No sound comes from the Command Center, no disgruntled thief or vagrant occupies the holding cell, but I think I hear something—like a soft murmur, a tiny whimper, a prelude to a scream. I look down into the wastepaper basket. Do the wet shadows in there seem to move? I stare at it for a long time and cannot decide if I am seeing anything real. I pick up the basket, leave my office, lock the door, go up the short flight of stairs and out into the dim, gray, narrow hallway, adorned by pipes, wires and water stains. It smells of dust, mold and French-fries. A haze of greasy smoke fills the air from a faulty ventilation system that has never been fixed, will never be fixed.

There is an incinerator chute by the elevator. I drop the waste-paper basket in there and hear it clang and cry all the way down.

Home

The building I live in is at the end of a dead end avenue called Transportation Avenue. Transportation Avenue didn't used to be a dead end street. It used to run down into the industrial section of town, but now a highway divides it from its former path. From one window of my apartment I can see over the highway, to the failing factories. From my kitchen window, above the sink, I can look directly at the kitchen window of another apartment across the common parking lot. This is the better view.

The sun has gone, leaving the sky a field of deep blue populated by pink clouds edged in gold. It strikes me as funny and hopeful that such a sky could still appear over a world so worn down and decayed. In the distance, Mortarville is just a jagged silhouette, a broken, black-toothed smile, with a small fire burning here and there, spouting from smokestacks or garbage cans.

A woman stands in the kitchen window of the opposite apartment. She is washing dishes. She looks sad to me, but maybe it is just her bottom lip that makes her seem so. It is fuller than the top lip and gives the impression of pouting concentration while she scrubs and rinses. She is young and pretty, and steam rises from the sink, occasionally obscuring her face like a veil. She looks like a Mary to me, or maybe an Amy, though possibly even an Alison or a Rachel. I imagine her as someone who is kind to animals and searching for love. The dishes she is washing will be from her own meal alone. Simple white plates. A single wine glass. A cat dish. Her hair, through the steam at least, is blonde or light brown. It looks soft. It looks as if it still smells of shampoo. She finishes the dishes and turns off the tap. The steam thins and disappears and she is gone.

Her light goes out and the sky left behind is dimmer and less beautiful. I go to bed, try for a moment to imagine the girl from across the parking lot laying next to me, try to imagine a life shared with someone, like I have seen on so many screens. I move an extra pillow so that it is beside me in the bed, but that is nothing like a real girl.

In the morning, when I park my car at work, a fresh school of dead fish floats by, their white bellies just breaking the surface, here and there a fin sticking out as if waving a motionless hello. It is, apparently, a morning thing: a fresh crop of them every dawn—a school of the dead—as regular as the dew, floating by on the slow and mucky scum of the winding river, beneath a blood red and Virgin Mary blue sky.

The stink of them rises from the water. I lock my car and check the lights. I walk up the stairs to ground level parking, go up the escalator into the mall, cross the food court and enter the damp and dusty corridor slanting downward, through a door, down a set of stairs, stealing a new wastepaper basket from the Command Center, unlocking my office, turning on the lights

I am startled to see it, sitting there again on my desk like a small, dead thing, no longer wet but now smoldering slightly, singed a little at the tips, a thin wisp of bitter smoke rising. I try to imagine the struggle—this strange creature of practical science pulling itself from the incinerator by its hair-like, silver highlighted tendrils. Slithering in shadows, sneaking into elevators, worming its way with imperceptible movements around corners, back to my office, up to the pinnacle of my desk like some misguided and ill-informed salmon returning to the place where its doom was spawned.

"Has someone been in my office," I call out to the guard in the Command Center.

He yells back: "Probably."

I sit down at my desk. Not too close. I poke the wig with the end of my pen. It does not jump or cry. It does not plead for its life. It seems impossible. Someone must have brought it here. Maybe Maintenance or House Keeping. Maybe they are telling me to be more careful with what I throw away.

"Do we have a garbage bag anywhere?" I yell, and the Command Center yells back: "Probably."

I find a bag in the bathroom and return to my office. The wig is still there. Has it moved at all?

I use the stapler to push it off the edge of my desk and into the bag. I take the bag, make my way down the usual stairwells and elevators to the parking lot by the river. I find a crumbling piece of pavement—which is easy enough to find in this lot—and pry a chunk of it loose, put the chunk into the bag, knot the top of the bag, and throw all of it into the river. It sits on top of the water's surface for a moment, puffing out with trapped air, teetering a little, trembling in a slight breeze or from the imperceptible struggle for life taking place inside. Then it sinks. A few bubbles come up thickly through the thick water.

I stand there for a moment, waiting to see what will happen next. A dead fish plonks its rotting head against the river's wall, a rusted expanse of corrugated steel. Other debris gathers there too: sticks, plastic milk jugs, the fragments of Styrofoam coolers.

I say a small prayer to no particular God. The Gods of Industry, perhaps. The Gods of Science. There but for the grace of my fathers, say I...

That night I dream about the wig. I dream it is my brother. I dream we are born from the same tank. We are there still, gestating, fully formed and suspended in jelly. Its tendrils are wrapping around my throat, clawing at my eyes, forcing their way into my mouth until I cannot breathe.

Her Honor

The Mayor comes to The Terminal Mall. She is here to announce big plans for saving our beleaguered city. She is a small woman in a sensible skirt and blazer, her white hair like spun sugar, her simple pearls, her circular red cheeks like a porcelain doll's. To see her you might imagine her to be quiet, motherly, even grandmotherly, sharing with you in a humble whisper her recipe for brownies or Dutch apple pie. But she is not quiet. She speaks always in something just below a scream. A happy scream, a smiling scream, the scream of an aging cheerleader, her voice high and always strained to the edge of breaking, but never quite breaking.

Standing at the top of the steps, overlookhing the sculpture of twisted steel, she adjusts a microphone she could probably do well enough without, and speaks with much spirit about the spirit of Mortarville, the greatness—even in these difficult times—of its institutions and traditions. She speaks to a small gathering of press, civic leaders, bored shoppers and derelicts that have collected on the floor below her.

"What other place in the world, in this great and vast country of ours, can be better described as the backbone of the nation! We forged that backbone! We mixed and set its bones!"

I am standing at the railing on the second level of the mall, looking down on the mayor and her audience. The Assistant Director of Security stands next to me.

"I think she's a dyke," he says.

The mayor goes on. She extends her metaphor: the rib bones and leg bones were made in Mortarville too. They were made from our cement, our mortar, our steel. Our trucks and trains are the blood of this great land, the highways its veins. Our cranes and kilns, our mixing drums and silos are the various organs.

It is a little like a high school pep rally and when she is done with the anatomical comparison portion of her speech, there is a smattering applause from those in the audience who have not wandered away to shop or pilfer coins from the fountain.

Then the serious part, delivered in a quieter, more somber shout: but our fair Mortarville has hit on hard times. We know this. We cannot deny this. We have seen, over these last few difficult decades, a decline in our productions, a diminishing of our quality of life. Our manufacturing base is struggling against the unfair odds of foreign competition. Our infrastructure is crumbling. Every year, fewer trucks and trains loaded with cement and cement products leave our factories, just as fewer workers enter the factory doors each morning, ready to do their honest days work for an honest days pay. But their spirit lives on, that great spirit that built Mortarville, the spirit of the men and women who carved from the raw and primitive wilderness a sort of paradise, the spirit of the men and women who fought and died and lived to protect it.

"I'll bet you anything she's a carpet-muncher," the Assistant Director of Security says.

I look at him for a second. "What do you base this theory on exactly?" I ask him.

He shrugs. "Those sensible shoes…"

The Mayor is still talking about our ancestors. I wonder when she will get to the point—the next big resurrection plan. And there is always a resurrection plan. Let us save Mortarville now by converting our rotting shore way into beachfront property, by planting trees down the center of blighted Silo Avenue, attracting tourists and a better class of business. The plans always come with artists' renderings and scale models. Tiny plastic people walking on green swaths of felt, beneath well-organized plastic trees. The tiny people do not shuffle or wear all their clothes at once or carry shopping bags from purchases made half a decade before.

The models and drawings always make me sad, a strange sort of sadness, as if it was nostalgia for an impossible future. The orderly white sidewalks, the calculated placement of unreal trees. The plastic figures usually walked in couples, and though their faces were small, indistinct blobs of hard flesh, there is always the vague impression of happiness and contentment.

But when the Mayor gets to the point today, it is not about changing the abandoned industrial section of town into a thriving neon land of nightclubs and restaurants, or cleaning the water front to provide playgrounds for the children of Mortarville (our greatest hope for the future). Her plans today are much less ambitious: to have a day honoring that great, indomitable spirit of Mortarville, to pay tribute to our past, celebrate our history, and embrace the promise of tomorrow. Spirit Day, we will call this new occasion, to take place later in the year, in the waning days of summer. There will be free balloons for the kids, free movies for the adults. Face painters and clowns on stilts.

"All I'm saying," the Assistant Director of Security says to me, "is that she has a certain cunt-lapping quality to her."

The Mayor finishes. She, her entourage and her audience leave. It may be on the evening news or in the morning paper. We will check. We will look to see if we are mentioned. Maybe our elbows or the backs of our heads will be recorded for posterity.

Now the mall is given back to its usual inhabitants. The sharp heels of women clicking on marble, going somewhere, away, determined. Teenage girls, all bones and bra-straps, shoulder blades poking out, poorly made flesh tents and soft white bellies. The boys in baggy pants, men in blue blazers. Frayed cuffs and collars. Ripped knees. The shuffle of lost souls. The hum of half-made talk.

The girl in the apartment across from mine is doing her dishes again. I stand in the darkness of my own kitchen watching. She pauses, looked down into the sink as if she might cry. Did she break something? Something valuable? Something loved? The steam is rising from the sink. Was it too hot? Has she scalded herself?

I suppose there is a long list of things that might make a pretty girl sad. A long list of details to a life completely alien to my own: love and family, health and finance, hormones.

She turns off the tap and stares down into the sink while the

steam dwindles to nothing around her. Stares down at what I
imagine now to be a lost engagement ring. She sniffs and wipes
her face with the back of her hand. Maybe she is wiping away tears,
but she wipes her forehead too, so I don't know. I imagine myself
wiping the dampness away with the back of my hand, and holding
her close, the way I have seen lovers in movies and TV shows do. I
imagine lifting her face by the point of her chin and looking down.
Everything will be OK, I will say. Or: *I understand*. Or: *I am here
for you*. Whatever it is the hero says.

I leave the kitchen, sit on the couch, turn on the TV. I think,
not for the first time, that I should get a cat. There are many strays
in the neighborhood and when I first moved here, I had thought
I would befriend one of these and rescue it from cruel winters and
heartless traffic. But they turned out to be a skittish lot, and ran
when I crouched to pet them, so maybe I will go to an animal
shelter someday instead, and save someone that way.

If I get a cat what will I name it? Probably Abigail.

I turn off the TV and go to bed, go to sleep imagining what
it would be like to fly above all of this, and then dreaming of small
scratching sounds and tiny feet in narrow tunnels, of pink whis-
kered noses pushing out through small spaces, sniffing around for
something like fresh air or sunlight. Dark dirt mazes. And maybe
it is me, and not Abigail the hamster, running through them, scur-
rying, looking for light or hope or love or cheese.

A Friendly Visit

The two men in black suits stop by my office. I don't know why. I ask them why and they say they are just visiting, that they are just being sociable. This does not put me at ease. They even give Richard pause—he is about to walk into my office when he sees them there, one sitting by the file cabinet in Richard's usual spot and the other one casually pretending to read something from my bulletin board. Richard says: "I'll come back later."

The two men smile at him. Even their smiles are frightening. Or maybe especially their smiles.

The man who had been at the bulletin board walks over and shuts the office door.

"So how's the job treating you?" he asks.

"Fine," I say.

"Adjusting to things OK?" the other one asks. In the corner of my eye, I see that he is examining the shape Richard has scratched into the file cabinet. He looks as if he is trying to make up his mind about it. Is it a penis, he might be thinking, or the state of Florida or random decay?

"I'm adjusting," I say.

"That's good," the standing man says.

"Have you heard otherwise?" I ask. "Should I be concerned?"

"*Should* you be concerned?" the man in the chair says.

"I don't know," I say. "That's why I asked you first."

The two men exchange looks.

"I guess you did," one of them says.

"I guess you did at that," the other one says, reaching into his jacket.

He pulls out a small yellow card and hands it to me.

"It's that time again," he says.

I read the card. I have an appointment to meet the Company Inspector next Friday at the shooting range. It's time to renew my license to kill.

Guns and Ammo

The Company Inspector sets a row of empty bottles along a piece of wood set against the bank of a hill. Our shooting range is a field on the edge of town, not far from the mile long divot which is all that remains of the secret facility where I had spent my formative years.

The Company Inspectors vary from year to year, but they are always the same type: tall, thick salt and pepper mustache, a gut and chest pushing out of a blue denim shirt like a full sail; they wear glasses that tint in the sun; they smoke cigarettes or chew toothpicks because they are trying to quit.

We exchange pleasantries about the weather (it looks like a storm) and the Company Inspector examines my gun. My gun is never as clean as it should be. I do not oil it properly and there are spots of something on the barrel that might be the beginning stages of rust. My gun spends most of its time in the far corner of my desk drawer and once an Inspector found a paper clip lodged in one of the chambers.

"Your gun is your best friend…your best tool," the Company Inspector says. "You should treat and store it as carefully as you would an expensive set of socket wrenches."

"Uh-huh," I say. His analogy is wasted on me; I do not even own a hammer.

I do not have the proper amount of affection for firearms to carry on more of a conversation with the Inspector than this. He is one of those guys—you can tell them by their belt buckles and bumper stickers—that knows the strength, weakness, and personality of every weapon, and follows their development and innovations in magazines as if they are characters in a favorite soap opera.

I shoot a number ten something or other that the company has given me and that's all I know about it. I pull the trigger, it makes a noise, a bullet flies out from the correct end and travels in the correct direction at a reasonable velocity. I shoot the bottles—enough of them to satisfy company requirements. He marks something down on a sheet of paper and I sign my name. He gets in his four by four and drives away.

When he is gone, I drop the gun into my jacket pocket and go for a walk through the woods, hoping again to see some piece of rubble or a broken steel bone jutting from the ground. Some bit of evidence should be here. How could so much disappear without a trace? It is here somewhere still, beneath the surface, black and rotting. The bones of my brothers, teachers, and captors.

The woods are new—the trees small and more like overly ambitious weeds than actual trees. The ground is low and swampy from a recent rain and a cold mud spills over the edges of my shoes. The sky is low and dark; a storm brewing, a rumble in the distance and then a blinding flash and I am thrown backwards against the ground and into a past that is not even mine.

John and Jonathon Smithee are carrying groceries into their lab. Glass tubes and beakers sparkle on shelves, and counters and card tables. A secret lab in a loft apartment in the warehouse district of Mortarville. The building had once been a textile plant, and after that, a restaurant—the large kitchen converted nicely for Smithees' uses.

A sky, seen in pieces in the large and numerous windows around them, is further split by lightening. Thunder follows and the glass rattles. Somewhere in the street below a car alarm goes off, a dog barks, etc.

John, whose arms are marginally less feeble than Jon's, carries the brunt of the order—the bags with milk, apple juice, bleach, laundry detergent, cat litter, and a twelve pack of sugar-free caffeine-free cola. He sets them down on the floor by the door, rubbing the red marks on the palms of his hands where the bags have dug in. Jonathon puts his own two small bags on the counter, between the Bunsen burner and a stack of Petri dishes.

"Don't squish the bread," John tells him.

"Yeah, yeah," Jonathon answers, thinking: *You're not my wife. And I'm not your wife either. We have no wives. There are no wives here...*

John puts the milk, soda and apple juice in the fridge, the bleach and detergent in the closet. He carries the bag of litter to their main work area, laying it like a body on the table next to the microscope.

The Smithees do not own a cat. The litter is just one of the many disparate ingredients they have discovered a need for in their most recent experiments. The same is true of the bread, but not the soda, (that is for Jonathon, who caffeine and sugar make jittery; he once shattered an entire tray of test tubes after only half-a-cup of coffee).

Not everything essential to the creation of life, it turns out, needs to be bought in specialty shops catering to mad scientists. The Smithees have had to venture, now and then, out into the world of grocery stores and all night convenient shops. The store they most often frequent is a block from their laboratory, a small mom-and-pop operation with a squeaking front door, rattling refrigeration and a display window cluttered with faded ads for defunct products. The Smithees have become familiar with the help there, and are almost known by name. It is assumed by the clerks, managers and assistant managers that the two scientists are brothers. A particular female clerk, with hair like a tangle of copper wiring, attracts the scientists. It seems to them that her smile widens when they enter the store and that she presses the keys on the cash register to ring up their sales with a particular and tender regret.

In conversations with each other, and in the privacy of their own thoughts, the two Smithees concoct elaborate fantasies about the romantic possibilities of such interactions and construct for her from their limited knowledge (her nametag reads: SUE) an enduring and affectionate personality. She would be amenable to their quirks, tolerant of their bodies and loving of their minds. She is studying physics or biochemistry at the community college. She finds intelligence the most agreeable of all human qualities and puts no stock in the vagaries or inefficiencies of body parts. To her, it is the size of their dreams that matter and their dreams are massive and throbbing.

John opens the cat litter and Jonathon opens a can of soda. John takes out a scoop of litter and begins crushing it to a fine dust with a mortar and pestle. Jonathon, sipping his soda, strolls over to the microscope and peers into the eyepiece.

Meanwhile, I float ripening in my corner aquarium. I gaze about through my neonatal fluids, through the preformed lenses of my eyes, at the vague and ghostly shapes surrounding me. The beginnings of my fingers amuses me. The strange soft scales of my fingernails.

And in the streets below, rumors are spreading, mobs are forming. Abominations to God and nature have been committed and torches are being handed out to an anxious crowd. The sky is nearly black and lightening flashes again. The atmosphere is set. *It looks like rain so let's get this over with*, says the mob. They break offending windows, overturn suspicious cars, batter down the door to the stairwell leading up to the secret warehouse lab. They start a fire. Smash and shatter. Tear and toss. Beat and murder my fathers. Burn their life and work and home.

I am carried away, poked and prodded until I reveal nothing but an ordinary child. Then off again to a hole dug into the world, lined with cement and iron. I am buried there like a seed. I grow. I am trained and taught. Like a vine. I rebel and am caught. I learn the ways of man.

I Am Saved

Who am I? I am that guy lying there on his back in two inches of muddy water. The upper part of my right leg feels as if it is on fire—struck by lightening with even now a wisp of smoke rising from the blackened hole in my jacket pocket. But the hole in my jacket pocket is not from lightening. It is from where the gun in my pocket has gone off. I reach down and feel the tear in my pants, and past that, the tear in my flesh where the bullet has entered me, the tear in the muscle, the blood and pain.

A drop of water the size and weight of a marble hits me square in the forehead, the first of many while I lay there, figuring the rain will put out whatever fire might still be smoldering on me or inside me. The raindrops appear from the distance like a hail of translucent bullets.

I finally struggle to my feet, limp my way to my car, sloshing through cold mud, stumbling and falling like Christ (three times). I get in the car, but do not start it. Instead I sit there, waiting for the dizziness to pass, for the world to right itself, for the rain to let up a little. I should go to a hospital, I know, but I won't do that. The dizziness will pass. The pain is not so bad. The rain will pass too.

Without even knowing, I have turned the key and put the car in gear. The road rushes out toward me, a black snake whipping in front of me. Cars, claws and traffic lights. I concentrate. I must concentrate. Hold the wheel. Mud and blood and pain, but how far is home? How far is a hospital? I want to go home. I can make it if I drive slowly, carefully, deliberately. It is a game of skill and dexterity. Pick up sticks. Red light green light. Dominoes. Consider every breath and blink and heartbeat.

I am holding the wheel. The road is still before me, but more like a photo of a road than a road. It is frozen, freeze dried, full stopped. A blurry photo, a video on pause with static lines and snow specks jumping like fleas. Then unpaused by an unseen hand.

Move forward. The light changes from red to green. Move forward. I can dimly hear horns blaring behind me. I will move. I am moving.

Somehow I make it this far and I am bumping down the broken pavement of my own dead-end street, swerving to avoid the ghosts that stagger in front of me, the living dead zombies with arms out-stretched, flesh and clothes and shopping bags rotting. I stop my car in my usual spot, turn off the engine, sit there for a moment, just breathing while mountains belch fire and smoke in the distance and an angel descends from a glowing gray wooden staircase.

The angel sees me. I wave to her and try to smile. I notice there is blood on my hand

"Oh God," the angel says in a voice muffled by the glass between us. With some effort, I roll down the window. I wave again. I say: "Sorry."

Then I hear sirens. Or I think I do. It could be these are sirens from the future—sirens that haven't even happened yet but will soon enough—they are just now rolling around like marbles at the bottom of my ear at the edge of existence, existence being the hole at the bottom of my ear. The idea frightens me and I can tell now that I am no longer smiling.

The angel is at my car window, like a waitress at a drive through window. For a moment I am confused. Is she a waitress? But she does not take my order. She looks into my car, a concerned frown on her face. She is beautiful and glowing. She is an angel.

"Don't call an ambulance," I say, though she hasn't said or done anything yet but look at me.

"I think I should," she says. "You look like you need it."

But I am afraid of that ambulance. A great flashing all-seeing red and blue eye screaming from the future. A clown car from which will pour an endless stream of men with painted faces and broad-brimmed hats. Electrified walking sticks that sprout fake bouquets of colored paper flowers and pain. They will take me back.

"Just help me get out of my car," I tell her. "It's just an accident. Target practice. I just need a little help getting out…"

What happens next is a blur. It has to be. What plausible scene can exist in clear focus? She is a stranger—not really an angel at all—helping me, another stranger. I am muddy and bleeding from a gun shot to the leg. She does not know my name. If she has seen me at all, it has only been fleetingly in the parking lot to or from work, or in looking up from her kitchen sink to catch me staring back. And now I am bleeding up three flights of creaking steps up to my apartment and her arm is around my waist. I leave behind a thin red trail that will have to be cleaned in the morning by some-one—although I know the maintenance people here and I know those drops will never be cleaned. They will dry brown and flake off in the wind, be worn away by feet or washed away by another rain.

It is nice of her and my point is this: for all she knows I am a robber of liquor stores. I could be a killer on the run. I am the most dangerous and most wanted. *Do not approach yourself but no-tify the authorities immediately.* Some men are like that and some women like that. Bad boys. Big bad wolves on the lam. I have a hole in my leg, a gun in my pocket and I am happy to see her.

I fumble my keys, drop them. She picks them up for me.

"Thank you," I say. "I just need to lie down."

"You need to see a doctor."

"A flesh wound…" This stikes me as funny—I don't know why. A flesh wound. Or maybe it is the one about the wolf on the lam. Lamb. I start to laugh.

The Scene Changes Slightly

"You were bleeding a lot," she says. "I put a bandage on it. I think it's stopped now."

I am on my couch. The angel kneels on the floor beside me. "You really should see a doctor," she says.

"Thanks. I don't like doctors. I've had bad experiences with doctors."

"It looks to me like you've had bad experiences without them."

I look down at my leg. My pants are off, which is a little embarrassing and hard to figure out. I am wearing my paisley boxer shorts—the ones that have a tendency to fall open. A pillowcase with tiny, faded daisies has been wrapped around my leg in a makeshift bandage. There is a bright circle of blood in the center. It doesn't seem to be getting any larger.

"Sorry about the bandage," she says. "You only had little one's in your medicine cabinet."

"I didn't think I had any that big or flowery."

"I found it in your hall closet. It looked like your leg needed it more than your pillow. But I really should call a doctor."

"I'm all right. You've been very kind, but I'll be OK."

I sit up. It hurts a little to do it, but not too much. My head is clearing. I look at her. She is both prettier and less perfect in person. The veil of distance and kitchen sink steam removed, I can see a small scar above her lip, a few stray hairs between her eyebrows. She has freckles and there is the slightest hint of a blemish forming at the tip of her chin. Her paleness seems now more a matter of poor health that anything ethereal, but I find these things comfortingly real.

"Is that a gun shot?" she asks. "On your leg, I mean. Is that from a gun?"

"Yeah," I tell her. "It went off in my pocket. I was at the firing range for work. I think maybe I was struck by lightening."

"I don't think the bullet is still there. It looks like it went through."

"That's a good thing, right?"

"I guess. I don't really get shot that much myself. Or know people who have. Are you a cop or something?"

"Security."

"Oh."

"Director of Security at the Terminal."

"Oh." Her second "oh" seems slightly more impressed which is what I am trying for.

"I have to qualify for marksmanship twice a year," I tell her.

"How'd you do this year?"

"Not as bad as you'd think. This happened after the test."

"When you were struck by lightening…"

"Yeah."

"You really ought to see a doctor."

"You live in the building across the parking lot."

"Yes," she says

"I've seen you."

"OK."

"In the parking lot."

She places her hand on my forehead. It is a soft hand, slightly damp.

"You seem a little warm," she says. "Maybe you should get some rest."

"Getting shot takes a lot out of a guy," I say.

"To say nothing of being struck by lightening."

"My name is Jack," I tell her. It seems like I should tell her that. It seems like it is time that she knew that.

"Get some sleep, Jack," she says.

She is smiling. I like her smile. I like her hair, which looks as if it would be very soft to touch. It is more brown than blonde, I now realize.

I don't know when she leaves, but she does leave. I am alone in my room. I close my eyes and sleep.

I dream I am being held in the brawny, bristly arms of the closest thing to a mother I have known. She pets my forehead with large black hands and licks my wounds with a rough tongue.

The phone rings. It is ringing in my dream. Where is the phone? I find it tucked inside the tire swing. I have to stack three blocks on top of each other to reach it.

"Nice work, Jack," the gorilla tells me. I feel very proud at this encouragement, but the dream peels back around me and I am on the couch and the phone is ringing on the floor. I reach over and pick it up for real this time.

"Did I wake you up, cocksucker?" the voice at the other end of the line says.

"Yeah…"

"Good. Bleuler's a no-call no show. What do you want to do about it? I'll give you a moment to spit the man-juice out of your mouth to answer."

"Fire him," I say. "Fire all of them. I don't give a fuck."

There is a long silence.

"Uh-huh," the voice finally says.

"Call someone else," I say more reasonably. "Try Johnson. He wants hours."

"OK. Johnson."

"And I won't be in tomorrow."

"Yeah?"

"I'm sick."

"If you say so."

"Yeah. I do."

"Whatever. You're the boss, bitch-boy."

"I am," I say. "Try to remember that a little."

I hang up, think about going back to sleep but stand up instead. I limp over to the kitchen window and look out across the lot. Her window is dark. Orange-pink clouds are shredded across the deep blue sky above her building. It makes me think of wings being torn apart.

There is a Knock at the Door

And I fall out of bed trying to answer it, crawl across my bedroom floor like it is a desert, struggle to my feet, shout, "Hang on!" I am damp, still covered with sleep like it is sickly dew. The hole in my leg aches, the pain radiating outward in concentric circles. How long have I been asleep? I should see a doctor, but I've had bad experiences with doctors.

"Just wanted to make sure you hadn't died in your sleep," she says when I open the door. I stare at her for a moment and manage a smile that I hope is warm, inviting, grateful.

"I haven't, thanks," I tell her. "Still alive."

"How's your leg?"

We both look down at my leg for the answer. I am wearing the paisley boxer shorts again, a fact I had not noticed or considered before answering the door. Also, I do not have a shirt on. I am neither fat nor skinny, but I am pale, and I am even paler standing in front of her now. The pillow case bandage is still around my leg, but crusted with yesterday's blood. I slide it aside to expose the wound. We both look at it. It does not look good.

"Jesus," she says. "That's not good."

"I think you're probably right." The hole in my leg is black, rimmed with red, the redness exploding outward in a network of thin lines like spider webs or broken glass.

Suddenly I feel dizzy. I stop looking at it but I still need to sit down. Or lie down. Or fall down. I stumble backwards toward the couch and she follows me in, places her hand against my cheek while I lay there trying to understand the sudden flock of green and purple paramecium that have flooded into the stagnant air of my apartment.

"You're burning up," she says.

"I feel a little funny..."

She removes the bandage. I try not to look at the hole in my leg. It makes me dizzy. The thought of it makes me dizzy. The air thickens. Everything starts to feel like it's a long ways off. I can barely see my feet, or the girl, or the room, and bits of the air around me seem to become like jelly for a moment before melting back into the general syrup of atmosphere.

"You need to have this cleaned," she is saying. "You need to see a doctor. I think it's infected or something. You're burning up. Do you have a thermometer?"

"I don't like doctors…"

"Do you have a thermometer? You don't mind those, do you?"

"No." At least I think I say no. It is hard to tell anymore.

"I'm taking you to the hospital," she says and I'm pretty sure I say: "OK."

"OK."

Somehow I get dressed. Does she help me? Do I match?

Then we are driving in her car. I roll the window down, stick my nose out like a dog. It helps some, but I get cold and roll it back up.

Her car smells of standing water. The back is filled with empty pop cans that roll across the floor when she turns, clinking against each other. I think there is a hole in the muffler, and maybe a hole in the floor as well. I smell exhaust and gasoline too. The car seems louder than it should be.

"My car's a mess," she tells me when I stoop to pick up an empty bottle that has been rolling against my foot. "I left the window open the other night." As if a strange wind had blown in the litter of a years worth of soda and fast food.

"So is my car," I say, but I'm just being polite. It is nowhere near this bad. Under the glass of her back window, is an old newspaper lying spread out. It is yellowing, and is held into place by three shriveled grapefruits

I roll down the window again. The litter stirs. A napkin rises up and flies out of the car; I watch it drift away in the mirror, caught by currents. It reminds me of a dove or a moth.

"I've been meaning to clean it out," she says.

"It's fine," I tell her.

Emergency Room

I give my name to the receptionist and she gives me a pen and a clipboard with several pages of forms to fill out.

"Everywhere where there's an X has to be completed," the receptionist says.

My neighbor and I find the last two empty seats in a row with a clear view of the TV. The TV is playing a tape of fish swimming about in an aquarium. If you watch the fish long enough, you can tell the moment when the tape loops into itself, where some tropical something or other passes some other tropical something or another in exactly the same way over the same bubbling rock bubbling the exact same bubbles.

"Prepare to wait," my neighbor says.

"I know."

I fill out the form as best I can. But there are blanks. I don't know the answer to everything.

"Do you think there is an all fish network somewhere that doctor's offices everywhere subscribe to?" she asks. On the TV a yellow and black striped fish is nibbling at something in the colored gravel.

"It's a tape," I tell her.

"Are you sure?" She is practically pouting.

"Pretty sure," I say.

"That's disappointing. I'd have paid for a station like that. I'd watch night and day just waiting for something to happen."

"You could buy the tape."

"Where's the fun in that? It's already happened."

"I'm not sure I know where the fun in fish is in any form."

She shrugs, then picks up the tattered remains of a golf magazine from the table in front of us. It is about three years old, but how much can ever really change in the world of golf? The same polo shirts, khaki pants, green hills must apply. The same sticks and flags and holes.

"I love golf," she says.

"Do you really?"

"No."

She puts down the golf magazine and picks up one about business. On its cover it has a picture of an old man giving two boney thumbs up. Underneath him reads: "Integrity is the way...to a better business!"

"I love business," she says.

"Do you really?"

"No."

She laughs. I smile.

Time passes. Names are called at slow intervals and various injuries and symptoms stand up to be placed in wheelchairs and rolled to a back room. A bloody nose, a ringing in one ear, double vision, a rash; the day passes like this. The fish repeat themselves.

A man with both eyes swelled shut begins heckling the patients called before him, though he cannot see any of them. The blind man's face is as red as a lobster. Around each eye is an unhealthy wetness, like a thick oil is being secreted, like he is crying oil. He is wearing an apron that says: Kiss the Cook. The apron has some singe marks on it. Whenever a name is called, he looks as if he is about to spit from anger. "What's he got?" he shouts. "What's he got that he goes before me? Is it a head cold? It smells like a head cold to me. Now that I'm blind, my other senses are heightened and this guy smells like he's got a fucking head cold to me."

A security guard sitting in the corner glances over at the newly blind man. The guard is big and solid, even sitting down. He makes a noise from somewhere in the back of his throat that seems to make the red-faced man settle down for a bit. Maybe the red-faced man does have heightened senses.

"You never told me your name," I say to the woman who has brought me here.

"Sure I did," she says.

"I don't think so."

"I'm sure I did."

Another name is called. Not mine. Not the blind man's.

"What has he got?" the blind man shouts. "A Charlie horse? The sniffles? A fucking strawberry? I'm blind, for chrissake! What does it take around here? Do I have to be holding my head in my goddamn hands? Do my eyes have to fall out of my fucking head and plop into somebody's fucking coffee? Someone lead me to a coffee cup then. These eyes offend me. I'll plop them out into your motherfucking coffee if it gets me some motherfucking service."

The security guard stands up, walks over, bends down and whispers something into the man's ear. The man sits down and shuts up. He wipes the oil from his cheeks with the back of his hands. He mutters something that the guard lets pass.

"It's a lovely place," she says. "I should come here more often."

"You don't have to stay," I tell her.

"I don't mind, really," she says and seems that she doesn't. "It's very colorful."

"So maybe you should tell me your name again."

"OK. It's Dora. Remember now?"

"Dora," I say. "No, I don't. But I will."

Somebody bleeding from his scalp goes to the desk for more paper towels. A man with a skinned knee gives up and goes home. A woman with a bloody hand comes in and takes his seat.

"I like that fish right there," Dora says.

"The striped one?" I ask her.

"The blue one."

Eventually they call my name. The newly blind man begins shouting again.

"What the fuck? I'm fucking blind here! You see my eyes? Does anyone see this shit coming out of my eyes? What the fuck is this guy's problem that's worse than that? Has he got eyes? I can't tell myself, because I'm fucking blind!"

The security guard rushes past me while I am limping to the desk. I hear scuffling but I'm afraid to look back. The blind man is shouting: "Fuck you! I can't fucking see!" as I am placed into a wheel chair and ushered through automatic doors.

A nurse gives me a bed, hands me a paper gown, tells me to take off my clothes and put on the gown.

She leaves, closing the curtain behind her. I take off my clothes and put on the paper gown. I sit and wait. The gown crinkles when I move and I have some trouble keeping it closed in back.

There are devices on the wall. Things made of the curving steel and chrome. They have meters, dials and diodes that are attached to the wall by spiraling black cords. What are they for? The usual poking, prodding I imagine. And I imagine worse than that.

The sound of moaning and consoling filters through the curtains. Someone has gotten some bad news or fears the worst. I imagine them rocking and holding their head in their hands while wheels squeak by. Machines are beeping, water is being poured into plastic cups.

I begin to sweat. Not from fever, but fear. This place has the stink of regimented decay—like something created a decade ago and left to wind down steadily into dirt and corruption ever since.

The thought occurs to me that I should run, run through the curtain, through the automatic doors, back to the lobby. Grab Dora by the hand, take her back to the apartment, pack my things. Pack her things. Would she come? Is that too much to ask of a neighbor? Run away with me. Flee these crumbling tombstone buildings, my job guarding the embalmed corpse of a train station dressed by taxidermists into a mall. Flee your own job, whatever it is, whatever assembly line you stand at, whatever parts you connect or pull apart. Flee office work, your position as clerk at a bank or grocery store. Even the grocery stores here smell of spoiled blood and decay. We will fill our tank and drive away fast, until the city is a broken toothed smile fading on the horizon in our rearview mirror. The rotting Cheshire cat—going, going, gone. And the sun before us, rising pink like a baby. Pink in an orange-Jell-O sky. Newborn above green mountains, winding roads, thick trees, a cabin—we could live in a cabin. We could live on nuts and berries in a cabin and sleep naked by the fire in a small bed stuffed with hay while friendly squirrels tap at the window.

But I am too late. I do not act, the curtain is pulled back and a doctor stands there now, smiling his bland doctor smile, holding his clipboard and pen at the ready. He is younger than myself, has pink cheeks and thin blond hair like the hair of a baby.

"Let's have a look here," he says and I pull the paper gown up a little to give him a look. He makes a face. "Ouch," he says. "And how did that happen?"

"A stick," I say.

He leans in close, looks into the hole, touches the edges of it with the end of a Q-tip. He changes the angle of his head to look at my hole from all angles and makes small, meaningless humming noises.

I study at the top his head—there is a thin, inch long scar on his scalp where no hair grows. Maybe his brain had been removed, rewired and replaced?

"It doesn't appear to be infected," he says. "We'll have to clean it out, but it looks OK to me."

"That's good," I say.

"A stick, eh? Is that what you said?"

"I fell in the woods," I tell him.

"Hmm."

"Yes. There are a lot of sticks there."

"I say 'hmmm" because it looks to me a bit like a gun shot. It wouldn't be something like that, would it, Mr. Smith?"

"No. I'm pretty sure it was a branch."

"A branch?"

"Or a stick."

"I see." He bends down and studies it some more. "Well, in any event, there's no bullet in there."

"There wouldn't be from a stick."

He squirts something on if from a clear plastic tube—water I suppose, some special, medically purified water; some water that had been boiled at specific mystical temperatures and run through the prescribed number of coiled tubes. It bubbles around the edges of the hole. It couldn't be water. Water wouldn't do that. He says "Hmm," again and begins to dab and wipe at the hole with a small cloth. Then he starts to dig at the hole with the corners of the cloth. It hurts.

"Want to make sure we don't leave anything in there," he says. "Sticks are full of germs, you know."

He digs deeper. It hurts worse. I wince, maybe I make a noise.

"Does it hurt when I do this?" he asks.

"Yes."

"Then maybe I shouldn't do this, huh?" He looks and smiles. It seems to be a kind of joke and I have heard something like it before. A long time ago. On TV. It may have even been funny then.

The fluorescent lights in the ceiling flicker. I can hear them humming. The humming seemed to get louder. The doctor stands up, tosses the cloth into a wastepaper basket marked with various warning signs. He says: "There's a couple more things I'd like to do. Just to be on the safe side."

He turns his back to me and begins going through the drawers of a cabinet. The lights flicker again and he pauses, looks up at the ceiling.

"Nice place, huh?" he says. "They are doing some work in one of the wards. Construction. Rewiring and that sort of thing."

I don't say anything. The air is growing thick again. He seems to be moving further away. He is doing something in the cabinet. His back is to me and he is plugging things in, turning knobs, flipping switches, pressing red buttons to alert the authorities. The lights dim again, the way they do in prison movies when someone is being executed down the hall. Or when someone turns on a large typewriter. The sound of electricity crackling, the smell of burning hair, a condemned man confesses and screams.

In Which I Relive a Portion of
My Past

I am returned to that cold table in the white room underground. My TV Mom floats above me, reminding me to wash my hands before eating, my TV Dad explains to me the mystery and sacrament of marriage. Also, he tells me about carburetors.

Do you understand, says Dad, *that when a man and woman love each other, and when they are old enough to know what they want in life, and within the sanctity of holy matrimony etc.* He actually says: *etc.*.

He drones on, also telling me about the Bernoulli Principle while taking puffs from his pipe and blowing out blue smoke that smells like butter and spice and the back of a closet. It is a new flavor he is trying. He hasn't made up his mind about it yet. Earlier, he was telling my TV Mom that he couldn't decide if it made him nostalgic or nauseous. Maybe a little of both, but definitely one more than the other.

Dad finishes his little talk with something he calls The Marital Embrace. *It is something sacred between a man and a woman, you understand*. He says. *Not a man and a dog, not a man and an elephant, only a man and a woman, you understand. This is nature's way, you understand.*

I answer that I understand and it seems that he responds. I go through the day responding with everyone responding as if the TV screen can hear my muttered words. Yes, Mom. Yes, Dad. That's nice dear. Elbows off the table, please. Pass the milk. How was school? School was fine. Have you done your homework? Yes I have. All of it? Pretty much all of it. Do all of it. I will. No TV until it is all done. OK.

But it is all TV. The world is TV, made up of glowing dots and lines, subject to static, jumps and skips, the occasional ghost. No commercials, no laugh track, no plot. The TV days come and go without act one, act two, act three. Without climax or dénouement, without a merciful editor, with only the dull, steady rhythm of a metronome, the seconds counting off, the muffled and distant beep of a monitor.

The white edges of the world beyond the screen disappear completely, as does the metal table against my back, as does time. There is only Mom and Dad, the kitchen table, my bedroom, school and all the places in-between, bouncing and jittering around in the first-person camera. Summers come and go, the floor and the cameraman's feet move farther away, the actors age, grades change, report cards and diplomas, notes from the teacher. I am such a disappointment.

Mom and Dad fight. They argue about money or me. My upkeep is expensive. The cost of heat and food. I hear their voices through the heating vent of my room as I lay in my bed, trying to sleep against a hard cold bed. What is to be done about me? What is the proper course of action?

Dad tries to show me again and again how to fix a car, but the parts whirring around beneath the hood—the belts and fans spinning, valves clicking—seem impossibly mysterious and deadly.

It will help you someday to know how to fix it yourself, Dad says.

I nod but do not agree. I secretly know that the gears, sparks and explosions that make everything run are best kept hidden and muffled beneath an insulated hood. The process of the universe is magical and filled with spinning parts and blades that should be left unexamined and untouched.

What do you plan to do with your life, son, now that school is nearly over? What are you goals? What are your hopes and dreams?

This is my dream. This is my dream and my hope is that it ends, that the audience applauds, the credits finally roll and the picture fades to black. I will take my bow at break or click of day.

A door opens, heels click softly, a woman's face hovers above me. The dark eyes, pale skin, yellow hair of the Head Administrator. Smiling and placing a soft hand on my forehead.

"You seem hot," she says. "Are you running a fever, dear?"

"Am I?"

She pets my forehead and says: "Yes. I think you are."

"Who are you," I ask, because I am feverish and confused and *Head Administrator* does not seem like enough of an answer.

"Who do you want me to be, dear?"

"I don't know."

"Then call me Mother. Or mom. Or mommy, if you really want to, but that seems a little juvenile, don't you think?"

"Mommy…"

She frowns.

"Mother…"

"My poor feverish boy. Do you mind being strapped to a table like that?"

"Yes…"

"Yes. I imagine you would. It's not very nice of us, I know, but it's for your own good you understand."

"OK."

"Such a good boy."

She holds my face in her hands and leans closer. She smells familiar. Vanilla, soap, rubbing alcohol. Up close, I feel I have seen her up close before, not just the peephole view I saw of her in the closet with Sterling. There is something more, bells ringing, sirens going off. Who is she? I know her, I have seen her on TV. Reflexively my eyes jerk up toward the ceiling, where the screen had receded to, where it might descend from again (they have not loosened my straps; I am still here). She follows my gaze, seems to understand its meaning.

"You're a smart boy, aren't you," she says. "My smart little man." She kisses my forehead and the place where her lips have pressed leaves a cool impression. Shaped like a mouth.

She leaves the room. The screen lowers, the show returns. I am a boy again, standing at the kitchen counter while the Head Administrator is stirring something with a wooden spoon in a plastic bowl. She is reading the back of a macaroni and cheese box, following along to a recipe. She pours milk, adds butter, reaches for a bag of mini marshmallows.

"Do you want to help, little man?" she asks me.

"Yes," I say, but do I say it on TV or from the table I am strapped to—I can no longer tell. "I want to help."

"Mother's little helper." She smiles. "Get me the mayonnaise from the fridge, then, Mother's little helper."

I or the camera do. We lope across the checkered tiles of the kitchen floor, reach a small hand out from behind the lens to take hold of the stainless steal handle of a towering white refrigerator. The door opens and the light comes on. A heavenly yellow glow falling upon chrome shelves, bright plastic containers, eggs, milk cartons, missing children and mayonnaise.

While I was Out

They have moved me to a real hospital room, not a temporary bed surrounded by thin curtains. I am surrounded by beige walls now and a reproduction of a painting of flowers hanging above my bed. A famous painting, I think. One of the impressionists.

They have attached something like an electronic clothespin to my finger. A wire leads from that to a machine in the corner. I cannot tell what the machine does. It has red numbers on small screens and a blinking red dot and the numbers change by fractions up and down. Is it my heart beat, my blood pressure, my sense of well-being that changes the number? I try a few things—I hold my breath or think of happy things, but I cannot see an apparent effect on the machine.

The young doctor comes in, holding another chart—or the same but thicker now by several pages. He is talking, but not to me; there is another doctor behind him not yet visible through the doorway.

The two men enter. The second doctor is the opposite of the first. He is older, but seems older than that even. The lines of his face are long and deep, like dried riverbeds. He wears a dark suit, a white shirt, a thin, dark tie. I look at him, then back to the young doctor.

"This is Doctor Millstone," the young doctor says to me. "I've asked him to look over your case with me."

I nod. Doctor Millstone nods back, the sort of nod you see on TV performed by actors playing undertakers. And in fact, he does not look much like a doctor to me. Where is his white coat? Where is his stethoscope or comforting bedside manner?

"You gave us a bit of a scare there, Mr. Smith," Dr. Millstone says.

"Sorry."

He chuckles. "No need to apologize," he says. "Do you pass out often?"

"I wouldn't say often."

"How often would you say?"

"Never."

"I see."

"When was the last time you've eaten, Mr. Smith," the young doctor says, as if to prove his own continued usefulness in the procedure.

"I don't know," I tell them. "Yesterday?"

The young doctor makes a mark on his chart. Dr. Millstone looks over his shoulder at the mark and then nods approvingly and says: "Well, probably just lack of food then, maybe a little squeamishness on your part, but we'd like to run some tests on you just to be sure."

"I'd prefer not to."

Millstone raises an eyebrow. They both raise an eyebrow. One each.

"No?" they say, exchanging looks to go along with the eyebrows.

"I don't like tests," I tell them.

"Tests would be useful," the young doctor says. "Just to be on the safe side. A lot of things can be the cause of fainting, Mr. Smith. We really should check it out, just to rule out some of the more serious possibilities."

I look around for my clothes. They were folded on a chair. I take the clip off my finger and all the numbers go instantly to zero.

"I really have to go," I tell them.

"We'd prefer you didn't," Millstone says, and I think I hear something more ominous, more threatening in his tone.

"I really have to go." The air is getting thick again, but I fight it, will it back to its normal density.

Millstone grabs the chart from the young doctor's hands, taking the young doctor by surprise. The young doctor holds a couple of fingers as if they have been hurt.

"You don't seem to have much of a family history, Mr. Smith," Millstone says.

"I don't have much of a family. I'm an orphan."

"All the more reason to run some tests. No family history makes it hard to rule out certain things…"

"I really have to go now," I say, trying to keep the panic out of my voice. "I really do."

The young doctor takes a reluctant step back while I retrieve my clothes and begin to dress. "You understand this is against medical advisement," he says, but he is shrinking from significance, disappearing into the corner beneath the TV.

Dr. Millstone moves to the doorway, stands there, his thin frame blocking my exit.

I am dressed now. I am facing him. I am close enough to smell whatever cologne or soap he might use. It smells like rubbing alcohol.

"I'm leaving," I tell him.

"We don't advise that," he says.

"So I've heard."

He smiles, then slowly steps aside.

Dora stands up as I limp toward her in the waiting room.

"All fixed?" she asks and I tell her that I am.

As we make our way to exit, through the crowd of the dead and dying, I brace myself for the alarms I expect to go off, for the Men in White to rush out from double doors to tackle me and bring me back, strap me down to a table, poke and prod. They wanted further testing. They have my permanent record now and I imagine that I can feel the eyes of Dr. Millstone on me as we walk, or hear the thin motor or security cameras turning to follow us.

The automatic door does not open when Dora steps in front of it and I figure this is it. I feel the cold sweat I have read about in books and the phrase, "Lock-down," pops unbidden into my head. There are flashing sirens outside the windows.

But it is a hospital and there are always flashing sirens outside the window.

I step forward and the doors open.

"Maybe I don't weigh enough on my own," Dora says.

"Maybe not." She is a small woman. Sometimes it seems like she is hardly there at all.

We escape.

Corrective Counseling

In the morning, the hole in my leg looks much better. Whatever the doctor had squirted in seems to have helped. The redness and pain have both faded and by the time I get to my office, I am only limping slightly. No one notices.

The usual problems have been waiting for me. Bleuler is late. Roberts was caught sleeping on post. Longstreet called in sick with a minor stroke. There was a water leak on the hundredth level and ceiling tiles falling on the fiftieth. The Manager of the Wig Shoppe has left several messages for me to call him. Cheswick left his gun in the men's room and a cleaning person found it and brought it to my office. I put it in the drawer next to my own gun.

Later, the Assistant Director of Security and I have a talk with Cheswick.

"You have to stop doing this," I tell him. Cheswick looks down at his feet, his fingernails, a spot on the floor.

"It's fucking ridiculous," the Assistant Director says.

"I know, sirs," Cheswick says. "I made a mistake. I know I have to do better, sirs."

"Better would be nice," Richard says. "Before someone gets their balls shot off."

"Um...yeah," I say. "That would be bad. Though balls *specifically* being shot off seems unlikely. The thing is, you're a good guard, Cheswick. We'd hate to lose you. But this is a serious issue. You can't go around leaving your gun places anymore, this is the third time..."

"More like the sixth..."

"I think it's only the second," Cheswick says.

"In any case," I say. "Once is probably too many."

A truck rumbles by overhead. White dust sprinkles down from the ceiling on all three of us

"It won't happen again," Cheswick says.

"It sure as fuck better not," Richard says.

And what more could I say? I hand him his gun and send him back onto the floor.

"Pussy," says Richard when Cheswick is gone.

"Why?"

"Because you are. You should have fired him."

"He's the best guard we've got."

"Pussy."

"I think he's learned his lesson."

"He's learned that you're a pussy. Was that the lesson you meant to teach him? Because, if that was the lesson then yeah. Loud and clear."

"You want me to fire one of our best guards because of a mistake." But Cheswick is not really one of our best guards and really, leaving your gun in a public restroom is a pretty big mistake. The truth is, I do not much like firing people. I do not like the weight of their lives in my hands. Where will they go from here? What exciting career opportunities are left in Mortarville? Every day I see people sleeping on sidewalks, on grates, in doorways and cardboard boxes. How have they gotten there? Had I fired them myself? I cannot always see their faces and can easily imagine it to be some guard or another who had once paced the Terminal, but had called off or showed up late once too often, or had been caught stealing from the wishing well. The great, unwashed and shuffling masses were people once too, driven mad from poverty, failure, loneliness, a lack of love, science.

Maybe I *am* a pussy.

Pasta Tuna Surprise

She brings me a casserole. That is what women do when you are sick and they are worried. They knock on your door with one elbow, while they stand there on the landing with potholders, holding a hot dish of something involving noodles, cheese and chicken or fish. That is what they do especially if they are the sort of women that wear aprons with matching pearls and possess a kitchen with sharp, perfect corners, well-organized shelves and all the latest, most practical gadgets designed to make the modern homemaker's life easier. Maybe they are concerned about your day at the office or worried about your ability to take care of yourself. You are their husband or neighbor, the nice young man who needs a good woman of his own.

"I brought you a casserole," she says and I thank her and invite her in. She is not wearing an apron or pearls, but the casserole smells good and her potholders are impressively large and shaped like lobster claws.

I realize I am hungry. When was the last time I have eaten? I can forget sometimes, and not eat for days, taking in nothing but coffee and water until I suddenly smell something cooking down the hall or on some balcony barbecue or in the food court at work. Then I will feel weak and jittery. I will crave something—something fried, with cheese melted over it. Or maybe even fried cheese. If I am not at work, I will have to get in my car and drive, because no place delivers to the end of my street.

"I thought you might have some trouble cooking for yourself," Dora says. "With your leg and all." She sets the casserole on the kitchen table. I get plates, two forks and a serving spoon.

"Also with my inability to cook and all," I say. "It smells good."

"So how's your leg?"

"Better, thanks," I tell her and give it a cautious tap. I scoop out two servings. "It smells good," I tell her again.

"Thanks."

"Would you like something to drink? Water or..."

"Do you have any diet coke?"

"Actually, I only have water. I don't know why I said 'or.' I just have water."

"Water would be nice."

I get up, fill two glasses, come back. She pokes at her serving with the prongs of her fork. An uncomfortable silence follows. I put some food in my mouth. It is good. I ignore the loose hair sticking to the edge of one noodle, discretely pluck it out while she is staring down at her plate.

"It's very good," I say.

"Thank you."

"Did you make it yourself?"

She laughs. "Like there's a fast-food place somewhere that serves tuna-casserole to go. In a dish."

"Yeah, I guess not."

"It's an old family recipe," she says. Clipped from a box by my mother."

"It's great."

"All her recipes came that way. From boxes."

"Mine too," I tell her.

We chew for a moment, then sip water, smile. I make an "mmm" sound once and reiterate the fact that it was very good a couple more times. I remember my fathers and their affection for the copper-haired clerk of the store where they bought their supplies. Was it like this? Was it like this growing but impossible feeling inside me? When they looked at her, did they feel they were not quite seeing her, but instead were seeing an overlay of everything they were missing? I wish I could be struck by lightening and ask them.

After we are done, I clear the dishes and clean them in the sink. She stands next to me. Her shoulder touches mine for a second. It is something of a thrill for me.

"Hey," she says. "I can see my apartment from here."

"Can you?" I say.

Rasputin's Hair

The wig is waiting for me in my office. On my desk again, its real/unreal follicles are somehow elementally changed by the chemicals of the river, or perhaps by the wig's own anger and sense of betrayal. Or it could be the result of some other unlikely combination of events—a lightening strike, planetary alignment, industrial waste. The wig is nearly red now, and the water that drips from it and pools upon the surface of my desk looks almost like blood.

I search the floor for its trail, some sludgy sign of the impossible struggle it had to have made to get from there to here. It must have been an epic journey for a wig—ripping itself free from the garbage bag, swimming like a mutant jellyfish through the unnaturally thick waters of the river, pulling itself onto the rivers bank, crawling up and up and up.

How could it not have been seen? I lean out the doorway, glance at the guard in the Command Center. He is rearranging photos of a pancake breakfast he attended last year. It is this particular guard's hobby. He takes pictures of different meals he has eaten on vacations or at family functions. If you ask him, he will show you a whole scrapbook featuring the buffets of Las Vegas. He keeps a picture of birthday cake in his wallet. Whenever possible, I avoid talking to him.

"Has someone been in my office?" I ask him.

"Not since I've been here, boss," he says. "Hey, did I show you these?"

I lie and tell him he has. I close my office door, sit down and stare at the wig. It is still now. Maybe it is resting. I take the plastic bag from my wastepaper basket and scoop the wig into it. I take the gun from my drawer and put it in my jacket pocket.

"If anyone asks, tell them I'll be back in a little while," I tell the Command Center guard. He starts to say something, but I'm not listening. I walk quickly and do not stop till I am outside and at my car. I skip the river this time. I strap the bag with the wig in it to the front passenger seat and drive to the shooting range. The sky is clear today—no chance of a storm.

While we are stopped at a light, I tell the wig that I am sorry. That it is nothing personal, though that is not the truth. It is completely personal. The bag does not stir. I cannot tell if the wig is listening, if it understands anything I am saying.

"It's better this way," I tell it. "Maybe you don't think so, but it is. There's no place for you here. It's not your fault, I know. They made you alive, but they didn't think it through at all. Where can you live? How can you fit into a world like this? All you can do is grow. OK, maybe swim and crawl to, but to what end? Why come back to me? I'm the guy that dropped you in the incinerator and threw you in the river. Where's your sense of self preservation? What were you thinking?"

The light changes. We drive forward. I continue to try and reason with the wig in the bag. I wish I knew if it was listening. I poke the bag a couple times with my finger, but still no movement.

"I think they made you wrong," I tell it. "Made you smart, but not smart enough to do any good. That's where they always screw up. Nature doesn't make mistakes like that, you know. Nature doesn't give a thing the ability to feel pain without giving it the ability to get out of the way of something painful. You don't hear carrots screaming when their being pulled from the ground. Nature doesn't give you features you can't use. Nature doesn't do anything half-assed."

We are there and I put the car in park, get out, go around, get the bag.

"I really am sorry," I tell it as I carry it to the end of the field. "It isn't your fault science is so thoughtless. Do you know there's a doctor who can do head transplants between two cats? I read about it. He can take the head of one cat and switch it with another cat so both cats are alive, but with their heads switched. He can do that, but what he can't do is connect any of the nervous system. So he makes two paralyzed cats out of two perfectly good cats. That's science. That's what science does. How do you think the cats feel?"

I set the bag on top of a plank of wood and step back twenty paces.

I say: "The cat would want me to do this," aim the gun and fire and keep firing until my gun is empty.

I walk back to the bag. I have missed every shot. I cannot even tell if I meant to miss or not. I pick up the bag and carry it into the woods. I release the wig into the wild. I open the garbage bag and stand back. When that doesn't seem to work, I pick up the bag and empty the wig onto the ground. It lays there dripping and sprawled out across the ground.

"You're free," I tell the wig. "I'm sorry about the shooting at you idea. I know it's not your fault you exist. It's not like you asked to be the product of science, is it?"

It still doesn't move. I nudge it a bit with the tip of my shoe, but no response. I hope it hasn't suffocated in the bag, but how could it? It had survived the bag at the bottom of the river, so how could it not be up for just a car ride?

I decide to go for a walk. Let it have some time to itself. Maybe it is a shy wig. Maybe stillness when being observed is one of its defense mechanisms.

I only walk about ten feet before falling into a deep, dark hole.

Homecoming

I fall a long way but do not shatter. A pile of ash softens the impact, sending particles of black and gray dust swirling into the shaft of light above me. The hole I have fallen through is like a too distant sun now, its brightness muted by the cloud I have caused.

Amidst the ash, there is something sharp and uncomfortable beneath me. I sift through it to find a dog's skull. I set the skull aside and struggle to my feet. It is like standing in sand or a very soft and dirty snow. I am sinking and must pull one foot than the other constantly free.

I seem to be at the bottom of a kind of concrete tube. There are steel rungs imbedded in the wall, forming a ladder leading up, but when I take hold of one of the rungs it crumbles in my hands.

At first I try to pretend this place is something other than what I know it is. I try to say to myself: maybe it's only a manhole to an abandoned part of the sewer system, or an unused access tunnel to a nearby utility plant. There must be a million reasons for people to build holes in the ground and then forget about them. Even squirrels cannot remember where they put all their nuts.

But I know this is none of that. I know this is my former home and prison, transformed by fire, catastrophe and time into these subterranean ruins around me. I have looked for it and I have finally found it, but having found it, what do I do now?

I will need a way out again. The rungs are no good. I search the walls around me and find a door, but the door is stuck. I pull and push on it, then slam my shoulder against it repeatedly until it hurts and my bones feel jarred. Even then it does not open so much as it falls forward off its hinges, clanging and clattering down a flight of cement stairs and disappearing into the blackness beyond.

I step through the threshold, moving cautiously forward into the darkness. Things crunch beneath my feet and I think of bones. Specifically, I think of finger bones, though why just finger bones I cannot say. I keep a hand against the wall to steady myself as I lose all frame of reference in the blackness. There is just the crunching beneath my feet and the smell of ash and dampness around me. Then I feel something different beneath one shoe—something that does not crunch but is hard and somehow familiar. I bend down, feeling through the dust and debris I don't even want to think about. I find a lighter.

I know it cannot work, but I try repeatedly anyway until my thumb is sore and then it does work. In the light of its flame, I can see the ruins around me, blackened walls, bits of decaying pipes hanging down, rust and ash and bones at my feet. I continue downward, to another door, enter from there to a hallway that opens up onto a metal floor I am less than comfortable walking on.

In the darkness, I can hear the drip of water, and sundry other small clicks and clanks that I cannot identify. At my feet, I find a bit of gray cloth, burned at the edges. Next to that is a femur bone. I wrap the cloth around the end of the bone into a make-shift torch.

By the light of the torch, I can see all the floors of the or-phanage laid out before me now in their current state, with metal railings and staircases collapsed against each other, jutting bars of steel, walls tumbled down, charred remains of architecture and anatomy all mixed together.

Even after the fire and intervening years of decay, there is a familiar smell to this place, and here and there a corner or burnt feature that I remember from before. I want to scream, but I don't know what it is I want to scream about and maybe I don't re-ally want to scream at all. It is an odd and indecipherable mix of emotions I am feeling. All of my memories are not bad. There were better times with Sterling, the occasional laughing fit, the TV shows in Popular Communications, my visions of Noreen.

I walk on, pick my way through the rubble, avoiding bits of floor more suspect than other bits of floor. The wood panel facades have all burned or rotted from the cell bars, revealing the rooms behind them—rooms that are blackened and reek of tragedy. I see the skeletons of young boys lying upon the rusting springs of their beds, or curled into a pile in the corner.

Nothing left on this level leads up to the surface, but I find a ladder going down to the next level. The ladder seems solid enough, and though one rung breaks off beneath my foot, I make my way down. From there I find another ladder going down, and from there I find a stairwell that seems relatively undamaged.

I walk up several flights before finding myself blocked by debris, then go down again, past the level I started on, taking the stairs as far as I can, which is a long way, a dozen floors maybe.. My torch goes out. I continue down by just the small flame of the lighter before finding something that looks like an old dishtowel on the floor and make another torch out of that.

As I go lower, the walls change around me from cinderblock to enormous stones. The fire had not reached here, but the walls are still black with age. The stairway ends in a door.

Going through the door, I am in a dark and ancient hallway, the stones forming an uneven arch above me. I hear a strange sound echoing in the distance—like a ticking, or a tiny scratching, like a miniature tin army marching, then running toward me. I hold the torch forward, trying to get a better look through the darkness and see only a vague shape on the floor, a glowing mist rolling in my direction. But as it comes closer, I see it is not a mist. It is a million white rats running toward me.

I finally scream, but even then it takes some time for the sound to work its way out of my throat, as if it had started out from a long ways away, and when it reaches my lips, it comes out deformed. The scream I want to make seems so big and my throat progressively smaller. The sound I make is strangled, abortive, ineffectual.

The rats take no notice of it at all. They run past me, lapping over my shoes like a liquid, continuing on down the hallway and through the door I have opened, as if they had been waiting for decades for someone to open that door.

When my heart has returned to a functional rhythm, I continue down the hallway, opening another door at the end, entering another hall.

And this is the infinite hallway—two parallel lines of white doors with white frosted windows. Most of the glass is still in the doors, most of the doors are still in their frames. The walls are not as white as they used to be, I can tell even in this dying light.

My torch goes out. I try the lighter, but it will not light again. I stand in blackness now, afraid to move in any direction—afraid of everything I can't see and everything I can remember.

The Help

Then the ceiling lights click on, one by one from the far end of the hallway moving forward toward me. Not all of them though—every third one or so is missing a tube, and every sixth one flickers weakly.

I stand there, waiting, still holding a femur bone in my hand. The bone is burnt on one end. I think better of this—what are the implications if I am seen like that?—and place the bone carefully on the floor. Then I think better of that—what if I need to hit someone over the head with something? I pick the bone up again.

I wait for something to happen, for Men in White or Black to run down the hallway like a swarm of rats, but rats that wouldn't just run past me this time; instead they would stop to beat and tear me from my unholy existence.

But nothing happens. Not yet. I walk forward down the hall toward the door that reads: HEAD ADMINISTRATOR. I look in the rooms that I pass—the ones with missing doors or broken glass. Inside some of them are empty desks, piles of paper, boxes of office supplies. Inside others are what look like outdated computers—the kind I have seen in old movies—as big as refrigerators, with reel to reel tapes and flashing lights. But the tape reels are empty now and the lights are not flashing and some of the computers are lying on their side.

I reach the end of the hallway, stand in front of the door marked: HEAD ADMINISTRATOR, and turn the knob. The door is not locked.

It has changed less than I would have imagined. No sign of a disaster here so much as just a hasty move. The desk is there, the lamp is there, there is a long dead fern in the corner and several boxes overflowing with papers. I go further into the room, expecting to be swallowed whole by it at any moment. And in one of the boxes I see a jar, filled with an orange liquid, and something suspended inside. I bend down to look closer. I don't know what I expect to find. It seems that it could be anything, a fetus, a turnip, a miniature replica of myself. It is none of these things either.

It is a set of teeth. What the fuck is that about?

And a man says from behind me: "Can I help you?"

I turn to see him, my femur bone ready. The man is about my own age. He is wearing a gray jumpsuit, holding a long broom and pushing a large, plastic garbage can on wheels. He looks both harmless and vaguely familiar. I lower the femur bone. I say: "I fell in a hole."

"It happens sometimes," he says. "They try to fix it, but it still happens. Can you find your way out?"

"I doubt it," I tell him.

"Follow me then," he says.

We leave the office. I follow him back down the hallway, through a different door, down a different hallway. We walk a long ways—so long it is awkward not to carry on some sort of conversation.

"So you work here," I say and he says: "Yeah."

"Doing what?" I ask.

"Cleaning mostly."

I look around. The place does not look very clean. I look at a piece of paper on the floor: a memo from five years before. I recognize the company letterhead. I have seen it on my own paychecks.

"Who do you work for?" I ask him.

"Blackpool Cleaning and Servicing."

"A division of UCI?"

"As a matter of fact," he says. "You too?"

"Yeah."

"I thought you looked familiar."

"I thought the same the same thing about you," I tell him. "Are you from around here?"

"I'm from almost exactly around here," he says, pausing for a moment to look upwards to the ceiling, through the ceiling, to the ruins above that. I know what he means.

We come to another hallway—this one green and narrow. A hundred yards in, it empties out onto a train platform. The platform is not new, but does not appear to be abandoned. "Are you heading back to town?" asks the man with the broom.

"I guess," I say.

"Then you want the blue line. Any blue line train will take you to the main station. From there, just follow the signs to the surface."

"OK," I tell him. "Thanks."

"Anything for a fellow graduate of Our Lady of Man-made Travesties," he says with a smile and the tip of an imaginary hat, then exits back through the green hallway.

I sit at a bench on the platform. I close my eyes for a few minutes and almost sleep. In my half sleep, I feel the slight tremble of ground, the screech of metal, a soft settling of dust around me. I open my eyes to see the train slowing to a stop in front of me on the platform.

The Underground

The train is empty. Like the platform, it is not new. The outside is tarnished, unpainted metal, the windows are caked with dirt and marred by scratches. Inside, the train car is furnished with what seems like the cast-offs of a Victorian era living room: overstuffed, high-backed chairs, ottomans, a few odd, banged-up, claw-footed end tables, all bolted to the floor. As far as I can tell, there is no one else on the train, but the chairs are placed at a variety of angles, making it hard to know at a glance.

I sit in a big leather chair in the back. I can see out a window from here, but I cannot see a driver or even a compartment for a driver, though this appears to be the only car of the train. A minute later, the doors close and the train continues down the tracks and enters a white tile tunnel.

I look out the window, at the white tiles blurring past, most of them still on. Though things here are old and somewhat rundown here, I am struck by the complete lack of graffiti or vandalism of any kind. Time is the only culprit here.

After awhile, we pass another station but do not slow down. The station does not look in use. Pieces of the ceiling plaster lay broken on the platform. The sign I read as we speed by says: PORTLAND STATION, and then the view becomes a white tunnel again.

It is maybe ten minutes later when the train slows again, this time to a stop. The sign reads: GYPSUM STATION.

A woman is standing on the platform. She looks familiar, but it takes me few seconds to realize it is the Mayor. She gets on the train, smiles politely when she sees me sitting in back, and takes a seat a few seats over.

The train starts again. After a minute I say: "Excuse me…"

She turns to face me. "Yes?" Her voice is no longer the cheery scream, but you can still hear the roughness in it, from years of

197

shouting.

"Where does this train stop?" I ask her

"At the Terminal," she says. "But you can go a few different directions from there. Where are you trying to get to?"

"The Terminal will do," I tell her.

The train is slowing again. I start to get up but the Mayor says: "This isn't your stop."

I look out the window. There is no sign, or sign of life, but the door opens and an old man is helped onto the train by two men wearing black suits and black shirts. The old man is one of the Vice Presidents—I know this, though I cannot really distinguish him from any of the other Vice Presidents. The Black Shirts I have not seen before, but they are cast from the same large mold as ever.

The Mayor smiles at the Vice President, who nods back without a change of expression. One gets the idea his muscles are like used up rubber bands incapable of pulling his face into any other expression.

The old man slumps into one of the high back chairs. The Black Shirts stay standing at either side of the chair, hanging onto it for balance as the train jerks forward and rocks along.

"The next stop is The Terminal," the Mayor tells me. I thank her. She is much nicer in person than I would have imagined. If I ever get the chance, I will vote for her again.

The Last Stop

The Mayor and I part ways on the platform. She shakes my hand and points me to the appropriate door. She tells me that it is just a series of stairwells from here—to just follow the arrows and everything will be clearly marked. I thank her again.

The two Black Shirts are struggling to get the old man down the train steps. At first they try to both do this at once, with one on either side of him, but they cannot fit through the doorway, so one Black Shirt exits and the other comes down holding the Vice President in his arms like a groom with his ancient bride.

On the platform, he sets the Vice President in a wheel chair that the other Black Shirt holds steady. From there, the old man is pushed through a nearby wooden door marked Private. I catch a glimpse of a wood paneled corridor before the door swings closed again.

I find my own doorway, taking the series of stairwells her Honor had indicated. Everything is as clearly marked as she had said and before long, I am in a back hallway I recognize. I pass by a delivery man. We nod and grunt hello to each other. I find my way back to my office with no further difficulty or adventure.

No one notices me enter; the Command Center guard occupied with arranging more photos of past meals. The holding cell is empty. I go directly to the bathroom where I wash the dust from my face and hair and brush as much of it off my suit as I can. Then I return to my office, sit at my desk, write reports, type memos, work on the next schedule. I make a rough draft of an Action Plan for the Spirit Day festivities.

Richard enters my office, sits in the corner by the file cabinet.

"How does my dick taste in your mouth?" he asks.

His dick is not in my mouth and it never has been. He is just saying that. What can you do with a man like that?

"I'm trying to do this schedule," I tell him. "If you don't mind."

He shrugs. "Don't let me stop you from pretending to work," he says.

I don't, and he is quiet after that. His heart does not seem to be in it today anyway, and for that I am grateful. When his heart is in it, he can go on for hours. He can call me twenty seven different words for penis. He can cast aspersions about my parents' hygiene, orientation and physical dimensions. But today he only adds a few scratches to the patch of missing paint on the file cabinet and leaves for the day.

Eventually, I quit trying and leave for the day myself. I have to take a bus home. My car is still at the firing range. The bus I take is crowded—not just with the people themselves, but the stifling heat they give off and the humid atmosphere they exhale.

I am lucky to find a seat, a place in back by the window recently vacated and not yet snatched up again. The woman sitting on the outside seat has to pull her legs to the side to let me pass. She is not a small woman and seems reluctant to let me sit down. But what can she do? I squeeze by, she makes some sort of noise of disgust, but allows me a few inches.

I recognize some of the people on this bus. I have seen them in the Mall. I have caught some of them myself stealing coins from the fountain and escorted them from the premises. I am relieved that no one seems to know who I am, who I work for, what I have done in the past.

I hold myself as close to the bus window as I can. The woman I am sitting next to cannot help but spill over her half of the seat; I can feel the bulge of her thigh pushing against me. For some reason it makes me think of tree roots breaking sidewalks.

I breathe the warm breath of my fellow man and become sleepy. Though the window is hard and cold, and the ride is not smooth, my head eventually rests against the glass and I fall into a kind of half sleep.

I know I am on a bus still, but other thoughts occur to me as well. I think: we are in this together. What? you ask. I assume you ask. Why wouldn't you? And I mean only this: all of this. Everything. The world, the universe, existence and all that. We are in it together, you and I.

And it is just like riding a bus, I think, I dream. Getting on a bus. A crowded bus. And you are not even sure it is the correct bus. You get on, find a seat where you can—by the window, by the aisle—try to find a spot to yourself at first, though you know that even if you do, someone will come along and sit next to you anyway. And who will that person be? That is the question. Will they smell funny or want to talk? If they have candy in their pocket, will they offer you some? Are they the sort that will fall asleep with their head against your shoulder or the type that will elbow you in the ribs for possession of the armrest? It is all fairly random. We get what we get.

So I am that person sitting next to you. That is what I think, what I dream I am saying. We are in this together. We are jostled along bumpy roads while the bus takes its slow and regular route around the sun. Here is our mutual armrest. Would you like to use it first? Are you sleepy? I am here. My shoulder is here. Hello.

But when I open my eyes, I have the seat to myself. The bus is nearly empty and the street outside the window is a street near my own.

"Last stop," the bus driver says and me and the small handful of others get up and stagger off the bus.

It is a couple blocks from there and I do not go straight to my apartment, but up the stairs of Dora's building instead. I knock on her door.

After a minute or two she answers.

"Can you give me a drive?" I ask her. "I accidentally left my car outside of town. I'll pay for the gas."

Oddly enough, she does give me a ride. Her car is still a mess.

"I left the windows down again," she says. "I've gotta stop doing that. I think a family of cats spent the night in here."

From the way it smells, she may be right.

"Thanks for the ride," I tell her when we have arrived at the firing range. She tells me that's what friends are for. As I watch her drive away, there seems to be something beautiful, promising and nostalgic in the glow of her taillights fading away into dusk and distance. Why that should be, I cannot imagine. They are only taillights. And what is more, when she stops at the corner I see that one of her brake lights is not working.

I get in my own car, drive home, look out the kitchen window before going to bed, hoping to catch one last glimpse of her—something to say goodnight too, like a pretend girlfriend, like the photo of a celebrity kept on the bed stand of a black and white teenager. But her apartment is dark. I guess she didn't go straight home, or if she did, she went straight to bed.

Cheswick

Richard is waiting for me at the door to my office. He tells me that Cheswick has lost his gun again.

"And this time," Richard says. "It is gone with the motherfucking wind."

We search the bathroom stalls, check Lost and Found, rummage through planters and garbage cans. Cheswick joins us. He is sweating. He tries to help but keeps dropping his radio and stammering about how he had only left the gun for a minute.

"It's a gun," the Assistant Director of Security says. "You're not supposed to leave it in the bathroom. Not even for a minute."

Eventually we send him back to wait in my office. He is no good to anyone now. After he is gone, Richard says: "I'd be worried he might try to shoot himself or something if it weren't for the fact he doesn't have a gun anymore."

So he sits there at my desk, waiting and sweating, while the rest of us try to find it, but we already know it is hopeless. A cleaning person has not picked it up this time and an upstanding and concerned citizen has not turned it into security, Mall Management or Lost and Found.

Having officially given up, Richard and I return, to find Cheswick with his head on my desk gently sobbing.

"Give it a day," I say. "Maybe someone…"

But no one. No day. We all know it.

"I only left it for a minute," he says.

"Go home," I say. "We'll talk about this tomorrow."

He leaves the office, carrying himself out like he is a bag of sagging groceries, wet and about to rip open. We watch him go up the stairs, wait for the door to close.

"You have to fire him," Richard says

"Well, yeah."

I spend the rest of the day, sitting in my office, waiting for that gun to go off.

It doesn't and I go home, watch the news, check out who was shot in the city that day, and whether or not there is anything mysterious about the circumstances, or some question about how the weapon had been acquired. And several people are shot, of course, but it is only bar fights, domestic disturbances and drug deals gone bad.

After that I go to bed, sleep dreamlessly and wake in the morning to the usual alarm.

Comic Book

Say a boy finds a gun sitting on the back of a toilet in a public restroom. Say the boy is fifteen and troubled. He comes from a broken home. It is actually broken; it leans to one side and there is cardboard covering several of the windows where the glass is missing. The water heater leaks and makes groaning sounds in the night. The foundation is suspect.

Maybe the boy has cigarette burns on his arms from an abusive stepfather or from his own self-destructive hobbies. As a younger boy he liked comic books; he liked men in tights with superpowers, flying over brightly colored city skylines, swooping down to save another perfect blue day. That is the same boy, now scarred and troubled, slipping the wayward gun into his school backpack, imagining what he can do with it. His backpack is old and frayed and there are the crumbs of stolen candy bars in the bottom of it. There are the remnants of stickers on the outside—peeling ghosts of forgotten cartoon characters he had once liked.

When he had liked comic books, he would spend hours in his room reading them. He would forget the world back then. He would see only a universe made up of bright dots, contained within the thick black borders of a square.

His favorite superhero was The Electron.

The Electron started his career in super-powered amateur law enforcement as a teenager. He was thin and weak, wore glasses and was picked on at school. A particular bully named Butch was fond of tripping him in hallways and locking him in bathrooms and lockers.

One day, after crawling out of a dumpster he has been thrown into by Butch and Butch's usual cohorts, the boy is struck by lightening. Molecules are changed by the intense forces of nature—a mysterious and unrepeatable recipe of DNA, garbage, the gravy from yesterday's school lunch, and chemistry class discards combine and transform under this unexpected catalyst. Our boy is elementally changed. He is engulfed by a jagged, thick-lined cocoon of pure energy. He collapses to the sidewalk and awakens three days later in a hospital bed, reborn a hero.

The boy who found the gun in the bathroom used to read comic books for hours. Sometimes he would sit in his closet with a flashlight and read them. There was no particular reason for this—he was not hiding, it was not past his bedtime, but he liked the comfort of closets, of being twice removed from an outside world that had already become a disappointment to him.

He had seen a movie on TV once that featured a bomb shelter. He did not remember the movie—did not recall or understand the cold war anxieties that had created the need for bomb shelters—but he liked the concept. He liked the idea of a fully outfitted room buried beneath the ground of the back yard; he could imagine living alone on canned food, saltines and bottled water in a place such as that. And a stack of comic books. That would have made him happy.

At night sometimes, trying to sleep, he asked himself the question: if I had been struck by lightening, if strange chemical reactions and alterations had taken place within my body and I had awakened with the powers to fly along arcs of electricity, to shoot powerful bolts from the palms of my hand, or intercept and receive TV and radio signals in some newly activated receptor part of my brain, what would I do?

He doubted that he would save the world. More likely he would spend his time flying far above it, looking down at the abstract patterns of a map beneath him.

Was he a put upon child? Picked on and bullied at school, thrown into dumpsters, locked into bathrooms? Not overly. No more than usual. His home is run down and leaning to one side, but nothing horrible happens there. His stepfather does not, in fact, torture him or treat him unfairly. It was the world itself that the boy has found impossibly dull and cruel. To fly above that, to destroy that with power-bolts, to be better than he was...That was his dream.

He was given detention one day for bringing a stack of his comics to school. It was against the rules. He was showing them to the closest thing he had to a friend—a boy who seemed interested and often encouraged him to do illegal things.

The teacher took his comics and did not give them back at the end of the day as promised. The boy was too afraid to ask. He sat in an empty classroom after everyone had gone home and drew pictures in the margins of his homework. He longed for a bomb shelter.

The Electron was cancelled after thirty-three issues. Poor sales. The final edition featured, in its last few frames, a half-dozen story lines—the villain, his secret, his parent's growing suspicion, the girl—tied up loosely in one unsatisfying knot.

The boy never bought another comic book after that. He read and reread his stack of The Electron's (the complete run) over and over again. In bed, in closets, on long car rides, always to the same unsatisfying conclusion.

The dots and borders wear away and now he is a boy—practically a man—with a gun clunking away in the crumbs and incomplete homework filled recesses of his backpack.

Something tragic must happen with all of this and so it will.

Cheswick is waiting for me in my office the next day. He has been crying. "I don't know what to tell you," is all I can think to say to him. "I don't know what to tell you," I tell him over and over again.

An Undeserved Award

Two Black Shirts show up in my office. They are there when I open the door and turn on the light. One is sitting at my desk and one is sitting in the corner. Not the two from the train—the two from before that, I think, but really, it is hard to be certain one way or the other. I cannot imagine how long they have been there sitting in the dark, or why they would.

"Long time no see," the one at my desk says. "How's everything been going?"

"OK," I tell them. He is fiddling with the keys of my typewriter, pretending to hit them, though the typewriter is not turned on so nothing is happening. The one in the corner is running his thumbnail along the patch of missing paint on the file cabinet.

I wonder why they are here. I say to them: "So why are you here?"

The one in the corner says: "Well, you don't stand on ceremony much, eh Jack? Just get right to the point, then, is that it?"

"No time for manners or anything," the one at the desk says. "No pleasant formalities, no hello how are you, just why are we here and all that."

And it occurs to me that they are big men and I am justifiably afraid of them. I do not know who they answer to besides the Vice Presidents—and only the Vice Presidents would be enough. I don't know much or anything about them or how much they know about me.

"I'm sorry," I say. "I didn't mean to be rude. I was just wondering why you were here is all."

"As well you should," one of them says.

"It is a legitimate concern," says the other.

It must be about Cheswick and the missing gun. What else could it be? But I don't want to say so myself, just in case it is about something else.

"Is everything all right?" I ask.

"You mean with us personally or with your job?" the man behind the desk says.

"Either, I guess."

"Now he gets sociable," the man in the corner says. "The Vice Presidents would like to see you," he says.

"What about?"

"I imagine that's up to the Vice Presidents."

They both stand up. They are both taller than me and take up more volume now that they are standing, as if they had not merely stood up but also swelled.

"Shall we go then?" they ask. I nod and follow them out of the room.

The Vice Presidents are slumped in their usual positions around their table in the hot shadows of the upper offices. I stand at the head of the table with the two men who brought me here standing at either side of me. In case I decide to run, I guess.

I wait for one of the old men to speak, or even look up. I try to pick out the one I saw on the train, but even now I can't tell the difference. Some time passes. I am not even sure all of them are breathing.

Finally one of the old guys tilts his head slowly toward me, like a turtle considering a leaf it knows it cannot reach. He says something. I have no idea what. The men in black escort me back out to the elevator lobby. They get on the elevator with me this time.

"I didn't hear him," I tell them. "What did he say? Am I fired?"

"We're not at liberty to say," one of them says.

"You're not fired," the other one says.

"Then what did he say?"

"Maybe he said you weren't fired," the first one says.

Then Black Shirt number two reaches into his pocket, pulls out an envelope and hands it to me. I open it, expecting anything: a termination notice, a tax form, a bill for parts and services. But what I find inside is a pair of tickets to a local comedy club.

"Compliments of the Vice Presidents," the men in black tell me. "So guess you're not fired," they say.

Comedy Club

Dora and I drive down Aggregate road, take a right on Slurry Avenue, follow that as it descends into the valley bordering the river. Every other streetlight is dead or dying. Weeds grow tall at the side of the road and the car rattles along on rough pavement. We hit a particularly deep pothole and Dora bounces up from her seat, bumps her head against the ceiling of my car. It makes a sound, her head against the ceiling, like a melon has been dropped on top of us from the sky. She rubs the top of her head and pouts.

"Ouch," she says.

"Sorry," I tell her.

"I blame the city."

We drive through this failing town, through the failing heart of its industry. Cement is still made here, it still crumbles here, it still feeds and entombs us. Smokestacks still billow, sludge still flows into the hardening rivers, but all is a little less than it was before.

The building we are looking for used to manufacture cinderblocks. Now it is a comedy club. Renamed the Ha-Ha Factory, roller conveyors have been replaced with tables and drying racks form the back of a bar featuring the largest selection of fine domestic and imported beers in Mortarville. The great kilns have been gutted and transformed into restrooms.

On a Friday or Saturday night you can go there to see any number of nationally known comedians passing through Mortarville on their way to oblivion. They will tell you about the differences between men and women, blacks and whites, people on the east coast and people on the west coast. Wednesdays are Open Mike Night and all the local up-and-comers tell you amusing things about the differences between men and women, blacks and whites, East Mortarville and West Mortarville.

We sit at a table near the back. It is not any particular night, not open-mike, not famous falling stars night, not ladies in for half price night, but we have free tickets and nothing better to do.

The man on stage tells a long story that has something to do with a pig, a wooden leg, and a flying horse. I have trouble following. It does not seem to be building to a punchline so much as piling up a supposedly amusing series of actions.

The joke ends anticlimactically to a smattering of laughter and applause. The man leaves the stage, looking only half crushed. The house lights come on.

I look at Dora. She looks pretty. I smile at her and she smiles back. All of this seems promising. The lights dim and another comedian comes on stage. With props. Brooms and plungers and power fans combined and converted to form punch lines. He spends his first two minutes bringing his things onto the stage in boxes as if he were moving in. Then he tells a joke involving a hammer attached to an alarm clock.

Dora laughs. I do not see the humor, but enjoy her laugh. Her nose wrinkles at the bridge. She looks at me and I smile.

"My wife won't have sex with me," the comedian says. "She's saving herself for her second marriage."

Everyone laughs again. I get the joke. Though I have no wife, I have seen them on TV. They are angels or shrews.

But where is *my* comedian? The one who tells jokes about being born in a lab, raised in a hole dug by the government, the amusing observations about being created by the manufactured miracles of science but working now in the lowly ranks of middle management? A funny thing happened on my way out from under the microscope, he might say, and launch into an uproarious two-minute routine comparing Petri dishes and test tubes, cages and prison cells, mothers and gorillas, Bunsen burners and the sun.

"He's funny," Dora says and I nod.

The act ends, the lights come on, a waitress comes over and we order drinks and appetizers. Dora gets a vodka and cranberry juice and I get water. We split the fried cheese platter sampler between us.

"You don't drink?" Dora says, eyeing my water a little suspiciously.

"Not much."

But really, not at all. I have seen too many after-school specials, or very special episodes of family sitcoms. Alcohol destroys lives, though it also, on occasion creates lovable drunks. And sometimes too, uptight business women might, after their nose has been tickled by champagne or their head walloped by spiked punch, undo one or two buttons on their crisp white blouse, or untie the knot that holds their hair in its coolly professional place. But even these benefits are followed by headaches, a morning sun too bright in the sky, and regret.

Dora drinks her vodka and cranberry juice very quickly, quicker than I drink my water. The fried cheese sampler platter arrives.

"I love cheese," she says. "And fried things in general."

"Then this is the platter for you," I say.

She chews happily. I take a bite of something—I'm not sure what. The plate is arranged with an assortment of fried shapes. They are all cheese, but it is impossible to know which shape will be which cheese. I mention this to Dora.

"It should come with a map," I say. "Like a box of chocolates."

But she tells me that there are no bad cheeses, that all cheeses are as good as other cheeses.

The lights dim. Another man gets on stage.

"I just broke up with my girlfriend," he says. "No reason, really. Things were going great, but I needed an intro for this act."

He goes on from there: the usual stuff about men and women. Our cheese platter is nothing but crumbs now and Dora's drink has been refilled several times over. I notice she laughs louder now, and sometimes even before the punch line. What time is it? I am getting tired. The comedy has worn thin. Dora is still pretty, but her movements have become sloppy and she spills her drink twice. It is promptly replaced both times.

I look at her face in the dimness of the theater lighting and wonder what it would be like to kiss her. I know it would taste like vodka and cranberry juice, but what else?

Another act ends and maybe it is the last act of the evening. The lights come on and already the customers are getting their coats and the waitresses are clearing off the tables. But the bar is still serving.

I put on my coat and Dora says: "Let's not leave yet. I'm having fun."

I take my coat off and look around. What fun is left to be had? Most of the people are gone.

"It's late," I say and she frowns.

"It's not late."

"I think it is."

"I don't."

She stands up and I am hoping it is her giving in and that we are going home now, but that is not the case.

"I'm going to the little girls' room," she says. "When I come back, I expect to see a little more enthusiasm for our date from you, Mr. Smith."

I smile. I will try. I am pleased that she has referred to this as a date. It seems like a good sign, though nothing else does anymore.

She looks around and asks: "Where is the little girls' room anyway?"

"I think it's the giant oven door over there."

"Thank you, Mr. Smith," she says.

She walks toward the door, bumping against several empty tables and chairs on her way. She struggles with the handle of the bathroom door for a moment, but it would be unfair to attribute this entirely to drunkenness. It is not a regular handle. It is a large, metal piece of hardware left over from when the bathroom was a kiln. Finally, she makes it inside.

I sip my water and wait. The waitress asks me if she should bring another vodka and cranberry juice and I tell her no.

"Mr. Smith," I hear a man's voice say behind me and I turn to see the tall, dark figure of Dr. Millstone.

"I thought that was you," he says. He is alone, dressed in a dark suit that does not seem greatly different from his work clothes and I wonder for a moment if he is here on official business.

"You a comedy fan?" he asks and I mutter something about the free tickets I got from work.

"Mind if I sit down?" And he is already pulling the chair away from the table. It is Dora's chair.

"I'm with someone…"

"Really?"

"She's in the bathroom."

"Ah…" He sits. "Don't worry. I'll be gone before she gets back. Just wanted to see how you were doing."

"OK."

"So how are you doing?"

"OK."

"The leg? Healing up OK?"

"Yes, thanks."

"Any more episodes?"

"Episodes?"

"Fainting spells, I mean."

"No. Everything has been fine, thanks. No episodes."

He nods, looks down at the table, at the crumbs on the empty plate.

"Well, you're eating now. That's good. Maybe that's all it was."

"Maybe."

He is still looking at the empty plate. I don't know why. Maybe he is hungry.

"The fried cheese sampler platter," I explain.

"Ah," he says. "Well, good thing I'm not your cardiologist."

I look over at the bathroom door. Why is she not back yet? It seems like long enough, but women can take a mysterious amount of time in bathrooms. There are processes involved that I do not fully understand.

Dr. Millstone follows my gaze. The door does not open, Dora does not appear, but he says: "Your girlfriend?" as if she is here now and I am about to introduce them.

"A friend," I say. "A neighbor."

"Ah."

"She brought me too the hospital," I tell him. "After the accident."

"I see. Very nice of her. That's a good neighbor."

"Yes."

"I don't even know my neighbor's name. I doubt he would bring me to the hospital."

"Her name is Dora," I tell him. "My neighbor, I mean."

"Dora is a nice name," he says and I tell him I like it too.

Finally, he stands up.

"Well, I don't wish to intrude on a first date or anything, Mr. Smith. Just wanted to see how you were doing."

"Thank you. I'm doing fine, thanks."

He nods and smiles. I watch as he gets his coat and leaves. The waitress comes by and tells me, "Last call for alcohol." She sings it a little, but with a tired voice.

"No thanks," I say, looking at the bathroom door. Where is Dora? How much longer can she take?

Quite a bit longer, it turns out. A different set of house lights come on, the ones that tell you it is time to go. Already someone is unwinding the cord of a vacuum cleaner and someone else is putting the chairs on top of the tables.

"I'm just waiting for someone," I explain to the waitress. "She's in the bathroom." Several of the workers are looking at me now, waiting for me to leave so they can finish their jobs and go home.

"I'll just check to see if my friend's OK," I tell a group of them leaning against the bar.

I knock on the bathroom door but the door is thick and made of iron. I open it a crack and call out to anyone inside that I am coming in.

Dora is in a stall, sitting on the floor in front of a toilet.

"Hey," I say tenderly, like a good boyfriend or a concerned citizen. "It's time to go."

"Something didn't agree with me," she says. "Maybe all that

fried cheese."

"Maybe that," I say, though I think it was the vodka.

I get her to her feet and walk her out of the club. The cool air outside seems to help her. She smiles and brushes a way a loose hair that has stuck to her mouth.

On the drive home, she holds her head out the open window like a dog.

"It feels good," she says and she seems much better now, or at least less drunk. I turn on the heat because it is not that warm out and the air rushing through the car's open window makes the tips of my fingers go numb.

We park in the lot between our two buildings. We stand outside looking from one building to the other. It seems like something must come next and finally she says: "Your place or mine?"

We go to my place.

Her mouth tastes like cranberry juice and vodka. Nothing else besides that.

Back to Work

Dawn and a mist the color and consistency of cigarette smoke rises from the thick, dull waters of the river. It rolls across the damaged white bellies of dead fish, the floating bones of broken trees, the gray froth pulsing against the steel banks, the cans and plastic bottles that rest upon the scum.

The sky is bruised, scarred and bleeding as if waking from a rough night; a night of binges, bar fights, car crashes. A night of runaways and domestic disturbances.

I have a headache. Dora tells me it is from drinking too much water last night. I don't see how this could be but maybe she is right. Her own head is fine—it is resting on my pillow while I get dressed for work.

"You should call off," she says. "That's what I'm going to do."

"I've called off a lot lately," I tell her. "What with the getting stuck by lightening and shot and everything."

She shrugs, sits up in the bed, pulling the sheet to cover herself. Her feet stick out the other end. Her shoulders are bare and white. Though I cannot see them now, I know there are scars on the inside of her thighs, like a small white ladder rising up from the smoothness of her flesh. Or a crude drawing of a small ladder, drawn with a steak knife or a razor some ten or so years before. I saw them last night. The lines had seemed to glow, the way the vapor trails of jets glow in a night sky. She must have noticed my stare, or the hesitation of my hand as it had brushed across her thigh.

"I did that," she says. "When I was younger. When I was a girl."

"Did it hurt?"

"Well, yeah. That was kind of the whole point, I guess. To feel something."

I trace the ladder with the tip of a finger. Gently. To show her I am not repelled, that I'm sympathetic, that I understand the traumas of life and the confusion of a violent youth, that all this only makes her more attractive to me.

"It's ugly, isn't it?" she asks.

I told her it wasn't and lean forward and kiss the scar. It seems like the thing to do.

Last night, after we were done, she fell asleep in my bed. In the middle of the night, I sat up and watched her. She was lit by a mixture of moonlight and street lamp and looked more beautiful and fragile than ever, as if she were made of frosted glass—a Christmas ornament I could almost see through. She whimpered from somewhere within her dreams and I touched the side of her face and felt the dampness of tears. The tears were cool like the moisture that forms on windows.

I wanted to hold her, but not here. I wanted to hold her inside of her dream.

I park my car and check the locks three times. Sometimes I doubt my ability to remember locks.

I stand for a moment by my car, look out over the mist and water, up at the sky as it brightens, the red sun turning orange, the mist burning away.

I check my locks again, check my keys, leave my car and make the long walk up and over and down again into my office.

I should have called off.

The usual fresh hell awaits me: no-shows, day-off requests, sudden vacations, family emergencies and reunions. The Assistant Director of Security thanks me for bothering to come in. I tell him he is welcome and close my office door. I turn on the typewriter.

Was I invented for nothing more than this?

Half-way through the day, the usual two Black Shirts come to get me. The Vice Presidents want to see me again. As we make our way through the mall to the tower, they ask me how I enjoyed the comedy club. I tell them it was fine. They tell me they are glad, that it is good that the tickets had not gone to waste, that they could tell right away that I was a guy who could appreciate comedy.

I stand at the head of the table again, looking down at the Vice Presidents in their shadows, their thick veined hands quivering like dying fish on the tabletop, their heads drifting downward like deflating balloons.

"Listen," one of them says—maybe a different one than before, maybe not. They are, as ever, indistinguishable from the shadows and the thickness of the air. They speak in one failing voice, with an old man's mouth—parts worn smooth or broken off sharp, all rattling, rubbing and scratching inside. I have no idea what they tell me.

On the elevator ride down, I ask the Black Shirts if I have been fired or rewarded. They answer me this time.

"They just wanted you to know they were concerned about the big day. About everything going smoothly," one of the black shirts says.

"The big day?" I ask.

"Spirit Day," the other one says.

"OK," I say.

"Are you ready?"

I tell them that I am.

"The old men hope so," the first Black Shirt says. "They've got a lot riding on this. They said Spirit Day will make or break us. There's going to be a lot going on. Clowns and balloons for the kids and all that. There's even going to be a carnival set up on People's Square."

"There's going to be a carnival?" I ask. The Mayor may have mentioned clowns and balloons for the kids, but at the time there hadn't been a carnival attached to it.

"A circus or a carnival," one of the Black Shirts says. "Which is the one with tents?"

"Either one," the other black shirt says. "Acrobats, exotic animal shows, and what have you. Are you ready for it, Jack?"

"Exotic animal shows?" I say.

"And acrobats."

"No one said anything about a carnival before."

"That's why they're telling you about it now."

"I may be a little under staffed," I say. "I had to let someone go the other day. I didn't know there was going to be a circus."

"Nice timing," one of them says.

"Right before Spirit day," the other says. "We'll scare up some replacements for you then. You can start interviewing next week."

I go back to my office. I think about a carnival or a circus setting up on People's Square. With tents, and freaks and exotic animals. Where will they put the elephants?

Dora

She is waiting for me when I get home, at the door, as if she lives here. I had expected her to be gone, to have my apartment to myself again, to be able to look out my kitchen window and see her there, across the lot, living her own mysterious life. But here she is in my apartment, greeting me with a kiss on the cheek as I enter my kitchen, put down my briefcase, say hello.

There is water boiling in a pot. The steam from it covers my windows. She asks me if I like spaghetti. I tell her I do.

Over dinner she says: "Tell me all about your day at work," and I tell her everything about work: about Cheswick and his missing gun, about my foul-mouthed Assistant Manager, about the Vice Presidents, the Black Shirts and the upcoming Spirit Day. To tell someone feels better than I would have imagined, like I am clearing out a room inside myself, emptying myself of a boxes of obsolete newspapers, magazines and TV guides.

"Wow," she says when I am finished. "A whole carnival!"

"I know," I tell her. "I was surprised to hear it myself."

"Do you think they'll have those monkeys that ride bicycles?"

"I don't know. I thought it was bears that rode the bicycles."

"I like the monkeys."

She follows me down the hall to the bathroom and stands outside the door while I do what I do, then wash my hands and face in the sink. I look at myself in the mirror. Dripping. I do not quite look real.

"Do you think they'll have monkeys?" she asks again through the door.

"I guess," I say. "I mean, carnivals do, don't they?"

"I think so."

"I think so too."

"Elephants?"

"I would imagine."

"Gorillas?"

I open the door, look at her. She reaches over, plucks a drop of water from my chin, wets her lips with it, smiles sweetly.

"Do carnivals have gorillas?" I ask her.

"I don't know," she says. "I was asking you."

I go to the living room now, sit on the couch. She sits down next to me, lays her head in my lap. I am thinking about gorillas, and the way she is resting her head in my lap reminds me of the way I used to rest my head in the lap of a gorilla. I pet her hair. It calms me.

"What do you want to do tonight?" she asks, and really, I have no idea. So we watch TV. It is nice—not just the TV, but the girl on the couch next to me.

She falls asleep to the news with her head still in my lap. I stay up and watch an old black and white show I have seen before about a man who lives with an alien from another planet. The alien looks human and passes for an out of town relative. He has strange telekinetic powers that he mostly uses for laughs. I fall asleep at some point while he is washing the dishes, with dishes floating from suds to dryer rack as if on invisible strings. I awake in the morning with cartoons playing and my alarm going off in the next room.

I lift her head from my lap, she stirs and curls up into the other side of the couch. I am sore in various places.

I shower, get dressed, go to work, and when I come back from work, she is still there and this time she has cooked fish.

"I hope you like fish," she says.

I tell her I like fish fine.

We eat the fish. It tastes good—if a little bland.

"Do you like it?" she asks me.

"Very much so," I tell her.

At night we go to bed. I kiss her scars. I almost love her.

Help Wanted

At work they are scrubbing the walls, mopping the floors, hanging the streamers for Spirit Day. The Black Shirts come to visit me on a nearly daily basis now. They tell me I will have job candidates soon. They give me a list of questions the parent company would like me to ask.

"No big deal," one of the Black Shirts says while the other nods and hands me the several pages of questions. "Just UCI policy."

"I don't recall having these before," I say to them, and they say: "It's a new policy, Jack."

I look over the questions. It is mostly the usual sort of thing: Do they get along well with others? What would they say the worst work situation they have experienced was? What was the best? Have they ever had a conflict with a coworker they could not resolve through management? Have they ever had a conflict with a supervisor? What would they say are their best qualities as a worker? What are their worst?

On page two, it gets a little weird.

"You want me to ask what their earliest memory is?" I ask.

The Black Shirts both say: "Yes."

"And which parent they preferred?"

"Everything on the paper, Jack, yes," one Black Shirt says. "That's why it's been written down for you. Ask them everything on the paper."

"It's a new company policy," the other one says.

"And what their favorite letter of the alphabet is?"

"Everything, Jack. Do you have a problem with that?"

"Do you have a problem with the new policy, Jack?"

I tell them both no.

"Just be thankful we're not asking you what your favorite letter of the alphabet is," one of them says. They both leave while I am still trying to figure out this last remark. It seems a little like a threat, but I cannot pinpoint where exactly the menace comes from. And what is my favorite letter of the alphabet anyway? It used to be E. Maybe it is the letter I now.

The next day I have my first interview. Richard and I sit in my office while our prospective employee sits in the only other chair we could scare up. It wobbles some and there are disturbing stains on the seat cushion.

We ask the prospective employee: do you get along well with others? What would you say is the worst work situation you have experienced? What was the best?

The first candidate is a small and nervous man—too small and nervous for the job at hand, though it is against company policy for us to point this out to him. We have to ask everything. We have to make notes next to all the questions. We have to fill out a comment section explaining why we have accepted or declined the candidate.

Every time the small man crosses his leg, the chair wobbles and the man clutches the sides as if to keeping himself from being violently thrown.

Then we get to page two. "What is the oldest dream you can remember having?" I ask him. He blinks at me. Richard looks at me too, leans toward me and looks over my shoulder at the sheet of questions.

"Really?" Richard asks.

"I guess," I say.

Then Richard looks back at the man in the wobbly chair. "Well?" Richard says. "Your oldest dream. Let's hear it."

The man says: "You mean, like my ambition? What I wanted to be when I grew up? A cowboy or an astronaut…that sort of thing?"

Richard and I exchange looks. Is that what we mean? The next question is: have you ever dreamt of falling and hit the ground?

"I think they mean regular dreams," I tell the man. "The kind you have when you sleep. The earliest one of those."

He is silent for a long time before saying in a trembling and nearly inaudible voice, "When I was a kid, I dreamt my mother shot me out of a tree with a pellet gun. She hit me in both eyes and I fell out of the tree and shattered like glass on the sidewalk."

Richard and I look at him. His eyes are wet, his lower lip is trembling. I skip the next question.

When I get home, Dora is waiting for me again. She is cooking spaghetti again. It turns out she has a pretty limited culinary repertoire. Spaghetti, casserole, and fish.

I tell her about my strange day, about the questions the parent company has given me to ask.

"It sounds like a psychological profile or something," she says.

"I guess so."

When I go to the bathroom, I see that she has added several things to the side of the tub. Various oils and lotions. Treatments I have never heard of for skin and hair conditions I have never heard of. While I am sitting there, I pick up one and unscrew the top. It smells like fermented rose petals. I try another and it smells like wet grass and crushed nuts.

When I am done, I return to the kitchen and sit down with her to our spaghetti dinner.

"I brought some things over," she says, pointing to a few boxes in the corner. "I hope you don't mind."

They are not big boxes. All three are labeled miscellaneous.

I tell her: "I don't mind."

Demons

The applicants begin to come in a steady stream. Richard and I bring them into the office, sit them on the wobbly chair, ask them questions from our two page list. Richard wants to add a few questions of his own—mostly involving first wet dreams, most painful erections, longest they've ever gone without any sort of release. He reasons that the parent company has already made things weird enough with all their do-you-dream-of-falling crap. I see his point, but tell him no anyway.

Most of the applicants we weed out immediately: the ones who mumble or shout, the ones that smell of liquor, the ones with incriminating burns on their upper lips or bruises on their arms, the ones who list working in the prison laundry room as part of their employment history.

One man, in response to a question on page two about feelings of supernatural oppression, tells us all about his personal experience with demons—how they occasionally push him out of bed as he slept, how he can feel them behind him sometimes trying to shove him into traffic. He is a young man, boyish looking but with eyes that remind me of fried eggs not completely cooked. He wears a suit that is too big for him and a tie that is too small. According to his application, he has worked in security before—six months at a warehouse before it was torn down to make room for a shopping plaza. The shopping plaza wasn't hiring. He had liked the warehouse job, he tells us. It had been nice and quiet, though sometimes he saw demons there too.

"So you actually see demons," Richard asks. "Is that what you're saying? I just want to understand this correctly."

"Oh yes," he says. "They're all around. They're everywhere."

"They're everywhere?"

"Yes, sir."

"We've never seen them here. Are they here too?"

"They're everywhere, but you have to believe in them to see them."

"But they've never pushed me out of bed," Richard says. "How come? I mean, if they're everywhere—"

"That's because you don't believe in them."

"But because I don't believe in them, they don't push me out of bed at night or try to shove me in front of a bus?"

"Exactly."

"But they do this to you."

"Yes, sir. They do. I wish they didn't but they do."

"That's fucking weird," Richard says.

"Have you ever considered not believing in them?" I ask him. "Wouldn't that be safer all around? My assistant and I can go through a day without getting shoved into traffic by demons just because we don't believe in them. Wouldn't not believing in them be the smarter way to go?"

He shakes his head. "It wouldn't do any good," he says. "They already believe in me."

Richard and I exchange looks. It is almost like a bonding moment for us.

The last applicant of the night comes in while I am getting ready to go. Richard has already left for the day. I had thanked him for his help—particularly for not swearing or calling me a cocksucker during any of the interviews. He said it was no problem and wished me well with my evening plans of ass-fucking the neighbors pet.

An hour later, the last applicant steps into my office without introduction.

"I seem to be the last one left," he says. "I hope I'm not too late."

I have already turned off the office light and the man who is standing there in my doorway is obscured by shadows.

"No," I say. "No...never too late. Have a seat."

"You look like you're getting ready to leave," he says.

"I was, but that's OK. Could you turn on the light?" I ask him. "The switch is by the door."

He finds the switch, flips it up, but nothing happens.

"That's odd," I say.

"Old building, I imagine," he says.

"Yes."

He sits down in Richard's chair. The office is not completely dark; the door is open and light from the Command Center is coming in. But even so, I cannot completely see the face of the man sitting opposite me. It's as if he has brought his own shadows with him.

He hands me a sheet of paper—his application. Most of it has been left blank. His name on the paper is illegible. Something starting with an S or a Z. His last place of employment is a company I have never heard of. He has personal references but the personal references have no addresses or phone numbers.

I reach my hand out to shake his and introduce myself. It is something I try to remember to do to create the illusion that I am professional and in charge, no matter how hopeless the applicant seems.

"My name's Jack," I tell him.

He leans forward and I still cannot see his face. This strikes me as very odd, as if he has managed to affix a shadow onto himself that was immune to the properties of light.

"Nice to meet you, Jack," he says. I can only see his mouth, grinning with teeth. They are good teeth—better than my own. Straighter, whiter, sharper.

His hand touches mine and there is a spark.

I remember Sterling. I see him again in a movie montage: Sterling as he peels potatoes, Sterling cleaning an animal cage, Sterling digging a hole beneath my bed, Sterling laughing, looking up at the light bulb in the center of our room as if it were a brilliant sun. Sterling growing from boy to man. A song is playing—the song is about growing from a boy to a man. As a man, Sterling is played by a famous handsome actor

The famous handsome actor says to me: "It's off now."

I say: "You're off now?"

And the famous handsome actor says: "No. You are."

I open my eyes. I had not known they were closed, but I open them now and see that I am alone in my office in the dark. Sitting in my chair. Who am I? Where am I? I am alone in my office in the dark.

I stand up. Leave. Lock the door.

The guard in the Command Center says: "Staying late?"

I say: "Going home now."

I go down the hallway, out the doors, down the steps to the river and my car. The smell of dead fish. Seagulls sit upon the river's thick surface. I pause to look at the birds, at the water. And suddenly the birds spring from the water and fill the sky above me. They fly over my head with a great squawking noise. White shit begins to rain down around me.

I get in my car and drive home. Dora is waiting.

Her Collection

She has three shoeboxes lined up on the bed. Each box has writing on the lid, in thick, careful letters. On one box is written THIS YEAR. On the lid of the other two, the words THE YEAR BEFORE LAST.

"This is my collection," she tells me. "I've never shown anyone before."

"I feel special," I say.

She says: "You are."

There is a tuna casserole in the oven.

She opens the first box—the one labeled THIS YEAR. It is filled with small, mummified things: an apple core, an orange, a daisy, and a moth wing. She lines them up in a neat row on my bed.

"I dry them on windowsills mostly," she says. "Or in the back of my car. Sometimes I get them started in the oven."

I ask her why and she says it's a hobby. "Everyone's got to have a hobby, right?" she says.

"I guess," I say, though I have no hobby myself. I am more the product of a hobby.

I pick up a mummified orange. It is light, and feels as if it would shatter in my hand if I made a fist. I shake it and hear seeds rattling around inside.

"Something, huh?" she says.

"It's something," I tell her.

I set it down, pick up the dried flower, which is much less interesting so I put it down again. The dried apple does not rattle like the orange, or look as much like as its original form. It is a small and wrinkled thing.

She opens one of the boxes labeled THE YEAR BEFORE LAST.

"Is this the same at the other box?" I ask, pointing to the third box.

"No. This is from the year before last. That one is the year before the year before last."

"How do you keep them straight?"

"That's why I label them."

"But you have two that say the year before last. How does that help?"

She is lining up the objects from the second box parallel to the first line on the bed.

"I know which is which," she says.

More fruit, a blade of grass, a mushroom, a small skull—like the skull of a mouse or hamster. The skull is bleached white. I pick it up. It rattles like the orange.

"I found it on the side of the road," she says. "Poor fellow."

"What is it?"

"I don't know. It's always just been that. As long as I've known it, anyway."

She takes the skull from my hand and places it back in the box. She puts the others away too.

"What about the third box?" I ask.

She says the third box isn't ready yet. I don't understand this, but let it go. Dinner is ready.

We go to the kitchen and eat. After dinner, we watch TV. After TV, we go to bed.

In bed she says, "Tell me about your family." Her face is against my shoulder. I can feel her mouth moving against my skin—lips and teeth and tongue. If I was deaf, maybe I could tell what she is saying by just the movement of her mouth against me.

"What about them?" I ask. "Why?"

"Everything. Because you never have."

I shrug. My shrugging shifts her face. She is no longer comfortable and props herself up on one elbow to look at me.

"Don't you think we should know about each others families? Haven't we reached that point?"

I guess we have. I tell her: "Mom always wore an apron. With pearls. Dad smoked a pipe. He liked to read the newspaper at the breakfast table. Sometimes I wouldn't see his face at all for the entire meal."

"How charming. Did he smoke a pipe at breakfast?"

"No. Just in the evening. He liked to work on his car too. Tinker with it. Make it better or something, I don't know. I guess he was just fascinated with how it worked…how things worked."

"Any brothers and sisters?"

"No. Just me."

"Who was your first girlfriend?" Dora asks.

"The girl next door," I tell her.

"The heart is a lazy hunter," she says, and kisses me on the nose.

I wake up in the middle of the night. The room is filled with the bluish light from a distant moon, making everything seem dim and black and white around me, as if seen on a fading TV set and for a moment I am unsure. Is this real or a TV show? Is this my present or my past? Am I a person or a character?

Then I see her black and white shoulder in the moonlight, her bare back, the slight ridge of her spine. It seems real enough. And she is like that, in any light; at times, it seems I have only imagined her, that the skin I touch is a dream I have willed into being, a skin made of memories. She is, after all, a girl who cannot even make automatic doors open.

With the tip of my finger, I trace the letters of her name between her shoulder blades. She stirs but does not wake. It is a short name and I am glad she does not wake. Who knows what pleasant and better world she is dreaming of now?

Something is Gone

At work we hire two new guards, give them uniforms but no guns. They will get their training for that after Spirit Day, when we have time. For now they are just warm bodies—a uniformed presence. They are unexceptional and unmemorable in every way. After they have left, I cannot even recall their faces.

I post a new schedule. I start another. I get a call from the manager of The Wig Shoppe demanding satisfaction. I tell him we would all like satisfaction. I tell him that everyone's satisfaction is our goal. I hang up while he is still sputtering something.

I put a piece of paper into the typewriter and write I am invented.

Something has changed.

I write it again. The typewriters hums, the words appear, but I receive no shock from pressing shift and I. I try again. I-I-I-I-I-I, I write. A whole page of I, but nothing.

I lift up the typewriter and look underneath, as if I could tell anything from that, as if I understood how any of it works.

Richard comes into my office and says: "What are you looking for, your dick?"

"Did you do something with my typewriter?" I ask him.

"Why would I do something with your typewriter?" he asks me.

"I don't know. I'm just asking. It's acting funny."

"How does a typewriter act funny? Is it typing?"

I set it back down on my desk. I hit the letter I, then pull out the sheet of paper and crumple it up before he can read it.

"Yeah," I say. "It's typing."

Later, two Black Shirts stop by to visit me. They say: "Hello."

I say: "Do the Vice President's want to see me?"

They say: "Not particularly."

Later that afternoon, there is a report of a man with chest pains in the men's restroom. A couple of guards respond and radio

back that it is Longstreet. I go down and see how he is. He is laying there on the floor with his back against the tiled wall and his
legs stretched out beneath a urinal.

"I don't feel so good," he says.

"I gathered," I say. The paramedics come in. They unfold their
gurney and check Longstreet's pulse, his pupils, blood pressure.
They ask him questions that they try to make seem like small talk,
but really they are trying to figure out what is wrong with him and
how likely he is to die on the drive back to the hospital. Longstreet
answers some of the questions and doesn't seem to hear the others. One of the paramedics points out that Longstreet is wearing
two different shoes. One is a dress shoe, the other a running shoe.
They are both left shoes.

"I haven't felt so good all day," Longstreet explains.

They load him onto the gurney and wheel him out. I ask the
paramedics what their unit number is and which hospital they are
taking Longstreet too. I walk with them to the street outside.

"I don't think I'm gonna make it in," Longstreet says.

"Don't worry about it," I tell him.

I watch the ambulance pull away, then go back to my office
to write the report. I use the four or five Ws. And an H. It feels
like I am writing an obituary, and when I am done, I check it over.
It seems cold and inhuman. It looks no different than any other
report. Man with chest pains. Transported to Mortarville General
by Unit Four. I write it again. I write it three times over and it
always comes out the same.

While I write, the sun jumps unseen across the sky, the light
fades, and at the end of the day, I leave my office to find the world
again transformed by the forces of time. Under a periwinkle sky,
I stand by my car, stare at the river for a moment, a long moment
that seems removed from measurement, immune to the clock. The
battered dead bellies, the mangled fins, the missing eyes.

From somewhere above me, I hear a sound like a muted trum-
pet and look up, up to a nearby road that runs along a ridge by
the river. I see a line of elephants marching by, a trail of brightly
colored wagons, a small brigade of clowns on stilts. I stand there
until the last one is gone.

I drive home past blowing trash and people, burning garbage cans, a soft snow of soot that falls on my windshield. I squirt washer fluid, smearing it across the glass in two arcs.   I go up the steps to my apartment, open my door to a darkness I do not expect. Why is she not here?

I step into the kitchen, banging my foot against something and nearly falling. I turn on the light and look down at the box on the floor. One of her boxes. It says "Miscellaneous," on the side.

I call out her name. No one answers, but in my bathroom I find an astonishing array of bath salts, oils and lotions. There is a foot cream made from frankincense and mirr.

There are more boxes under my bed and some of her clothes in my closet. In my bedroom I can smell her shampoo, but I cannot see her.

I undress and crawl into bed. The day seems suddenly endless and exhausting, as if I have lived my entire life in this day. I lay naked on the bed and feel myself collapsing into the folds of the sheets, spreading out like a puddle, absorbed by the mattress as if I were a drink spilled onto a sponge. Where is she? I stare up into the darkness. I want to sleep but am too tired to sleep. And sleep is not safe, with power lines above me and the clouds brushing their woolen shoulders together. Christ knows what will come to me if I close my eyes now. I am tired of the past, tired of this day and afraid of the day that will come tomorrow.

I pray: *Save me from this buzz and noise, this incessant murmur of electricity, its shouts and laughter. Its frothing mouths and chatter, cackles, coos. The chunking of the clock. The punching of the card with fading ink. Faded ink and floating ash. Crumbling cement. From dust to dust. Deliver me from filthy hallways, pipes and wires dangling. The water stains and peeling paint of my present, past and future. My Holy Trinity. Rescue me from robberies, beatings, threats, and memories. From the addicts and derelicts, disgruntled employees, the gray corner sameness filled with heaps of sleeping men and ghosts. Preserve me from the flotsam and jetsam, the detritus and decay, the ebb and flow, the discarded ephemera, the unwashed masses, the untold millions, the unwanted, unloved, and unmade. Mr. and Mrs. Christ, who sent their only frog down to be crucified on a board with pins and dissected for our sins, save me. Adopt me. Carry me from here in golden, bristled arms of light. Rest me upon Your holy mantel, constructed of clouds, polished into marble. Set me there, next to an urn, an hourglass, a clock, a snifter of brandy. Deliver us from Mortarville.*

And finally I sleep and mercifully, I do not dream or remember. My prayers, for once, are answered.

I wake up alone. I would have guessed differently, and almost thought from my dreamless sleep, that she had crawled into the bed and curled up next to me, her lips touching my back and breathing warmly. She likes to nestle her small face against my back, the tip of her nose sometimes tickling me awake.

But I am alone. I rise from the bed, dress from a pile of clothes in the corner and walk to the kitchen. Where is she? I feel suddenly lost, disoriented, alone, as if awakening from a dream into a room without light.

But there she is. She is standing at the kitchen window looking out. She is wearing one of my shirts and nothing else. In her bare feet she seems particularly small, but she is here and I am happy to see her.

I ask her what she is looking at.

"You can't see my apartment from here anymore," she says.

I stand behind her, look over her shoulder and out the window. The building is gone. It has been taken away in the night, but how? How with such efficiency and silence and so little warning? As if it had never been there at all. I look at the ground where it once stood. There are a few scattered piles of bricks, a yellow truck, and gouge of raked over earth where her building used to be. There are a couple of guys in hard-hats standing around and I want to open the window and shout down to them: *How can this be done? How did you do this?*

But I don't open the window and shout this—partly because that window is painted shut.

"How the heck can they do that?" I ask her.

"I don't know," she says.

"Wow," I say. It is all I can think of to say. I put my arm around her, pet her hair, tell her everything will be all right.

Spirit Day

Pink, red and black balloons like clusters of alien fruit hang from all the railings and pillars of the mall. Banners drape from the ceilings, praising the history of Mortarville with enormous black and white photos of the city when it was bustling, when the smartly dressed people of yesterday moved to and fro with a sense of purpose and accomplishment. The men wore hats. The women wore heels. That world is lost and unfamiliar, but the archways and columns that surround them in the pictures can still be seen slightly rearranged throughout the mall today. If you close your eyes, you can imagine the people as ghosts, rushing to catch trains that no longer run.

Displays are set in a circle around the sculpture on the main floor, the history and uses of cement are fully explained with scale models of cement plants sitting in glass boxes on plastic pedestals. Miniature silos, kilns, conveyor belts, pump houses, batch houses, central mixing drums, and tiny trucks waiting by the bins for their hoppers to be filled, like orphans waiting for their daily dose of gruel. *Can I have some more, please sir?* Little plastic men point to the silos, the trucks, the glass walled limits of their tiny universe. They are frozen in time beneath plastic trees.

Already the crowds are forming, more than I imagined—they must have bussed in from the other towns and villages. They are milling about in the food court, sitting on steps, setting their coffee cups on the twisted steel rails of the sculpture. I see men in black shirts, traveling in their usual pairs, checking the shine on banisters, the placement of waste receptacles, the workings of door hinges and handles.

Except for Longstreet, who is still in the hospital, we are fully staffed. But I have no confidence in our recent hires and cannot even remember their names. I recognize them only by the newness of their uniforms. There is one standing by the cell-phone cart.

There is another, standing by a different cell-phone cart. Who are they? Why did I choose them? One seems the same as the other, and they themselves do not seem greatly different than anyone else I have ever hired or fired.

Richard and I stand at the railings looking down at the growing crowds. Someone's kid is attempting to climb the statue of the man with the hammer.

"Five-twelve, you've got a kid on your statue," Richard says into his radio, and one of the guards steps forward, tugs at the kid's shirt sleeve, has a word or two with the mother.

"Another disaster safely averted," I say to my assistant.

"Should have let the little cocksucker get to the top then crack his head open on the floor," he says.

I say: "Yeah, well…"

It will be another long day. I would like to spend it in my office, pretending to do reports or working on next week's schedule or payroll but it is Spirit Day and I must be seen. I must show myself to be a concerned and attentive manager of men. I must show my Mortarville spirit.

"I'm going to check out level fifty," Richard says and I am happy to see him go. I stay at the railing, watching the numbers multiply, thinking again what a lot of work the fact of my existence must have been and for what? For nothing more than this.

Directly below me, a tall man in a dark suit looks up and waves to me. It takes me a moment to recognize him as Dr. Millstone. I wave back. He stands there, looking up, not moving as people swarm and flow around him. A woman bumps against his elbow, dropping her bags, and he looks down for a moment, then stoops to help her pick up her things.

I take the opportunity to back out of sight. I do not want to talk to Dr. Millstone. I do not want to tell him how I am doing today.

I go to the food court, find another railing and look down at the crowds from there. The air smells of grease and cheese and it occurs to me that I cannot remember the last time I have eaten. Dr. Millstone would not be happy. I could buy something now—a burger or fries or whatever—but the lines go on forever. They are like a slow parade of humanity stopped at a dead end.

I should have eaten this morning. I could have made toast—or maybe there wasn't any bread, Dora may have taken the last slice to dry out on the windowsill to add to her collection. She is staying home from work today to keep the ants off it. I don't know what sort of job she has that she can take so many days off. She says she has an understanding boss. I tell her it must be nice and she says she is sure I am that sort of boss as well.

"I guess," I tell her.

"You should come with me today," I said to her on my way out the door this morning. "It's Spirit Day." But the bread needed protecting, so she stayed home and here I am alone. Though not really alone, of course. I walk around the mall killing time until the Mayor's speech.

I meet a clown walking through the mall. He has black eyes framed in white circles and a bright red smile painted over his regular mouth. He is carrying a bunch of balloons.

We are walking directly toward one another and instead of getting out of the way or letting me get out of the way, he does some clown business where we end up repeatedly stepping in front of each other as we try to pass. I try to get around him again. He steps in front of me again.

"Just let me get by," I tell him in a low voice. People are starting to look. They have stopped and gathered in a clump around us. A few laugh, a few others point. The clown grabs me, pulls me close, pretends we are about to dance. He says into my ear, quiet enough so that no one else can hear: "What's the matter, buddy? Don't you like clowns?"

Then he gives me a peck on the cheek. His nose squeaks. The people laugh. I shake myself free, push my way through the crowd, wiping the red and white make-up from the side of my face as their laughter fades behind me.

I do not look back for five minutes as I walk away, afraid he is following me. When I finally do, I am relieved to see only the anonymous throngs closing behind me. I really don't like clowns.

There is something patently dishonest about them—about having a mouth painted over a mouth, and eyes painted over eyes. To say nothing of painted on tears and shoes that go on twelve inches past the ends of their real feet.

Later on, I meet a couple of the Black Shirts in front of The Wig Shoppe. They are wearing silver pins on their chests, and I think for a moment it is the emblem of some club or army that they are a part of, but I get a closer look and see that the pins are stylized depictions of the skyline of Mortarville itself—minus its fires and flaws.

"You like it?" one of the Black Shirts.

"Sure," I say, though I don't really.

"You should get one," the other Black Shirt says. "They're three bucks in the front portico. Go show your Mortarville spirit, Jack."

"I just might do that," I tell them, but when they are gone I head in the opposite direction, working my way back through a crowd determined to go in the opposite direction, and am relieved to meet neither clown nor doctor as I go.

The Mayor is standing at the podium on the steps, overlooking the main floor and the now densely packed crowd. The people and the press, with balloons floating up from the hands of children buried beneath them. I imagine the perspective the children must have of all this, a deep forest of knees and shins, a thunder of voices overhead like an ongoing storm.

The Mayor smiles at her adoring public, making eye contact here and there, nodding, waving, adjusting the microphone. She is about to start screaming.

"The world ends one mall at a time!" she yells. "A mall ends one store at a time! A store ends one customer at a time!"

It strikes me as an odd beginning for her Spirit Day speech. I look around to see if this uncharacteristically grim note throws anyone else. The crowd stares blankly up at her; they are either not listening or patiently waiting to see where she is going with it.

"But looking out at all of you, at these wonderful masses

in front of me, I know that this mall, this world, will not end! Mortarville is strong! We are alive and vibrant! Vibrant with commerce, with industry, with energy! We are filled today with the indomitable spirit of our fair city! The spirit of that boy, who more than two centuries ago faced an invading army with nothing more than a flute! That is the spirit of Mortarville! That is the courage and pride in the face of everything that this day has been set aside to honor! So we honor those before us! We honor the monuments they have left behind! The city they have built. O Mortarville, O Mortarville! Thy beauty of we sing!"

I half expect her to break out into song. She does not. She continues.

"But I will not bore you with a long speech on this day! We are here to celebrate and not listen to me ramble! So celebrate! Enjoy what this city has to offer! Enjoy this fine and shining example at the heart of this great place! Thank you and God Bless! Free movies all day at The Terminal Cinemas today! Free balloons for the kids!"

There is applause. Flash bulbs go off as the Mayor waves to the crowd and steps backwards out of sight. The crowds disperse, spreading out like water across the floor of the mall. They pour up and down escalators, fill the glass cages of stores, crash against walls and pillars. It is more people than we are used to. And I see an expression of panic growing on some of the guards. They finger the butts of the guns in their holsters, playing with the snap. They are backed against the walls now, hiding behind planters.

I am a little nervous myself. There are too many of them and not enough of us. They could turn on us in a moment and already there are reports of shoplifters being phoned in to the Command Center by frightened clerks, a woman having trouble breathing in the food court, unruly teenagers in the front portico. Exhausted shoppers are sitting on the floor and people are tripping over them, then turning back to curse. Children are losing their balloons and crying.

From above, you can see the current of the masses as it pushes and pulls through every opening, or is damned up by some impediment and must go around or over or wash the impediment away.

A balloon pops and everyone looks around nervously for the source of the explosion.

There is Dr. Millstone—himself looking less confident than usual, and though his head and shoulders rise several inches above anyone around him, he is being carried away in a direction that is not of his own choosing. He looks back longingly at the store he had intended to visit or perhaps the nearest exit.

Things get really bad first at the Terminal Cinemas. Not all the movies, it turns out, are free on Spirit Day. It is only a select few: documentaries on the history and pride of Mortarville. Locally made opuses entitled *Mortarville Lives! Our Fair City! Concrete and You!* This is a disappointment to many, and particularly to the large group of young men and their dates who had planned on enjoying a popular new film featuring explosions, breaking glass, car crashes and a city on fire.

They throw their soda cups into the face of a frightened ticket taker, topple the popcorn machine, steal several boxes of Junior Mints. Then they run down the walkway from the cinema, screaming of injustice and occasionally pausing to punch the face of an unsympathetic onlooker.

They will make reality into the movie they did not see and start fires in several of the garbage cans on their way.

And what can security do? We respond to the noise, the panicked calls, the cries for help. We swim against the restless currents of humanity and arrive in time to see it spill over. Tables are knocked aside, chairs thrown, burning garbage cans upended. The air is filled with smoke, shouting and coughing. Where is our enemy now? They surround us. They are pushing and pulling in all directions. They are no longer the angry young men and their angry dates. They are the people that the young men have pushed and punched on their way. They are the people that sympathize with the angry young men or sympathize with their dates, or they are the people that hate them for what they have done, what they are doing, what they might have done in the past. These could be the very same punks that stole their wallets, keyed their cars, left tire marks in their tree lawns, dated their sons and daughters.

The crowd surges forward against a row of tables and the tables give way. Smoke alarms are going off now and the emergency ventilators kick on, spitting out a gray dust from the ceiling that falls onto our heads like clumping snow.

In the food court, I see Richard fall under a wave of old women swinging shopping bags and walking sticks, an unlikely gang in tan coats and red hats, unnaturally rosy cheeks and lips that look painted in blood. He screams but his scream is engulfed. I think he is screaming: "Mother Fucker!" Or maybe, "Back the fuck off you stupid cunts!" Whatever, it is an unwise choice for final words and his scream becomes a muffled, strangled sound and he is gone. I hear the walking sticks smacking at his flesh and bone. I hear the bloody meat of him being ground into the floor.

I try to push my way toward him but the crowd reacts against me and pushes me back in the opposite direction, forcing me out onto the main floor of the mall, where I am banged by elbows, shoulders, fists.

A man in a suit and hat climbs to the top of the statue of the hammering man, perches like a monkey in a tree on top of the statues looped-rail of a head. The man has a box of jellybeans with him and begins tossing them one at a time onto the heads of the people below. I yell for him to stop, but really, it seems such a small point by now. My assistant has been trampled to a pulp a hundred yards away. The world is crushing in around me. Glass is being broken, drinks and free popcorn spilled and people are being run over by other people. The faces around me are red and shouting, the corners of all these mouths are specked with foam, and I feel the spray of them hit my face, while I yell at a man throwing jelly beans.

"Stop that!" I yell. "Stop throwing those!" I cannot even hear myself.

There is a bang—it could be a gun, or it could be another balloon popping. I see, by a planter, a guard draw his own gun in response but he is promptly washed over by the angry ocean. The gun and guard both fall to the floor, are pushed and beaten by an undertow of feet until they disappear, they are swallowed, they are gone.

A cell-phone cart is overturned and a chair from the food court is thrown through the window of the Wig Shoppe. Somebody knocks over a potted tree.

A boy stands at the top of the escalator, pulls Cheswick's a gun from his backpack, waves it around. At least I think it is Cheswick's gun. It looks like it from here and the boy looks like the boy I have imagined. But the crowd is rushing up toward him. They will not stop. They cannot. The Electron himself could not turn back this tide. I try to go to him but am caught again in the current. It carries me up the escalator. I see the boy ahead of me, I see him fall beneath us screaming. He is swept over and lost.

I am carried forward, past the boy, or where he was but is no more, past storefronts and around corners. I struggle to keep my head above them, above their heads and shoulders, away from their grinding heels.

A man is on the floor beneath me. Blood, and a hand reaching feebly up. I see him as I am almost carried past. I grab hold of the railing, pull myself free of the mob, hold myself close to the edge like I am clinging to the narrow banks of a swollen river. The fallen man is revealed in flashes between the rushing legs of the crowd. He is old and dying. His teeth have been kicked in and he is blowing red bubbles from his mouth. I try to reach my hand toward him, but it is like sticking my arm into a flame, a flame that crushes, that stomps, that consumes with weight and mass.

I shout something to the man. I don't know what. My voice no longer exists. People slip on his blood, more fall—the young and the weak. They join him on the river's bed, form a bank of broken flesh. I can do nothing. I have lost my radio. My gun is in my desk drawer, gathering dust.

I see Mr. Millstone carried past, struggling, flailing, thrown to the side, pressed hard by the mob against the window of a store specializing in fake nails and temporary tattoos. I try to go to him, but am swept up again in the surge. The glass cracks around him, falls down in lethal shards but I do not see the results. More people fill the space in front of me. A foot bangs against my head, and then another.

I hear a crashing, more screams, the sounds of hooves on the marble floor as a horse runs at full gallop against the crowd, crushing those beneath it to slow to get out of the way. The horse is dragging the body of its rider, the bloodied and misshapen remains in a sequined tuxedo.

I struggle to my feet and am immediately carried away. I see one of the Black Shirts thrown over the railing, falling onto a cart selling umbrellas and silver pendants.

A man dressed in a white suit runs screaming out of a store holding a cash register over his head. He crashes the cash register down on top of another man's head.

We pass a clown—maybe the same clown. Someone is punching him repeatedly in his red-ball nose. The nose stops squeaking and begins to gush blood.

There is blood everywhere—on the floor, on the walls, on the knuckles of all hands. The crowd pushes on. I feel something hard—a fist, a brick, a stick—hit me in the back of the neck. I fall forward, hit the ground on all fours as other feet go through or around me.

Smoke and flames, and the sound of things cracking, crumbling, popping, columns toppling. Shouts and screams and hacking coughs. The whinny of a dying horse, the trumpeting of frightened elephants. The smell of things burning: wood, paper, plaster, wigs.

I crawl, fighting against the onslaught of shoes and shins, pull myself again to the side, sit panting and bleeding with my back against the railing. Maybe now it is finally thinning, weakening. I can see spaces between the people as they rush by. I can see individuals again, hear their separate voices cry and moan and shout. Has it ended, or started to end? It has not. It has found its way out. It has burst free and spilled out onto the streets, where the bright colored and tattered remains of the carnival are burning. Tents are collapsing, horses and elephants are stampeding now, over people and vehicles alike, disappearing down city streets strewn with debris.

The mob still rages and police in riot gear—with clubs and helmets and plastic shields—arrive in cars, pour out of black vans, hover above the city in silent helicopters. Men in Black shirts charge from the exits, scatter into the mob. Park Rangers arrive in green jeeps, point their sticks at a raging elephant

The world is revolting against an unknown or unnamable oppression. The people have it in for all windows, all vehicles, for anything that can be tipped or broken or lit on fire. The police form a line and move with clicking steps toward the raging mob.

The city is falling. Shots are fired. Screams and sirens and all the accompanying sounds of destruction and I am finally destroyed by an errant bullet. It pierces my shoulder or chest. I stagger bleeding and surprised back toward the door. I will go back inside where it is only rubble and stragglers and victims left. I will die like that, like an animal returning to its lair.

Inside, the hordes have abandoned us, leaving blood and broken glass in their wake. The ambulances will come now or soon. The stretchers will carry us away. The blood is leaving me quickly and I imagine all the veins and arteries whose Latin names I cannot remember being severed now and spilling forth.

I cannot make it to the door. So instead I crawl behind a pillar, a nice quiet spot. I look up into the sky, for help from there, but only see the silent helicopters, hanging in the air like dragonflies. I wonder if I was I shot by Cheswick's gun? Cheswick's gun wielded now by the angry mob, fired randomly into another angry mob. Or fired by the entire mob at me, their communal finger pulling the lost trigger and sending its dusty, ill-cared for bullet into my flesh. From flesh to flesh, shirt sleeves to shirt sleeves, dust to dust.

It is falling. Soot and ash and bits of the burning carnival. A bearded lady runs by, swinging a tire iron. On the corner, a white tiger goes down in a hail of rubber bullets. I think of Dr. and Dr. Smithee and all their hopes and dreams bleeding now into the cracks of the pavement, seeping into a toxic soil. I am unmade and the blood flows. Is it fatal blood? Is it essential? Is it real? It is red like blood.

None of this will do.

I try to think of Dora, but her face will not come into focus and my memory of her becomes entwined with my black and white memory of Noreen Cochoran and the TV show I loved in my imprisoned youth.

I wish I could crawl, and imagine myself crawling, crawling into a hole, for the comfort of darkness.

Then I feel a warm breath on me, feel thick fingers touching my hair. I know it is her without opening my eyes. I do not want to open my eyes. What if this too is a memory, the work of a dying machine, the images that flash upon a fading screen? What if she is not there? What if all this is just my mind shutting down as the oil spills out and circles the drain? Are all my wires sparking and fusing together? Is this the present or the past? I keep my eyes closed and maybe it will not matter.

But then I do open my eyes, and it is Abigail. Her fur is peppered with gray now. Her wrinkles are deeper, there is a scar in the black flesh above her thick brow, and one of her eyes is nearly solid white. Time and medical research have not been kind to her. Her journey from government lab to traveling circus is unimaginable.

"Abigail," I say and I think she mouths the word John. I almost hear it--carried not by sound, but by her hot breath.

I try to crawl toward her, though I do not really crawl so much as lean. She scoops me into her arms, holds me gently, licks my wounds. She presses me to her broad and graying chest, surrounds me with her still muscular arms. Her hairs are like wires. She pushes soft, thick lips against the top of my head and her breath is warm and smells of chewed leaves and cotton candy.

She lifts me from the ground, carries me close as she climbs the pole of the nearest street light. I hear shouting beneath us, guns are fired, bullets whir through the air around us, but we are not touched by them.

She roars down at them. It is a strange roar. Her vocal chords have been removed. Her roar is like air being pushed through black leather bellows.

The city is in flames. Abigail holds me close, leaps toward the next streetlight, swings from that to the next, and then the next. She carries me like that, like a baby cradled close to her breast, as we swing from lamppost to lamppost into the sunset and the old world burns around us.